Diamonds

in the

DIRT

Angela Geurin

5 Fold Media
Visit us at www.5foldmedia.com

Diamonds in the Dirt
Copyright © 2013 by Angela Geurin
Published by 5 Fold Media, LLC
www.5foldmedia.com

Scripture quotations are taken from the Holy Bible, New Living Translation, copyright 1996, 2004. Used by permission of Tyndale House Publishers, Inc., Wheaton, Illinois 60189. All rights reserved.

ISBN: 978-1-936578-66-5
Library of Congress Control Number: 2013940025

For my daughters:
May you come to understand the truth of Jeremiah 29:11.

And for my husband, Rob,
without whose encouragement this story would have stayed
hidden in my computer.

Contents

Preface

So, Esther Rose, what is your story?"

Inwardly cringing at the sound of my birth name, I paused in the middle of drinking my tea and raised an eyebrow at the woman across from me. "My story?" I asked curiously. "And please, call me Scout."

I am known as Scout Rose, but for all official purposes my birth name is Esther Aileen Rose, after my great-grandmother. Scout is the nickname my father gave me at age four because I could name all of the players on the St. Louis roster, along with their batting averages for the season. He said I was his "little baseball scout," and since Esther was such a grown-up name, it stuck.

Fresh out of college and armed with a degree in journalism, I believed I would land that perfect job, scouting and writing up recaps for local and national baseball games. But every sports department I had interviewed with said the same thing: I had an amazing talent for writing, but was just not what they were looking for in a sports writer. Translation: wrong gender.

Although the male-dominated profession of sports writing had cracked the door and allowed one or two females to sneak into the department, overall they were still not ready to embrace the thought of a woman sports writer. I had faced and defeated that egotistical line of thinking before, but I needed a job now, or I would be forced to move back to Booneville and live with my sister: again. So, after about four rejections, I decided to broaden my options and send resumes to every newspaper opening that I could find. But I never thought I would actually receive a call from the Human Interest Department at the *Houston Times*, the largest circulated newspaper in the state of Texas.

This job seemed completely out of my league. What did I know about human interest?

I took a deep breath and studied the stoic face of Charlotte Anderson, a.k.a. Editor-in-Chief of the Special Interest Department at the *Houston Times*, known simply as "Life," and pondered a response.

My typical smart mouth comments eluded me, while inwardly I patted myself on the back; many a time I had shoved my foot in my alligator mouth. But this time, my mind was completely blank. Truth be told, I was intimidated by the woman across from me: something that had never happened before in my life. I prided myself on being the intimidator, but she had me completely stammering from the moment I received her call. This was so surreal. The Life section of the *Houston Times* was among the most notable in the country. The writers there were award winning, and one of the most decorated journalists was interviewing me in person, not taking the word of some assistant. Also, this "first visit," as she described it over the phone, was not at her office, but at Antonio's, the most expensive Italian restaurant I had ever visited. The cost of the appetizer alone could buy my groceries for a week.

Everything about her breathed high-class and total sophistication. From her pale blue linen business suit, to the beautiful pearl-drop necklace that dangled just below her perfectly painted face, Ms. Anderson was a sharp contrast to my plain, boring 6 foot 2 inch frame draped in a slightly wrinkled brown pant suit and scuffed leather pumps. Other than my towering height and thick, wavy auburn hair, my appearance was forgettable.

The smile that raised the corners of her pink lips didn't quite reach her dark brown eyes. "Scout," she tried out my name. "We are in the storytelling business," her sultry voice began, "and what better way to ascertain your skills than to listen to you tell your own story?"

"What makes you think I have a story?" I asked seriously.

Angela Geurin

"Everyone has a story. Everyone has something significant in their past that changed them, helped them grow, defined who they are today. That is our business after all: life, achievement and overcoming unthinkable odds. We tell these stories. We inspire others through the examples we provide, the lessons we learn." Delicately, she lifted her fork and asked again before biting into her salad, "So, what is your story?"

I sighed heavily and thought about my story. There was not just one defining moment, but several that were all connected, woven like a tapestry that brought me to this very time and place. To condense it would leave it broken. I couldn't tell one part of the story without the other, and the complexity of my life could take hours to explain.

"How much time do we have?" I asked.

"Take all the time you need."

Chapter One: The Shoes

Nine Years Earlier

It was a dark morning in November. A sense of sorrow filled the air as huge drops of tears poured from the gray clouds above. All was silent and still, even the blistering Kansas City wind. Only stifled cries echoed through the cemetery, rising from beneath the sea of black umbrellas.

There were about fifty of us gathered to honor Daniel Rose, my father: a widower, a professor, a grandfather, and my hero. My dad was a rare gift to the world. He never met a stranger, was never too tired or too busy to help someone in need, and never, ever gave up—no matter how difficult or impossible the circumstances may have seemed. He just always found a way to make it all work out.

That was up until five days ago.

Five days ago I watched my hero fall. He lost his final battle with cancer. I still couldn't believe it, and had I not witnessed it myself, I would have sworn it hadn't happened.

It was just after my sixteenth birthday. I was sitting in my dad's hospital room with my oldest sister Mary, and her husband Brian, listening to the doctor explain that the results of the exploratory surgery showed that the cancer had spread into his kidneys, his liver, his intestines and stomach, despite the four months of chemotherapy and radiation he had just completed. There was nothing more they could do for him but make him comfortable. He estimated that Daddy had maybe another month to live.

We were stunned. It was like the cancer was devouring his body one system at a time. I heard Mary gasp and glanced over to see her eyes glistening with tears. Brian cursed and ran a hand through his hair, but Daddy grinned and cleared his throat.

"Well," he said, "we'll just have to see about that, sir. I believe that only the good Lord can number our days and we'll just have to wait for His perfect plan to unfold."

His confidence warmed me. God was in complete control. I reached over and squeezed Daddy's hand. "I agree with Daddy. God knows what he is doing."

Daddy winked and Mary rolled her eyes. "Do you two not hear what the doctor is saying? He can't do anything else. They can't cure your cancer! They have tried every known treatment and nothing has worked! It's over! Now we just wait until you die!" She choked out the last word, tears flowing down her cheeks.

Daddy laughed, "You sounded just like your mother there."

Mary huffed and looked at Brian. "Denial. Complete denial."

Daddy realized then just how upset she was and his face softened as he straightened himself in the bed. "Mary, Mary, quite contrary, sit by your father's side," he sang in his beautiful baritone voice. It took a moment, but gradually her face brightened and she walked over to the other side of the bed. He took her hand and continued. "Have no fear, Daddy is here and everything will be just fine." She leaned over and kissed his cheek. Daddy turned his attention to his doctor. "Thank you for all that you have done for me, doc," he said seriously. "But if you would be so kind, I believe we need a moment to digest this news."

"Absolutely, Mr. Rose," he answered. "I wish this news could be more positive. I do hope that I am wrong." He turned and left.

The doctor was off by a month. Daddy lived just two months more.

The day he died, my school counselor pulled me out of gym class, saying only that I needed to go home, my father was asking for me. I immediately rode my motorcycle straight there. Minerva, the home health nurse, ushered me through the front door into my dad's bedroom as fast as she could. I barely had a chance to notice all of my siblings, minus David, milling about the family room.

With a deep breath I opened the door to Dad's room, bracing myself for signs of death, but surprisingly, he didn't look like he was on his deathbed, just tired. He was sitting up in his flannel pajamas, grinning ear to ear.

"Scout," he said in a scratchy, breathy voice, so different than what I was used to hearing. "Come here, girl." He reached his arms up as I approached, and pulled me down to sit beside him. "It's not looking good, baby," he said without reservation or fear. "I don't know how much time I have left, but I want to say good-bye while I am still myself and strong enough to do it."

I scoffed. "Daddy, what are you talking about? This is just like all those other…"

"No, baby, not this time," he interrupted. "This cancer is all over my body now. There's nothing else they can do and I don't want to spend my last few hours tied up to machines." I opened my mouth in protest, but he raised his hand and I stopped. "I have already talked to the other kids, even David…It's time to say good-bye."

I tried to swallow the lump rising in my throat. Gently, Daddy brushed a strand of my auburn curls away from my face and tucked it behind my ear. It was the same soft touch I remembered from his calloused fingers.

Minutes passed before I digested what he was saying. "You're giving up?" I questioned. "I-I don't understand. Why are you giving up?"

"It's over, baby," he said breathlessly.

"No it isn't, Daddy!" I exploded. "You just have to fight harder! That's what you taught me. You would never let me quit anything when it was too hard! You can't quit! You just can't! You have to keep fighting!"

"It's time, Scout, I can feel it," he said quietly. "There is nothing short of a miracle that can save me and I just don't feel that is what God has in mind for me now."

Tears formed in my eyes, but didn't spill over. He was right; I knew he was right. This cancer was like a hungry parasite eating away his body, moving from place to place until its appetite was satisfied, but it was never satisfied. It only wanted more.

I couldn't respond. Still fighting back the tears as he pulled me into his warm embrace, I leaned my head against his shoulder as he spoke.

"You know, for a long time now, it's just been me and you, kid. Your sisters and brothers grew up and moved out and they missed a lot of your growing up. I wish they could have had the same chance as me to see you grow into such a beautiful young lady. You look so much like your mother, but your determination and drive is a lot like your old man." He chuckled and then turned serious again. "You were your momma's miracle and she fought hard to bring you into this world. I know she would have been so proud of you." He coughed slightly and continued with a sigh. "You are smart, talented, and you can do anything you set your mind to do. You are the complete package: beautiful, strong, independent, fun. Why, if I were a young man trying to find the perfect woman, you'd be what I'd want. Stay true to who you are. I am so proud of you, honey. Always remember that."

His voice cracked on the last sentence and I could hear the tears of pride and joy in his words. They were a validation of my life. They were full of love and pride, but at that moment they were not the words I wanted to hear. They only confirmed my worst fears.

Diamonds in the Dirt

"Daddy, please," I said, blinking away the tears resting at the corners of my eyes. "Please don't give up." I turned to look him in the eye, hoping to find some glimmer of strength, but all I saw was defeat.

"It's time for me to move on, Scout."

"No, it's not! It's not time. Just go to the hospital, they'll fix this!"

Without realizing, I pounded the bed with my fists. Tears ran down my face as his weakened, but firm, arms wrapped around my shoulders and held me tight against his chest. I lay in his arms sobbing uncontrollably.

"Daddy, don't leave me," I whimpered.

"Scout, I'm not leaving you," he said softly. "I am going to live on with you forever in your heart and in your mind, just like your momma."

"Daddy, I never knew her," I whispered through my tears.

I hadn't known my mother, at least not the same way I knew my father. My mother had died of cancer when I was two years old. They said she actually found out she had breast cancer when she was eight months pregnant with me. She held off her treatment until I was around 6 months old, but by then it was too late to make a difference.

My memories of her were simplistic, like the smell of her perfume, her warm smile, things that were pieced together by the stories of others. I really didn't know my mother, not the way I knew my daddy. I loved my mother, but not the way I loved him. I had no memory of my mother's death, but my father's death would shatter my heart.

I hated cancer.

Daddy was silent for a long moment. I could hear the wheezing deep in his chest as he tried to continue. "You knew your momma better than you think, Scout. You may not remember her the way you'll remember me, but you speak her words often enough. She is there inside of you and I will be too. You just got to let me go, baby."

A siege of grating coughs convulsed his body at that moment. They lasted so long that I nearly called for Minerva, but Daddy waved me off as he fought to control the force that was striking his body.

I hated cancer.

With strength and determination, he wrestled it under control and spoke in a much weaker voice, breathy, dying, "I love you, Scout." Then he closed his eyes.

"I love you too, Daddy."

I squeezed my eyes shut. Maybe he was wrong. He was just tired and he would make it through just fine despite himself, but with every shallow breath he took, I knew it was inevitable. My dad was going to die today, and it wasn't fair.

What had he ever done to deserve this? Daddy was great man—a strong Christian example for this lost world. He had so much life left to live, so much more to give to God's people. Why would God take him like this? How could He just let him die after all he'd done for Him?

"How can God do this?" I voiced my thoughts.

His eyes fluttered open and he shook when he spoke. "Don't go blaming God, Scout. We can't possibly understand His plans. We just have to trust Him. He knows what's best for you. He created you and loves you more than I ever could."

"How can I trust God in this? He is taking you away from me! The only parent I have left. How is that possibly the best thing for me?"

"You can always trust God, Scout. He is your heavenly Father," he replied. "When your momma died, I didn't think I could ever raise you kids all by myself, and I was right. If I had turned my back on Him, you would have been taken away from me, but God was there every step of the way and He will be there for you, every step of the way for the rest of your life. Don't turn your back on Him, honey. Run to Him. Run as fast as you can into His arms. He will give you comfort and strength, just as He did for me when your momma died. Run to Him," he pleaded, "and let me go."

With those last words, he gently eased his head back against the pillows. His breathing became slow and even, but much weaker. He closed his eyes and completely relaxed.

Tenderly laying my head on his shoulder, I pulled the quilt up over us both and curled into his side. For that moment I imagined that I was a little girl again and daddy was as strong as a superhero. He wrapped me in a gentle hug, and automatically I snuggled as close as I could get.

It seemed like hours had passed as I watched my hand rise and fall rhythmically on his chest. Then he whispered softly, "Mariah, it's you."

I lifted my head. His eyes were open and he was staring at the ceiling. "Mariah," he whispered, "I missed you." I stared with him, unable to see anything but the white popcorn speckled ceiling, but knew that he was seeing my mom in whatever glorious state her death had taken her.

Fresh tears stung my eyes and I wrapped my arms around him. He inhaled one final deep breath and as he released the air, it sounded like a sigh of relief. He was gone. It was not overly dramatic. There was no sign of pain or struggle. He just stopped breathing.

Vaguely, I remembered hearing Minerva's quiet footsteps enter the bedroom followed by a stifled cry as she quickly left to let the others know that Daddy had passed. The corners of my eyes pooled with tears again as I reached up and kissed Daddy's cheek. It still felt warm beneath my lips. Ceding to his wishes, I climbed out of the bed and whispered, "Goodbye, Daddy. Tell Momma hello."

Sitting under the shelter of the canopy, I squeezed my eyes shut against the memory and tried unsuccessfully to concentrate on Pastor

Angela Geurin

Harris. It was difficult to listen. He struggled to keep his voice steady as he spoke the words Daddy asked him to share. Not only was he our pastor, but he was my daddy's best friend. Although the elderly man had spoken at hundreds of funerals in his ministry, none was more personal than this one.

As he spoke of my dad's many accomplishments, my eyes drifted unwillingly to the gray box encasing his remains. I couldn't help but cry. By nature I am not one to wear my heart on my sleeve, but this was such an emotional roller coaster ride that no matter what I did, I couldn't stop the tears—they flowed like the Mississippi River.

I tore my eyes away from the cold coffin and idly picked at the hem of the black dress and mid-thigh coat that Mary had insisted was appropriate funeral attire. I had planned to wear my black slacks and combat boots, but she argued that black slacks were for tea parties and evenings at church. I was really too tired to fight with her over clothes, so I gave in, but had I known that she would also insist that I wear panty hose, I probably would have fought harder for my slacks.

My eyes burned from the tears, and I crushed them with the palms of my hands in an attempt to slow the flow. My two brothers, David and Danny Joe, stood at the podium preparing to recite Daddy's favorite Scripture: Matthew 5, the Sermon on the Mount. They were both younger versions of my dad—tall and athletically built. David had my dad's blonde hair while Danny Joe had auburn hair like me.

Even though I knew this was going to be a part of the funeral service, I was not prepared for the amount of anger and animosity that welled up inside me as they began to speak. Neither of my brothers had any business reciting Scripture. They were both selfish and arrogant, nothing like daddy at all.

David and his wife, Emily, lived in Atlanta in a yuppie suburban house. Emily was from a wealthy, stuck-up southern family that had groomed her to follow their path of haughtiness. On more than one occasion, I had heard her refer to the Rose family as "David's redneck relatives" and she rarely allowed David time to visit. Emily and David had no children despite seven years of marriage and couldn't even

17

make the time to come visit during the last four months while daddy was fighting for his life. Yet, there David stood, speaking on behalf of the family.

Danny Joe was even worse than David. Black sheep was an understatement for him. He got arrested for shoplifting at age fifteen, married Sadie when he was seventeen, had his daughter Adalie by eighteen, divorced Sadie at age nineteen, and then remarried her at twenty-two. Danny Joe had caused daddy much heartache. He hadn't even gone inside a church until about a year ago. Daddy always had to pick him up from bars or jail, get him a job, buy him a car, and pay his rent. He had no business speaking for our family, let alone reciting Scripture!

My chest burned in anger as I unconsciously clenched and unclenched the hem of my dress. Before it boiled over, I tried to imagine my father reciting the Beatitudes instead of my hypocritical brothers.

David started to break down. His voice cracked as he attempted to complete the reading. Danny Joe tried to carry on, but eventually he stopped too, and they both bent their heads, unable to continue. I felt momentarily satisfied and in my head, continued listening to Daddy's lovely baritone voice.

Out of the corner of my eye, a flash of porcelain perfection that was Mary rushed to the rescue of our brothers. She slid in between them, wrapping them both in her sympathetic arms. Together the trio began reciting the passage again, much to my disappointment.

Mary, in her designer funeral regalia with big oversized hat and black spiked-heeled shoes, squeezed both of their necks as she spoke. She was tall and beautiful with long flowing strawberry blonde hair that cascaded down her back like a golden waterfall. Everything about her was perfect, and she would never let anyone forget that fact.

My oldest sister grated on my nerves more than any one of my four siblings. She dropped out of college to become a model in New York. After two years of modeling for an exclusive lingerie company, she married Brian Zamora, a partner in a large law firm in Houston, Texas. Even though Mary visited often, she was constantly interfering with Daddy's care. She argued with every doctor, nurse, even the cleaning ladies that came into his hospital room, as if a year and a half of nursing school made her more knowledgeable then any of the professionals caring for him.

It would have been tolerable if she would have just stuck to managing our father's care, but she felt it her place to straighten me out as well. With me, she was relentless. My clothes were never right. My hobbies were all wrong. My dreams were impossible. My nickname was juvenile. She was the only person in the family who insisted on calling me Esther. She refused to even acknowledge that the rest of the world knew me as Scout. And softball—she couldn't fathom why on earth a girl with such outward beauty would waste so much time on something as dirty as softball.

Mary continued reciting the passage in a strong voice, tears streaking down her cheeks seeming to glisten rather than smear her painted face. Obviously she remembered her waterproof mascara.

Off to the right, I saw my other sister, Ruth, slowly rise out of her seat and join the others. She was average height, but much shorter than the rest of us. She made up for it, though, with the four-inch heels she always seemed to have strapped to her feet. Her short, straight hair was blonde like David and Daddy, and she casually brushed it out of her eyes as she put her arm around Danny Joe. Mary looked to her and smiled, and Ruth began to read the passage with them.

The spark of anger inside my chest grew steadily hotter with each pulsing moment.

Ruth was such a follower!

Just eight years my senior and five years Mary's junior, Ruth thrived in Mary's shadow. Like Mary, she had graduated and immediately left home. But unlike Mary, she couldn't get into modeling school. So she headed to some university in southern Florida. She only called when she needed money. She hadn't returned home in two years. Then, last year, Ruth showed up unexpectedly, to announce that she had run off to Key West and married Julio Villalobos, a minor league pitcher who was not only a Cuban defector, but spoke very little English. Ruth, fluent in Spanish, acted as if she were announcing a new tattoo, not a lifelong commitment to a foreign baseball player.

The blaze in my chest burned like an inferno, threatening to engulf my insides at any moment.

Staring at each of their tear-stained faces made me sick to my stomach. Hypocrites! Every one of them knew nothing of what daddy had gone through in the last four months, or what it was like to watch him die a slow and painful death. I was the one who cared for him when he was too sick to get out of bed. I took over and made sure the bills were paid and that he got to his chemotherapy appointments. Their lives were never affected by any of this, but there they were, pretending to be something they were not. It was infuriating!

In my peripheral vision, I caught sight of Mary waving me up to join them. Her singsong voice addressed the crowd, expressing gratitude for their attendance; and I pretended not to notice as the anger spread within my chest.

There was no way I would stand alongside my siblings and play their charade. The audacity of Mary to think that the way they had treated daddy these last few months was worthy of this attention! I stared off into the distance, trying to ignore the gestural demands of my oldest sister.

"Esther," Mary whispered loudly and motioned again with her hand.

I bristled at the sound of my birth name.

"Esther," she spoke with as much force and sophistication as she could muster, "Come join us." The way she articulated each word with precise enunciation was so belittling. It made me feel like such a child. I shook my head and turned away, but she didn't stop, she just kept motioning for me to come.

Angela Geurin

My anger was close to the boiling point and I tried to calm myself with some deep breathing, but I made the mistake of looking down at my shoes and snapped.

The shoes!

Just the sight of the shoes fanned the flames. I glared at them as if they were the cause of my problems. They were not the comfortable black boots that served in my wardrobe as dress shoes, but rather the delicate, strappy, peep-toe high heeled *Mary look-alikes* she had insisted had coordinated with my entire funeral dress. I hated high heels. They made me feel like a freak. Mary knew that, just as she knew that I hated being called Esther.

With fire in my chest and Mary beckoning, I decided enough was enough. I looked at my dress, the pantyhose, the shoes and then up at Mary. This was not me; this was her! It was all Mary! I slipped off the high heels in disgust.

"Esther Aileen Rose!" Mary spoke through gritted teeth.

Taking both shoes by the heel straps in my right hand, I abruptly stood and slung them in Mary's direction, shouting at the top of my lungs, "MY NAME IS SCOUT!"

I didn't wait to see if the heels reached their intended target. All I could think about, all I could hear, were daddy's words: "Run to Him…and let me go."

That is just what I did. I ran as fast as I could. Pushing my way through the crowd, ignoring the gasps of the unfortunate onlookers, I just kept running. As I burst through the back of the canopy, I stripped off the black coat and tossed it to the ground, never breaking stride, dodging head stones all the way to the cemetery exit. The rain was letting up, but the rocks and mud were sloshing beneath my feet, slowing my pace. Raindrops mixed with salty tears on my tongue as I hiked up my dress, allowing my legs to stretch into a full-out sprint.

In the distance, I heard David and Brian shouting for me to stop, and I spared a glance back over my shoulder. There was no sign of Mary, but David and Brian were pursuing as fast as they could.

21

I snickered. They would never reach me. They couldn't. Not only was I the fastest catcher in the county, but I could run for hours, days even. Running was second nature to me. There was nothing like it. I felt free from the pain, free from the anger, completely and blissfully free. I stepped up my pace as my feet hit the street and decided right then that I would just keep running until the pain subsided. Yes, a good long run was just what I needed.

Chapter Two: The Knockout Blow

T hump! Crack! Thump! Crack! Thump! Crack! From the moment I stepped up to the plate in my first little league game, I loved hitting. There was just something about standing, bat in hand, a ball hurtling in my direction at lightning speed. Every muscle in my body coiled like a snake, ready, waiting for that perfect moment to unleash and crush the ball. It was exhilarating!

For that reason, my run led me all the way to the Grand Slam indoor practice center. I had spent nearly an hour every day after school for the last two years perfecting my swing in the long batting tunnels. Because of that, Sid, the owner, gave me unlimited tokens on Saturday mornings and after all, it was Saturday. I figured this was as good a time as any for a little batting practice.

My appearance spoke differently. Still in my black dress and remnants of the black shredded panty hose hanging loosely around my bare feet, I had tied my long hair into a tight knot at the base of my neck, using some blue pre-wrap from the first aid kit. I may not have been particularly dressed for batting practice, but I hadn't been dressed for a thirty-minute run either, and at the moment I really didn't care.

Thump! Crack!

I completed two circuits of drills and was now well into my tenth round on the automatic machine when I heard Sid approach.

"Rose! What are you doing in my batting cages?" he asked harshly.

Sid was a widower and had opened the practice facility shortly after his wife had died. He was a simple-looking man with remnants of jet black hair smoothed over the top of his nearly bald head. Still dressed in his Sunday best, having just arrived from the funeral, he looked uncomfortable, like he couldn't wait to return to his jeans and T-shirt.

Thump! Crack!

I figured someone would eventually show up here looking for me, and I was relieved that it was Sid, and not David or Brian.

Thump! Crack!

"Trying to work out this hole in my swing, Sid," I grunted in reply.

Thump! Crack!

"We have rules about proper batting cage attire," he returned coolly. I spared him a quick glance. His tweed jacket was now slung over the crook of his arm and he was loosening his tie.

Thump! Crack!

"I'm wearing a helmet," I fired back.

"I don't care about your helmet!" he retorted, anger seeping into his voice. "You're wearing a dress! You know my rules. No tight-fitting tank tops! No shorts! And definitely no dresses! And where are your shoes?"

Thump! Crack!

I smirked. "Planted firmly in Mary's forehead."

Thump! Crack!

My last comment received no reply, but I saw Sid walk along the right side of the batting cage, heading toward the pitching machine. Apparently, he had other ideas. He bent down behind the machine and switched it off.

Thump! Crack! Thuuuuump!

Angela Geurin

The last ball died, dribbling out of the mechanical throwing arm and rolling to the plate as the machine lost power. *Crack!* In frustration, I took a golf swing at the rolling ball and sent it flying back in the opposite direction.

"Taking up golf now, huh?" he remarked nonchalantly. Then after a moment's pause, he stated, "You need a break."

I rested the bat on my shoulder and tilted my chin up in defiance. "You said that I could practice anytime on Saturdays as long as I wanted. I'm not finished yet!" I yelled.

By nature, I am not a disrespectful teenager—especially to adults like Sid. It's just that my anger consumed me. I had never felt such hatred towards anything in my life. I wasn't angry at him and I think he understood that; but I was angry nonetheless, and it was definitely getting the best of me.

"You need a break!" he repeated, matching my tone. "Go to the showers. I am sure there is a change of clothes in your locker. I want you out of this building in an hour!"

I stared down at my dirty bare feet and the frayed hem of my knee length black funeral dress. I was a mess! My feet were nearly black with dark red patches where the rough surface of the street had cut them. My skin was soaked with sweat and grime. Slowly, I removed my batting helmet, releasing the wild untamed ringlets of hair and wiped the sweat from my brow with the back of my grimy hand.

"Go on! Get out of here!" he said harshly and walked away.

I shifted my weight and glared at his back. He paused suddenly and looked over his shoulder. "You can come back tomorrow, Scout, and hit as much as you want, but that's enough for today. Go rest," he added gently.

To my relief, he didn't say another word, just strode back toward the entrance of the building and left. He probably was afraid I would break down and cry. Sid never was an emotional man, and he wouldn't know what to do with a blubbering teenage girl.

25

Diamonds in the Dirt

I stepped out of the batting cage, put my helmet and bat on the rack, and headed to the locker room. Hardly anyone ever used the women's locker room, so I had grown accustomed to the solitude and turned it into my own private space—which was why I nearly jumped out of my skin when I rounded the corner and found Mary sitting on *my* bench.

She sat, legs crossed with her big ugly "funeral" hat lying next to her. My gym bag sat on the floor at her feet. Just the sight of her chewed at my insides and made me feel nauseous. *Why did it always have to be Mary picking up the pieces?*

"What are you doing here?" I spat.

"Sid found out you were here and I thought you could use a change of clothes. I came in here while you were, um, practicing." She covered her nose with her delicate hand and sniffed in disgust. "How can you stand it in here? It reeks of sweat."

"It's a locker room, Mary," I remarked. "What do you expect it to smell like in here, a flower garden?"

She waved off my comment with a flick of her hand. "Look," she said in the pompous little voice that I loathed. "We need to discuss this. You have to understand, I only want to help you deal with daddy's death."

The flame of anger and resentment began to boil up inside me again. There Mary sat, fulfilling her self-proclaimed role of family savior, coming to the rescue once again, saving the day as only Mary could. I didn't need to be rescued, and I didn't want her help.

"I don't want to talk to you, Mary," I stated flatly.

I turned back and headed around the set of lockers toward the showers. Mary stood, her designer shoes *click clacking* to attention. Quickly, she rounded the opposite corner of the lockers, and cut off the entrance.

"Get out of my way, Mary," I growled.

26

Angela Geurin

She stood her ground, both hands planted on her hips. "I know you are angry right now, and I really don't care if you take all your frustrations out on me at the moment because I can handle it, but we seriously need to talk."

"That's just it, Mary," I exploded. "You don't want me to talk. You want me to listen and do! Listen to what you have to say, and do whatever you think needs to be done!"

"You are terribly emotional right now and acting very defensive," she returned soothingly, her voice raising an octave but still controlled. She stepped aside. "You need to calm down. Go get yourself cleaned up and we can try this again when you are in a better frame of mind."

I balled my hands into tight fists. "My point exactly. I was headed to the shower on my own and I was wrong, but now it's your idea and it's suddenly okay? So, no, I'm not taking a shower until you get out of my locker room."

"You have the wrong idea, Esther," she answered, "and I am not leaving without you."

"No, *you* have the wrong idea, Mary!" I yelled. "All my life, you have treated me like your child! Stand up straight! Put on a dress! Fix your hair! Take a shower! Wear *these* shoes!" Emphasizing the last, I did my best Mary impression, waving my finger in the same manner that she always did. "There is nothing wrong with me, Mary. I don't need to be fixed. I am fine just the way I am. I am not your child. And the name is Scout!"

Mary shook her head silently for a moment. There was something in the way her posture changed that gave me a sense of dread, like a prelude to a knockout blow that came at me in slow motion.

"I really didn't want it to come out like this," she muttered, and then with a resigned shrug of her shoulders her next words did, in fact, blow me away, "but you don't really leave me any other choice. Brian and I are your legal guardians. Daddy signed the papers two weeks ago."

27

"What? Daddy signed me over to you and didn't say anything to me?" I asked through my shock.

"After that last hospital stay, we all sat down and began making the arrangements just in case. We made sure all of his affairs were in order, went ahead and made the funeral arrangements, met with his lawyers, everything. That way we would be ready. We all agreed that Brian and I would take legal guardianship of you and we signed the paperwork the next day."

"Who is *we*?" I asked.

"You know, us kids and daddy."

"Am I not one of the kids? Why wasn't I included? Don't I have a say in anything?"

"It's not like that," Mary explained. "You're only sixteen years old. Daddy didn't want you burdened by all of this."

I was stunned. I just sat down on the bench and shook my head in disbelief. "You? Why you?" I questioned, as for the hundredth time that afternoon, tears fell from my eyes. "I have been getting along just fine the last few months without any of your help. I don't need someone to take care of me. I work, I go to school, and I pay daddy's bills."

"And what other sixteen year old has that responsibility?" she asked respectfully and matter-of-factly. "Is that really the life you want?"

She was absolutely right. It had been really hard balancing everything and I had to give up so much, but there was no way I was going to give her the satisfaction of agreement.

"I don't need you to take care of me, Mary."

"Daddy didn't want to be your burden. He never wanted you to do all of that. He wanted you to grow up and live a normal teenage life. Go to parties and dances, and date."

Angela Geurin

Parties, dances, and dates? That didn't sound like Daddy—that sounded like Mary. It all sounded like Mary. Daddy loved playing ball and riding motorcycles together.

"I don't need to date! And I don't like parties or dances." I started fuming again. "That's all the stuff *you* want me to do, not Daddy! All you have ever done is tried to change me into your idea of a proper lady!"

"Do you think I was doing that on my own initiative?" she asked. "Right after you got your first period, Daddy asked Ruth and I to help him teach you to be a lady!" Mary *click clacked* her way down the bench and sat down next to me. "After all, I had mom and Ruth had me. We were all out of the house by the time you became a woman. Daddy really didn't know what to do. He tried, but then finally called for help."

"Ruth never tried to help me. She was too busy learning Spanish and chasing her own dreams, and you, all you did was disappear for months at a time and then unexpectedly show up just so you could show me the errors of my ways."

"Ruth tried to be there for you, but you always pushed her away," Mary explained. "That's why she stayed out of your way. You pushed me away too, but I'm not like Ruth, I see through your defensiveness. You try to act so intimidating and self-confident, but I know you; I see your fears, your insecurities, and I am not afraid of you. I can put up with your attitude."

Attitude! Oh, I would show her just how big of an attitude I could have!

"Yeah, right!" I fumed. "I don't need Ruth's help and I definitely don't need yours. I can take care of myself, and I am not moving in with you."

"You are not getting rid of me and I will never stop trying to help you. I promised Daddy," she answered with narrowed eyes as her temper began to flare. "The sooner you accept this, the better off you will be."

29

"I'm not doing it! Daddy wouldn't have done this without talking to me first!"

"This shouldn't be such a shock. Daddy tried to get you to move in with me months ago, but he didn't want to force you; he had hoped you would see reason and realize that you would be better off with me." Mary continued. "Unfortunately, he forgot that you're really stubborn."

Tears were streaming down my face now. I was angry at everything. Clenching and unclenching my fists, I fought off the urge to hit Mary as hard as I could. "I'm not moving in with you!"

"You don't have a choice in the matter!" Mary said.

"I have other options!" Although in reality I had no idea what those other options were, there had to be something better than moving in with Mary. "I'll just rent…"

"What?" Mary asked gently. "Stay here in Kansas City all by yourself? Get your own apartment? Even if you could somehow manage to stay here and finish high school, how are you going to pay for an apartment? What about a social life? How are you going to do all of that? What about your precious softball? You honestly think you can run a household, go to school, and still travel around the country playing softball?"

As ambitious and determined as I could be at times, it was ridiculous to think that I could make all that work. Recently I had taken over the household, paying the bills, buying groceries, and it was almost a full time job! Although I had made it work with school and ball for the time being, I knew I couldn't keep it up on a daily basis. Something would eventually have to give.

But why Mary? What was Daddy thinking?

"Why you?" I spat.

"Am I really that bad of an option?" Mary quipped.

"Well, we do have two brothers and a sister," I stated flatly.

She looked hurt. "You really hate me that much?" she asked softly, her shoulders visibly bristled. It was more of a statement then question, but the pain was fleeting and she straightened her shoulders and looked me in the eyes, returning to her contrite, perfect model posture. "Let's look at your alternatives here for a moment, shall we?" She began to pace back and forth in front of me, *click clacking* the whole way. "You could move in with David and Emily, but he travels all the time and Emily is so enthusiastic about us, isn't she? But I am sure it wouldn't matter. She is rather busy with all of her social events. Maybe you could help her organize her social calendar? Although, I am pretty sure you wouldn't be allowed to wear combat boots there either. I hear Atlanta is quite the baseball town."

I frowned. I hated their baseball team, not to mention that being with Emily would be worse than living with Mary.

"I'll take it from your expression that David and Emily are not an option." She remarked and continued her *click clack* pacing. "Well, Danny Joe and Sadie live in that lovely one bedroom trailer with little Adalie; that could be nice and cozy, don't you think?"

I rolled my eyes.

"Let's not forget Ruth and Julio in their cozy apartment in little Havana, and well, Julio is a baseball player and that fits with what you like. Although there is that whole *No habla Ingles*, factor, plus, he is always being sold to another team."

"Traded," I corrected.

Mary didn't falter. "But we did meet all of those cousins at the funeral today; surely one of them would be more than happy to take you in. Although after your whole shoe-throwing incident, they may be a little worried about your emotional state."

"Mary, stop it!" I shouted.

"So," she said, her *click clacking* abruptly stopping as she sat back down on the bench beside me, "I guess that just leaves me or foster care. And I do hope you would consider me a slightly better alternative than a foster family for the next two or three years."

Diamonds in the Dirt

I buried my face in my hands and tried to erase the reality staring back at me. Everything was spinning out of control. My whole world was changing right before my eyes and all I wanted to do was stop time, so that I could catch my breath. More than anything, though, I wanted Daddy back!

Mary just didn't understand. After today, she could return to her life—return to her happy little home with her husband and friends. But I was losing everything I had ever known, and to make matters worse, I was moving in with someone that for as long as I could recall wanted me to change. I was afraid of losing myself and being forced to comply with Mary's ways. I understood that there were no other options, but I just wished it wasn't Mary that had to point it out to me. Why did it always have to be Mary?

Defeated, I raised my head and looked into the face of my sister. No, my legal guardian. "How soon do I have to move?"

"The fall semester is over in two weeks. That should give you enough time to get your things put together. Brian and I have already cleared out the mother-in-law room for you, so you will have your own bathroom, sitting room and bedroom. We all agreed that you could take whatever furniture you wanted from the house. We have plenty of storage and everything is completely unfurnished in your area so you can decorate it however you would like. We're going to have to sell everything else."

"Everything? Even our motorcycles?"

"Probably; no one else rides besides you and Danny Joe, and he can't afford to keep them right now." Mary shrugged.

I choked down a sob. "You can't sell them, Mary, they are classics and Daddy and I spent a year and a half restoring them. If anything, I should get to keep them."

"You know you have no business riding a motorcycle, and besides you don't honestly think you can afford the upkeep of two motorcycles?"

Angela Geurin

"Daddy showed me how to take care of them, Mary," I returned evenly. "He didn't just hand over the keys without making sure I knew how to ride safely and keep up with the maintenance. He wasn't stupid."

"I'm not saying he was stupid, but you are my responsibility now. I promised Daddy I would take care of you and I meant it." Mary responded sternly. The corners of her deep blue eyes sparkled with unshed tears as some memory passed before her mind's eye. "I don't know, Esther," she said thoughtfully and her voice cracked as she continued. "I know how special they were to Daddy. We'll just have to see what happens with the estate. They are worth a lot of money."

"But *Angelfire* is mine! Daddy gave it to me!"

"I said we'll talk about it later," she cut off any further argument. She bent her head and composed herself. Then, politely, she smiled and reached out to rest her hand on my shoulder. "Daddy told me all that you did to keep things going around the house. I don't know how you did it. We are all very grateful for how you cared for daddy. It showed a great deal of maturity on your part."

It was a rare compliment and I swallowed my pride. "Thanks," was all I could manage to get out before the lump in my throat choked off the rest of the words.

Mary ran a hand through her flowing hair. "I will be staying here for the next two weeks with you, boxing stuff up, and tying up the loose ends, selling whatever I can." She tilted her head. "Then, it will be off to Booneville. Brian has already enrolled you. You should be ready to start school as soon as the break is over."

"Has he talked to the softball coach?" I asked. "When does their season start?"

"About that," she started slowly. I braced myself for the knockout blow. "Booneville High School doesn't have a softball team. The only girl's sports they have are basketball, track, and cheerleading. So you will just have to do one of those other sports."

33

Diamonds in the Dirt

My stomach dropped. "Mary, I don't play basketball. I have never run track, and there is no way that I will ever be a cheerleader. I play softball. It's the one thing I love more than anything else. I can't give it up!"

"I figured you would say that too," she responded not even trying to hide her disappointment. "Brian said since they do have a boy's baseball team and no girls' softball team, they have to let you try out for the boys' team or we could sue them because they would be in violation of some kind of title thing."

"Title Nine," I corrected her.

It was the 1972 act forbidding any kind of discrimination based on gender, race, or religion from federally funded programs. I knew all about this law because I had written a paper at Daddy's urging for my government class last year. Since athletics was included in most educational institutions that received federal money, they couldn't deny me an opportunity to try out for the boy's baseball team. But could I really play high school baseball? I played baseball all through my elementary years, but made the switch to softball when I was in junior high.

"Coach Ryan thinks you could make the team and so did Daddy," Mary stated almost as if reading my thoughts. "In fact, Coach Ryan already contacted the assistant baseball coach."

That was all I needed to hear. If they thought I could do it, then there was no question what I needed to do. "Good, then tell Brian to do what he needs to do to convince them to let me try out."

"Wait a second," Mary interjected. "I am not sure you should do this."

"I am not giving up ball," I stated vehemently. "You can sell my motorcycle before I do that."

"I know, but do you really want to start out with a reputation like that?" she reasoned.

"A reputation like what, Mary?"

Angela Geurin

"Like a rabble rouser."

"A what?"

"You know, a rabble rouser, a trouble maker."

"If that's what it takes to get them to give me a shot at making the team," I began, "then I will become a *rabble rouser*." The new word tumbled off of my tongue in an acrobatic display of linguistics.

"But..." Mary began.

I interrupted her with a wave of my hand, "I am not quitting ball, and I don't care if I sit on the bench all year. They'll eventually come to the point that they need me and I'll be ready."

"So I guess I can't change your mind?" Mary asked.

"Not a chance," I stated flatly.

"Well, I guess that's that," she sighed.

"Yep. Sounds like you have everything planned out and ready to go as usual," I muttered. "I'll just sit back and try to enjoy the ride." I added under my breath.

"Not quite," Mary returned, "there's one more thing." I groaned. Slowly, she reached into the duffle bag at her feet and pulled out a small leather bound book. "This is for you. Daddy was supposed to give this to you on your sixteenth birthday, but for obvious reasons it slipped his mind."

I took the book and eyed her curiously. "What is this?"

"It's a gift from Momma," she stated. "It's one of her journals. We each have received one at a special time in our life. David and I received ours when we graduated high school. Ruth's was for her sweet sixteen. I think Danny Joe got his when he turned 18. Yours is the last one. I'm sorry Daddy forgot to give it to you."

I smiled. My sweet sixteen hadn't been all that sweet with daddy fighting cancer. "I guess I can forgive him. Fighting for your life is a pretty good excuse." Carefully, I unsnapped the front cover and opened it.

35

Diamonds in the Dirt

The first page read:

For Esther Aileen, God's beautiful miracle,

God opened my heart the day you were born and showed me that all things are possible for those who love the Lord. May you find comfort and assurance in the arms of your heavenly Father all the days of your life.

Love Momma

August 16, 1978

August 16, 1978 was my birthday. She had already made plans to give me this journal the day I was born! Tears formed in my eyes. That meant she was already preparing to die! The day I was born, she was dying of cancer! How could God do this to her? How could he do this to Daddy?

Quickly, I slammed the book shut. Even though this was a gift from the mother I never knew, I couldn't handle any more talk of faith and God. He took away my parents. He took away my life. He gave me to this stuck-up sister of mine. It was His fault and I didn't want to hear anything else about how much He loved me, because from my side of the fence, He sure had a funny way of showing His love.

Regaining my composure, I straightened and replied with a short, "Thanks." Then, I tossed the journal back into the bag.

"You're welcome," Mary answered, rising to stand next to me.

With her high heels we saw eye to eye, and to my surprise, she kissed my grubby cheek and wrapped her arms around me in a strong warm hug. "I love you and we will survive this."

I let her hug me and then reluctantly returned her embrace. "I hope so."

"Now will you please go take a shower?" she asked, wrinkling her nose.

"All right," I huffed and turned toward the showers.

"Scout," Mary called.

Freezing midstride, I turned slightly just in time to see her wink. *Did she just call me Scout?*

"Sorry about the shoes," she said quietly.

I snickered. "Yeah, me too."

Chapter Three: Alligator Mouth

Welcome to Booneville,
The charming town you'll love to call home.

"Boy, is that a stretch," I mused as I read the welcome sign on the way into town.

"You say something?" Mary asked.

"No," I glanced over at her quickly and shook my head. Her large sunglasses were pulled slightly down the bridge of her nose and she peered over the top of them in my direction. For the umpteenth time, I wondered how in the world all of this had happened. Slowly, I turned my attention back out the window of Mary's luxury car as we headed to the Booneville High School athletic complex.

I had been here in Booneville, my new home, about a month. It was still winter break so I had yet to start school, but adjusting to life in this small "charming" town proved to be as hard as adjusting to living with Mary. Located just southwest of Houston, Booneville had a quaint appearance with a pretty little downtown that housed an antique shop, a small grocery store, a post office, a restaurant, and of course, a fancy coffee shop. There was even an old-fashioned drive-in joint called Frosty's just outside of town, but that was about where the charm of this town stopped.

Booneville seemed more like small town for the rich and famous. The population was rather high class, made up of wealthy executives who commuted to urban jobs in and around downtown Houston. Few people who lived in Booneville actually worked in Booneville. In

Angela Geurin

fact, all the businesses, with the exception of the antique shop and the drive-in, were owned and operated by people who commuted from neighboring towns.

It was the perfect town for Mary though, and I could see how my brother-in-law convinced her to move away from big city life. Booneville actually suited them both. Brian got his acres of land, unavailable in the Houston city limits, and Mary got her high-class life, complete with snooty friends. I, on the other hand, still felt like a square peg being forced into a round hole.

I missed Kansas City. I missed the snow and the chilly winter winds. Booneville was hot and humid. I missed the plaza with all of its fountains and bright lights. The only aesthetically pleasing site here was the golf course in Mary's neighborhood.

I loved walking through downtown KC. People were friendly and they smiled when you passed by them. People in Booneville seemed to walk around with their noses in the air, looking down at those who were not so *charming.* Then again, my pursuit of a tryout for the boy's baseball team at Booneville High School didn't really help my charm factor.

Initially, the head coach and the principal refused to allow me to try out, but just as Mary had suggested after dad's funeral, they offered tryouts for all of their wonderful girl's teams, one of which involved cheering and dancing. It wasn't until a very official letter from Brian's law firm suggested that the school's athletic program was in violation of the 1972 statutes of Title IX that I even got a chance to plead my case with the athletic director. The letter, so eloquently written, suggested that unless this policy was changed, a legal action would be pursued on my behalf, Miss Esther Rose. The athletic director stepped in at that point and for the first time in Booneville Bearcat history, tryouts were open to all students, including girls. I had to hand it to Brian; he knew how to play hardball.

Needless to say, the coaches, and the whole town for that matter, were less than enthusiastic. Like most small towns, the rumor mill started up right away and had successfully made me the scrutiny of every person in town. There were whispers that I was on steroids, that I was a lesbian, and, my personal favorite, that I was really a boy, but thought my chances for making the team were better if I could do it as a girl.

Since most of the women there were like Mary, they didn't seem to understand why a girl would have an interest in sports, let alone want to play on the same team as the boys. They looked at me as if I were from another planet, like I had some kind of disease and that if they made eye contact for too long, I would infect them and their little girls with the seeds of my craziness.

Yet, even with the knowledge that the district was breaking the law, the town still disagreed with opening the try-outs to all students regardless of gender and subsequently painted me as a troublemaker, a "rabble rouser" as Mary had put it weeks ago. I had quickly become the most controversial figure in town and had even been featured in an editorial piece in the local newspaper, *The Booneville Times*. Daddy had always said to leave my mark wherever I went, and I had definitely accomplished that in my first month in Booneville.

Mary was less than enthusiastic, of course, but she was pretending to be supportive. I know that deep down she was frustrated with Brian for stepping in on my behalf, but she had never said it out loud. It was more like she went out of her way to change the subject anytime Brian and I started talking baseball or my case for a tryout. Add that to the fact that any conversation Mary and I had always ended in a fight over me doing things that were more "ladylike." She was relentless, going as far as offering to buy me a car if I would sell the motorcycles and stop trying to play baseball.

"Esther, are you sure this is what you want to do?" Mary asked, interrupting my thoughts. "You know it's not too late to change your mind."

I glared across the console. "Please, Mary, you promised!"

"All right, *Scout*," she rolled her eyes as she exaggerated my name. "Are you sure you want to do this? I mean you saw the newspaper

40

article. You have very little support and you could end up making more trouble than this is worth. What happens if you don't make the team?"

Exasperated, I rolled my eyes in her direction. "We already talked about this. All I need is a chance to show them what I can do, and I know that they won't be disappointed with what they see. They will have to put me on that team."

"Right," she was saying, "but are you sure you want to start out your semester like this? Small towns don't like change. I just think it would be safer to explore other alternatives, like cheerleading. You know cheerleading is very athletic now. It's nothing like when I was in high school."

"Cheerleading!" I groaned, "Honestly, Mary, can you really see me out there flipping around, smiling and screaming 'Go Bearcats!'?"

"It would be better than swinging clubs and tackling boys," Mary responded.

"We swing bats, not clubs, and there is no tackling in baseball. Geez, Mary, I swear on Daddy's grave, I don't know how we're related!"

"Hey, watch your mouth, sister!" she waved her hand as she continued. "All I am saying is that you should seriously think about trying out for another sport. They do have other sports besides cheerleading."

"Yeah, sports that I have never played."

"Well, at least, you would be playing with other girls," she retorted.

"Whatever!" I groaned. "I'm so sick of this argument! You'll never understand."

What she didn't understand, and I doubted that she ever would, was that baseball was a huge part of my relationship with Daddy. We followed our favorite team religiously. When we couldn't talk about anything else, we always had baseball. He coached my little league teams until I switched to softball in junior high, and even then, he never missed a game or practice.

Now that he was gone, baseball took on a whole different meaning. Playing was the only way to stay connected to him. I needed to keep playing, to keep going, in order to fill the void that his death left in my life.

Mary continued without a hitch. "I don't think you understand the situations that you will find yourself in with playing with a bunch of boys," she was saying. "The boys could totally take advantage of you. And the girls at school…well, how are you going to make any friends?"

Then it hit me like a slap to the face. All the pieces to the puzzle slid together in one moment of clarity. Her mention of friends reminded me of a conversation I had overheard a few days ago between her and Brian. It was right after the editorial piece; she was frustrated because her friends had left her out of Bunco. The reason Mary was pushing so hard to convince me to drop this whole thing was not because of concern for my reputation, but concern for her own. It all made sense now.

"Wait a second!" I turned an icy glare in her direction. "You are not worried about my social acceptance if I make the team. You are worried about your own!"

"What are you talking about?"

"Oh, you know that the only reason you are trying to discourage me is because all your snooty friends at the coffee shop excluded you from 'Ladies Latte and Scrapbooking.'"

"Seriously, Esther, I don't know where you come up with this stuff!"

"Oh, don't act like I can't figure anything out! As soon as I became the talk of the town and they put together that we're flesh and blood, they took away your tiara, princess."

"You know just when I think we are making progress, that alligator mouth of yours shows up again."

"Better an alligator mouth that speaks truth than an ostrich who buries its head in the sand."

"I most definitely will not be excluded from any of my social groups because of you. That's absolutely ridiculous!"

"Yeah right, keep telling yourself that. I heard how upset you were when you found out that Bunco had gone on without you."

"Is that what you think? Really?" She actually rolled her eyes at me. "For your information, I explained at the last meeting that I was taking on a new project and would no longer be able to attend after the first of the year. They thought I meant immediately."

"Project!" My temper flared. I was so tired of this constant song and dance, and had no desire to be Mary's clone or even her protégé. All I wanted was acceptance. "I am not your project, Mary! I am not..."

"Oh, get over yourself," Mary hastily interrupted, "You are so conceited. You think the world revolves around you?"

"No, your world revolves around you. And conceited!" I added, "Mary, you wrote the book on that one!"

"You're being defensive again, Scout," she replied in a singsong tone that fueled the fire.

"You're avoiding the truth, *Mary*," I fired back, my alligator mouth on a roll now. "Like I said, truth hurts and now you are an outcast in this town, just like you were in New York."

It was a low blow. I knew it before the words came out of my mouth and immediately regretted it. I had heard the story many times and it was cruel of me to use it against her, but what can I say—alligator mouth.

Mary's modeling career had ended not by her choosing, but because her modeling agency let her go. They had said that she no longer had the look they were after and that it would be better for her to seek other career options. She was absolutely devastated, but everything happens for a reason, because that afternoon, as she was drowning her sorrows in the biggest piece of chocolate cake she had ever seen, she met Brian and they lived happily ever after. At least until I came along.

Mary didn't respond as we pulled onto the main road toward the high school leading to the athletic complex. I saw a tear trickle from beneath her sunglasses down her cheek and felt guilt wash over me like hot coals. With the air hanging thick, I finally broke the silence.

"So, if I am not your project, what is it?" I asked quietly.

I could see a cycle of internal dialogue cross her face. It began with confusion as she judged my sincerity, which gave way to fear concerning my reaction no doubt, and then finally delight, as she decided to share her little secret with me.

"I am going to go back and finish my nursing degree," she said at long last. The excitement rang clear in her voice, but her face revealed nothing. "I start in two weeks."

"What made you want to do that?"

Mary turned towards me. "Daddy." Tears sparkled in her eyes and her voice cracked, but she was smiling with absolute satisfaction. "He supported my modeling career, but he always wanted me to finish college, and now that I've left modeling, I think I need to move on and finish my degree. You know, start a new career that doesn't feed my vain habits," she joked.

"I think Daddy would be happy no matter what you did," I replied.

I meant it too. As far back as I could remember Daddy had always been there for each of us kids. He was always our biggest support, no matter what we did. I remembered when Mary had announced that she was moving to New York to be a model. He sold the first motorcycle he had ever restored, took the money, and started a bank account for her. He had helped David pay for Emily's engagement ring when he didn't have enough money, but wanted to propose on her birthday. Daddy had gone with Danny Joe and Sadie to explain to her parents the reason they wanted to get married, and he even went with Ruth to pick out the perfect dress for her senior prom.

I smiled as I remembered the ultimate test of his fatherhood when the dreaded day of my first period arrived just after my twelfth birthday. He didn't have Mary or Ruth to help since they had both moved out, but he marched into that grocery store anyway and bought every kind of tampon and maxi pad they had on the shelf, and then took me out to dinner at our favorite restaurant. He really was the world's greatest dad.

"I miss him, Mary."

"I do too. You know I sat down to call him last night and tell him that I'd been accepted into nursing school." She stifled a sob. "I guess old habits die hard."

"I wish I had him here right now. He would be up in those stands cheering louder than anyone else…"

Mary took my hand and gently squeezed it. "He'll be there," she said, and then touched my chest. "Right there. Always."

I smiled again.

She pulled into the parking lot of the athletic complex and guided her car into a parking spot in the second row. There was a long silence as she stared at the baseball stadium, looming beyond the windshield before turning to face me again. "It's not too late," she said one last time. I didn't respond and after a moment she nodded her head. "Well then, good luck," she said at last.

"Aren't you going to watch?" I asked.

"Do I have to?"

The sweet talk from before and my hope of understanding left in a rush of bitterness. We always took one step forward and two steps back, me and Mary. "Never mind," I said in disgust and started to open the car door.

She grabbed my arm. "Hang on. Do you even want me there? "

"Look, don't do me any favors, Mary!"

I jerked my arm free and stormed out of the car, retrieving my bag from the backseat and slamming the seat back to its upright position.

"Scout, that came out so totally wrong. Wait!"

"Don't bother," I spat. "I would hate to inconvenience you any more than I already have."

I slammed the door and stormed to the main entrance to the athletic offices. Mary got out as well.

"That's not what I meant, Scout. You are not an inconvenience. I just didn't realize you would want me to be there, that's all. I figured you'd think I would embarrass you or pose a distraction for you. I'll be there."

I turned. She leaned over the top of her car door, her sunglasses propped on the top of her head. Her eyes were sincere and I nodded. This was the first of a thousand moments in my life when I would wish Daddy was here with me, but having Mary there was as close to him as I could get, and I wasn't about to let my pride push her away. "All right...Thanks."

Booneville High School's athletic building looked simple on the outside with its two-story brown bricks made into a giant cube. But inside, it was a rat maze with hallways and dead ends everywhere. I thought I could find the girl's locker room on my own, but fifteen minutes into the labyrinth and I ended up back where I started at the front doors. With it being the Friday before the spring semester would begin, the building was completely deserted. I wandered the halls, striking out at every corner. At last, I noticed a partially opened door and started to knock, but paused mid-air when I heard two men in a heated discussion.

"If she is really as good as she looks on the books, does it matter that she's a girl?" I heard one say. "You know we are pretty thin at

Angela Geurin

catcher and there really is no one coming up that can handle Acer's fastball."

"Of course it matters! Ed, we can't have some prissy little thing behind the plate!"

The argument was similar to the many I had overheard over the past week and a half. I took a moment to look at the nameplate on the door. It read: John McNicholson, Head Coach, Boy's Baseball. Immediately I pulled my hand back.

That was just great! I had only met with the head coach and principal one time, and I didn't have to say a word because Brian handled everything. I was hoping to completely avoid any further contact until the try-out when I could actually show them I could play.

"What if she breaks a nail?" He continued. "Will we have to call time-out? What if some big ogre barrels in for the game-winning run, Ed? Do you think she'll stand in there and take him out or will she get run over and cry? And I don't even want to think about all the woman issues. Can she even play when it's that time of the month?"

I couldn't help but laugh. *Woman issues! Really? Does he think we go into hiding when Aunt Flow arrives?* I turned to head in the opposite direction and inadvertently bumped my elbow against the door.

Suddenly, the conversation on the other side of the wall stopped. Two graying heads popped out of the door and at first, looked in the opposite direction before swinging back towards me. I recognized one of the men as Coach McNicholson.

Recognition shown on his face as well, but it was followed by a shake of his head. "Speak of the She-Devil!" he muttered and abruptly returned to the office.

"Excuse me," I said politely. "I didn't quite catch that, Coach McNicholson."

Ed studied me for a moment and then politely offered his hand. "Ed Haywood, assistant baseball coach."

47

I accepted his hand and gripped it firmly. Like nearly everyone I met, he was shorter than me and I looked down at him when I replied arrogantly, "Scout Rose, your new catcher."

"I don't think so!" Coach McNicholson hollered from inside his office.

I knew my remark walked a fine line between confidence and disrespect, but I had to show these two that I was not easily intimidated, and judging by his reaction, it had just the right effect.

"Well, Scout, I have heard a lot about you," Coach Haywood remarked as he glanced up and down my 6'2" frame. "They sure didn't exaggerate anything about your size. I'm sure you hear it a lot, but you sure are a tall drink of water."

"Only every other day of my life, Coach Haywood," I smiled sincerely as he gestured for me to enter.

"Come on in, Scout." The older man flashed a polite thin-lipped smile and led me inside the office, leaving the door wide open. "You come here all by yourself?" He feigned looking up and down the hall for an escort.

"My sister dropped me off and my brother-in-law is in Houston today and will be unable to attend the tryouts."

"Oh, I see," was all the assistant coach offered, but I could see relief written across his face. The pressure Brian had put on the athletic department to comply with the law was enough that everyone was on high alert now.

I strode confidently into the office and glanced around. It seemed like a typical coach's office, littered with buckets of baseballs, bags of equipment, and mounds and mounds of paperwork. On the adjacent wall, hung team photographs, a framed newspaper article and a glass trophy case that stood mostly empty.

I gathered from the newspapers and talk around town that Booneville's baseball team was legendary for feeding great talent to the small colleges and even some minor league teams, but lacked the leadership to win. The team had far more losses then wins over the last decade, but Coach McNicholson was such an important figure in the town that his job was secure.

He was the town's pride and joy actually. He had graduated high school and skipped college to play two years in the big leagues. When he blew his arm and had to have the infamous Tommy John surgery, he took up coaching in the minor leagues, and decided to go back to school. As soon as he graduated, he headed back to his roots and had been in Booneville ever since.

He must be frustrated sitting in this office day in and day out staring at such a bleak trophy case. I imagined it was like having your nose rubbed in it the fact that you really hadn't lived up to your potential on a daily basis.

Coach Haywood directed me toward two very plain brown leather padded chairs opposite a long brown desk littered with stacks of paper, but I remained standing behind one of the chairs. He mirrored my action, standing as far away from me as he could. Coach McNicholson, on the other hand, stood behind his untidy desk, hands on his hips, back to me, staring out the window.

His posture sent a message of annoyance. He tapped his fingers on the sides of his hips impatiently. When at last he turned to face me, he scowled, showing his crow's feet, and crossed his arms over his chest.

"So," he finally spoke, "you like this hornet's nest you stirred up in Booneville? We are the biggest joke in the state of Texas now!"

"Now?" I replied. "The way I understand it, Booneville hasn't had a winning season in a decade. You could use a catcher that's familiar with winning."

"What makes you think that I am going to let you play on my team?" he spat.

"Because you need me on your team. You need me behind that plate. You need my glove. You need my brains. You need my stick. Your all-star catcher graduated and your back ups are mediocre and have no experience. I can come in as a high school All-American with varsity experience and a solid batting average of .350, and," I paused, "because without me, you'll just keep staring at an empty trophy case." I jerked a thumb towards the glass trophy case against the wall.

"You played softball," he sneered. "It's not the same game."

"I know. It's a lot faster. You have to be quicker. And I did play baseball up until three years ago. It won't be that big of an adjustment."

"For your sake, I hope you have the stuff to back up that mouth of yours."

"Oh, I can assure you, I do."

"We'll see," he answered.

"Yes, you will," I agreed.

The air was thick as silence fell between us. Finally, Coach Haywood cleared his throat and asked, "So, Scout, I know you didn't come by here to chat; can we help you with something?"

"Actually, I was trying to find the locker room and..."

Coach McNicholson interrupted, "All my boys run a 3.9 home to first and my catchers have a 2.7 pop time."

I shrugged my shoulders and fired back. "Like I said, your backups are mediocre."

Abruptly, he leaned over his desk and sneered, "Our outfield is 350 dead center."

"I can hit 350," I returned. It wasn't a complete fabrication. I had hit 350 feet one time during batting practice last season.

"My ace tosses an 87 mph fastball. You think you can handle that?"

"So compared to the 65 mph fastball I'm used to catching from forty feet, your pitcher is a little slow," I said, crossing my arms.

He paused for a moment, letting the silence fill the air.

"What is it that you want?" he asked. "What are you hoping to accomplish after all of this?"

Angela Geurin

I sighed. "I just want a chance to continue playing a game that I have loved since I was five years old. Maybe along the way, help a team that's spent most of its existence in the cellar, win a championship."

His hard-leathered skinned face softened just a little, just enough to show a hint of understanding. His eyes sparkled and his jaw relaxed. I had found his heartstrings. He understood the motivation that lies within the heart of every player who has ever crossed those chalk lines. The hallowed spirit that flows all across America, whispering to the hearts of anyone who has ever picked up a bat and ball and pretended to be Babe Ruth or Mickey Mantle. It was a common bond that all baseball players shared, the love of the greatest game on dirt. For a fleeting second, we were standing on equal ground.

Then his face hardened again and he spoke, "Well, I'm only giving you one shot at this, and when you screw it up, you'll know that this diamond is not for girls."

"Oh, but Coach Mac, everyone knows that diamonds are a girl's best friend," I replied.

He turned his back to me and looked out the window again. "Ed, show her to the girl's locker room."

"Sure," he replied. "If you'll follow me, Scout."

I started to follow him out and heard Coach Mac mutter, "We'll be the laughingstock of Texas!"

I stopped and called over my shoulder, "Don't worry, coach; they won't laugh when they are dodging my line drives."

"Humph," he responded. "You sure are cocky."

"Confident, coach; I am just confident."

"Well, try not to be too *confident*. These Texas boys are a different breed."

I grinned as I stepped out into the hall, "Well, I'll try not to embarrass your boys too much."

51

Diamonds in the Dirt

After leading me to the second floor of the building and pointing me to the third door on the left, Coach Haywood disappeared back into the stairwell. When I pushed the door open, I was immediately hit with the scent of strawberry shampoo and overexaggerated attention-drawing laughter.

"You saw her at the New Year's Eve party?" I heard one of the girls saying, "Like I'm not going to notice that she is wearing the same formal that I had on at the Christmas party!"

I walked around the corner and spotted a group of eight blonde beauties standing around in matching white sports bras and hot pink shorts.

Cheerleaders! This just couldn't get any better!

The navy blue lockers were arranged in two large squares around the room with one set of lockers serving as a dividing line. Long benches ran parallel with each set and the doorway that led to the showers and toilet area was situated in the middle of the opposite wall.

There was an empty row of lockers down the middle and I quickly chose the locker furthest away from the other girls and began emptying my bag. It was then that I noticed that the conversation had suddenly dropped to a whisper. I really didn't feel like making any new friends today so I concentrated all my efforts on changing my clothes as quickly as I could. I was in the process of removing my pants when I heard a trill "Mary-like" voice say *"Excuuuse* me!"

Blinking my eyes deliberately, I turned my head nonchalantly and answered, "Yes."

The hot pink beauties moved in my direction as one like a pack of lemurs.

"What are you doing here?" the blonde in the middle spat.

I rolled my eyes. *Ordering a cheese pizza!* "I'm just changing for practice." I tried to sound cheerful and pleasant, but it sounded a bit sarcastic, almost like I was mocking them.

"I can *see* that!"

Angela Geurin

Pulling my shirt over my head, I turned and stared down into the face of a blonde beauty queen with bright blue eyes and pouty pink lips caked with enough make up for a Kabuki dancer. Her highness wore her hair pulled back in a pony tail at the crown of her head and secured with a large bright pink bow. Little wisps of curls lay in perfect formation in front of her ears.

"Then why did you ask?" I questioned.

She rolled her eyes and thumbed her nose before she replied. "Because I think you're lost?"

I looked around at the girls and the lockers and then back at the queen. "No, this looks like the locker room," I answered with a shrug. "I'm in the right place."

"Uh, no! We keep all of the dyke basketball players on the other side." She waved a hand toward the square of lockers on the opposite side of the room. "We can't have them watching us change."

As I expected, her comment was immediately followed by a series of annoying girl giggles. It's like there is some kind of cloning plant for cheerleaders. It was the same in Kansas City. Little pretty robots wearing too much make up, giggling too loudly, and picking on any non-cheerleader they could find.

I took a deep breath. "Good to know, I'll be sure to avoid that side of the room since I don't play basketball. I would hate to give people the wrong impression."

"Well, then why are you here? This locker room is for athlete use only," she scowled placing her hands on her hips.

I literally had to bite my tongue to keep from remarking that jumping and screaming for the football team did not make someone an athlete and instead sat down and started putting on my cleats. "Obviously, I am an athlete or I wouldn't be in here, princess."

"*Princess*? Aren't you funny?" she said sarcastically. "For your information, my name is Kiley!" she snapped, turning slightly and pointing to the embroidered letters on the rear end of her shorts that spelled out K-i-l-e-y in black script. "You better remember that too."

I burst out laughing. "How cute! Your name is stitched on your shorts! Is that so you don't forget who everyone is while you're flipping around?"

Kiley rolled her eyes to the ceiling. "What a loser. Come on, girls." Just like that she spun around, followed by the rest of the squad.

"Wait a second," a taller girl with curly blonde hair and not-so-bright pink lips spoke up. "I know you from somewhere."

"I seriously doubt it," I replied, still chuckling slightly. "I'm not from around here, uh...Bonnie," I said glancing around at the name on her shorts.

"That's right! You're that girl from Kansas City that's trying out for the boy's baseball team! I saw your picture in the paper!" She shouted enthusiastically.

Suddenly interested again, Kiley and the rest of her squad turned back around. She pushed her way to the front.

"Oh, so you are a dyke after all." Kiley remarked followed again by the giggles.

"Why, because I'm a real athlete? Not some cheap imitation cow town beauty queen?"

Kiley fixed me with an icy glare and pointed her finger at me. "You have no idea who you are messing with."

"I am really scared now," I replied sarcastically. "What are you going to do? Stab me with your lipstick case?"

"You are going to wish you never came to Booneville by the time I am done with you this year!"

"Hate to disappoint you, Kiley, but I already do." I stood and grabbed my gym bag and hoisted it over my shoulder. Rounding the lockers, I thrust open the door, ignoring the catcalls and outbursts that were directed my way. "What a charming little town!" I muttered and hustled out to the baseball field.

Chapter Four: History in the Making

I t looked like a beautiful day for baseball. The sky was painted a brilliant blue, dotted with cumulous clouds. A tropical breeze blew across the infield, kicking up an occasional miniature whirlwind of dust as it passed. In all appearances, it *was* a beautiful day for baseball, but appearances could be deceiving. The air around Kenneth Traylor Stadium was thick with tension.

Already, the stands were full of curious onlookers. It seemed that everyone in town was showing up to see this historical tryout. As strange as it was to be the talk of the town, it was stranger still to think that there were so many people taking the afternoon off to watch a high school baseball tryout.

"They should have sold tickets," I mused as I strode through the main gate.

I bet they don't even get this many at their regular season games. There had to be at least fifty or more. It seemed crazy, but I guess this was what happened in a small town.

Both coaches stood deep in conversation at the pitcher's mound. My fingers trailed along the back of the dugout on my way to the gate on the first base side. As I rounded the corner, a short overweight middle-aged man, wearing a hunter green lightweight jacket and a matching baseball cap, blocked my path to the field.

"Scout! Davis Freeland from the *Booneville Times*," he said enthusiastically, "Mind if I ask you a question or two?"

Startled I jumped back a step. "No comment!" I shouted.

His neck flab wobbled as he continued to hurl questions at me, ignoring my declination. I ducked my head and stepped around him and through the gate. He followed me through anyway. This guy would not take a hint! Ignoring him, I continued along the right field fence where the rest of the players were milling around.

"Get the *Booneville Times* off the field, Ed!" Coach Mac ordered. "This is a high school baseball tryout, not a three ring circus. Ridiculous!"

I mentally thanked him for saving me from all the attention. But as Coach Haywood jogged over and cut off the reporter's path, I knew his only motivation for sending the reporter away was to save face in the Texas baseball community. The less attention this tryout received, the safer his reputation.

Scanning the faces in the crowd, I started to unload my gear. Mostly the stands were full of students, but there was a healthy complement of adults in business attire, too. Too many, in fact, to assume they were watching their sons try out for the baseball team.

"Look at the dyke on spikes!" It was the voice of my new cheerleading friend, Kiley. She and her group of lemurs were just outside the right field fence, doing heel stretches.

I fought hard not to roll my eyes and instead flashed my best smile and turned my attention back to scanning the crowd in the stands. Mary had said she was going to stay and watch; and silently, I hoped she hadn't changed her mind. As much as I hated to admit it, I really needed to know that at least one person was there to support me, even if that support was somewhat reluctantly given.

Keeping a wandering eye in the stands searching for Mary, I tried to ignore the attention that I seemed to be drawing from everyone else. I finally spotted her at the top of the bleachers directly behind home plate. She looked so out of place sitting with her legs crossed, her bright red high heel shoe bobbing up and down with her leg. Preoccupied with filing her nails, she didn't seem to notice me like those around her. It was obvious she would rather be anywhere else but here.

Oh well! At least she is here.

I bent down and pulled a hair tie out of the front zipper pocket of my bag and started braiding my long hair when I heard *the whistle.* I hated the whistle. It was not a coach's whistle, calling everyone to attention. It was not a fan whistle, congratulating an accomplishment. It was the whistle that said: *you are just a piece of meat.*

I never understood why a guy just couldn't keep his thoughts to himself or at least have the decency to look a girl in the face and say, "you look pretty." Out of the corner of my eye, I spotted the whistler and ignored him, until he did it again this time loud enough that everyone along the fence looked in our direction.

Deliberately, I turned to my left to find two boys, both shorter than me, one scrawny, and the other a little on the stocky side, laughing and nudging each other in the ribs. I finished my braid, thread it through the back of my cap and secured my hat to my head. "Need something, boys?" I asked politely.

"Yeah," the scrawny one said, "a piece of you."

He winked the kind of perverted wink that only sleazy pick-up artists would give. His stocky buddy avoided throwing any looks, but nudged his friend again and chuckled. The onlookers were laughing too.

"Oh really, just a piece," I taunted in my best imitation of a Texas drawl, "well, why don't you come over here and I will give you a piece of my fist!"

The crowd erupted in a series of "oohs!"

The scrawny one spoke again. "So, you're a tough girl, huh. I can handle that," he jeered.

Great! A wise guy!

Instinctively, I wanted to pile drive him into the dirt, but that would just give everyone the ammo they needed to keep me from playing. On the other hand, if I didn't set boundaries right here and now, every jerk on the team would think he could sexually harass me the entire season. I searched for a quick and more appropriate solution, and at last spotted it lying on the ground behind *the whistler*.

"I don't know if you're tough enough for me," I returned and took a step toward him. As I expected he backed away half a step. So, I just continued sauntering toward him slowly a step at a time watching him retreat, matching me step for step. "You know, I am really tough," I said playfully. "I don't think you can handle it."

Both boys were backing away a slow step at a time, the scrawny one smirking all the while. "Oh, yeah, I can..." he started to say.

Splash!

In a tumble of arms and legs, the scrawny boy tripped backwards over his bag and fell into the water cooler, knocking it over in the process, and ultimately giving himself an unwanted bath. His buddy stepped just out of the way of the river of water.

A fit of laughter coursed through the crowd of onlookers as well as some of the people in the stands. Everyone was having a great laugh, but I did my best to remain stoic as the coaches jogged toward us.

I offered the scrawny boy my hand. "Cooled off now?"

He stood on his own, ignoring my hand and fixed me with an icy glare. Wringing out his shirt, he didn't respond, neither did his friend, as the coaches approached. The rest of the group began to back away and soon he found himself alone and sopping wet.

"Son," Coach Mac said exasperated, "What are you doing horsing around in the water cooler?" He didn't wait for a reply and looked at the rest of the hopefuls who tried to look busy doing other things. His gaze lingered on me for a moment, sending a silent warning. "The rest of you, head down to home plate. Apparently you've got some excess energy to burn off."

Without hesitation, I grabbed my glove out of my bag and sprinted towards home, leaving the others in the dust trying to catch up. I stamped my foot firmly on the plate as I arrived and turned to watch with satisfaction as the others finally caught up. They were all at least five steps behind me. The first to arrive, a young, dark-skinned boy only slightly shorter than me, came to an abrupt stop on my right.

He leaned in. "You better watch who you pick a fight with," he commented with a slight Hispanic accent, "You don't embarrass the mayor's son in this town and get away with it."

"Thanks for the tip," I returned dryly.

Mary would not be pleased. I stole another glance up in the stands and shook my head. She was completely engaged in painting her fingernails now! Apparently, she missed the whole show.

"Cade Traylor really doesn't even have to try out," he continued, "He makes the team no matter what because his dad built this stadium. He's only out here so it looks fair."

"This just gets better by the minute," I mumbled.

"It's kind of the same reason you're out here," he said, "Coach might look like he's being unfair if he doesn't let you try out."

"Look, I am not here to meet quota for the coaching staff," I spit out, glaring at him. "I am here to play ball and…"

"Hey, take it easy," he lowered his voice, "I'm on your side. Every year, I try out hoping to make the team, only to be turned away because I am too dark. I am just letting you know how things work. Cool?"

I shrugged. "Yeah, cool."

He smiled, his teeth bright white against his dark skin. "Cool," and then added, "By the way, the name's Jose Medrano."

"Sorry," I apologized. "Nice to meet you Jose, I am Scout…"

"Rose," he finished. "I read the papers. Were you really a high school All-American as a freshman?" he asked.

I nodded and quickly turned my focus to the coaches jogging towards us.

"If you think you can lollygag around this field with no hustle and make this team, you might as well walk away right now, because that is not what this team is about," Coach Mac barked. "As a Bearcat, you will run everywhere on this field. Am I clear?"

"Yes, Coach!" I yelled back in reply. I felt everyone's eyes snap to me and a couple followed my lead and echoed my reply.

Coach Haywood nodded his approval, while Coach Mac shot daggers my way.

I didn't care. The only way for me to get on this team was to put on the greatest show of my career. I needed to look so good that it would make him a fool not to include me on his roster.

"We are in for a long afternoon, boys…and girl," he hesitated and then in frustration ordered, "Drop your gloves and line up!"

After a short jog around the outfield, we ran bases for the next half hour. I didn't feel as fast as usual, but I was confident my times were faster than most of the boys there. We went into fielding and throwing exercises next. Coach Haywood hit us five ground balls and three pop flies

As expected the balls I received were tougher than any of the other hopefuls. The first ground ball he hit me was up the middle, but my first step was quick enough that I cut it off behind second base and made a solid throw on the run. The next one was in the opposite direction, and I had to dive down the line to get a glove on it. I turned and made the throw to first from my knees. It wasn't nearly as hard as I could throw, but it was still on line. The next three were screaming grounders that short-hopped my approach. I was able to snag them all and make good throws.

The three pop flies weren't any easier and again I found myself sliding under one, catching one over my right shoulder in left field and sprinting over to catch the final one in foul territory. Clearly, he wanted to challenge me to the point that I failed, but his plan didn't work.

My face revealed no emotion as I jogged across the field, but inside I was grinning ear to ear. He tried to make me look bad, but instead I finished looking like a superstar and we hadn't even gotten to hitting and catching yet.

Before we started hitting, the coaches told us to get a drink. I jogged down to the water table along the right field line and grabbed a cup. Cade, sucking wind like a vacuum, went out of his way to bump my elbow as I tilted it back and the water spilled down the front of my T-shirt. I looked down and groaned. Why, of all days, did I have to wear a white T-shirt?

"Whoops!" he sneered as his eyes lingered on my chest.

"Get a good look, Cade!" I growled. "This is the only action you'll ever get."

"I always get what I want," he retorted. "I'll get what I want from you, Red."

"Maybe in your dreams."

His eyes were creepy, the way he leered in my direction as if I were some kind of fabulous steak. The others started laughing. I grabbed another cup and stepped as far away from Creepy Cade as I could.

"I'd say we are even now," he retorted, gesturing to his own shirt.

"Not even on your best day will we ever be even. If I were you, I would focus more on improving your game than worrying about what you could do to irritate me."

"Don't you get it? Nobody wants you here. You'll never make the team. The school is only trying to please your idiot brother-in-law."

"Then I guess I have nothing to lose by trying out, but you, on the other hand, are getting beat by a girl." I straightened out my hat and tossed my cup into the trash. "Don't worry though, Cade, I am sure your dad can afford a really nice position on the bench for you."

"At least I have a dad."

Silence.

The silence spoke volumes. Everyone recognized his comment for what it was: a cheap shot, a low blow. Tears stung my eyes and I took a deep breath, shocked at how cruel his comment was, and then mentally kicked myself for allowing the verbal sparring in the first place.

I had two choices. Give into the hurt and wipe the smirk off of his arrogant face, or take the high road and walk away. Somewhere in my mind Proverbs 12:16 rose to the surface: *A fool is quick-tempered, but a wise person stays calm when insulted.* I blew out my breath and settled for the high road.

"Yes, you do," I replied and walked away.

"All right, boys and girl," Coach Mac barked. "Get your helmets and bats and line up on the first base side."

Thankful for the interruption, I mentally rubbed my hands together in anticipation. Crushing some leather was just the remedy I needed for Cade. I didn't see a pitching machine so it looked as if we would get to hit some live arm, which excited me even more.

Jose sidled up next to me. "I heard they are bringing in someone to pitch to us so they can really see what we can do."

"Really?" I responded, "Who is it?"

As if on cue, a tall, long-armed college-aged man trotted in from the left field bullpen. "You may recognize Jeremy from last year's team. He is here visiting his family during the break and has graciously offered to help us out with tryouts before he returns to Gregory State for the spring semester," Coach continued.

"This is bad," Jose mumbled, a little shaken. "My hitting is so weak. I struggled to hit off Coach Mac last year and he has a rubber arm. I can't hit a college pitcher."

"Relax!" I encouraged, "He is a freshman at a division two school. Just think of him as a senior from a losing team."

Jose cracked a smile.

"Line it up," Coach barked. "Who's first?"

Several players jumped, but no one moved toward the plate. I looked around at the faces of the worn out hopefuls. It appeared that everyone was as intimidated as Jose.

"I'll go," I responded striding toward the plate.

"Be my guest," Coach Mac replied with a smug look.

Taking a few warm-up swings, I watched as Jeremy continued tossing pitches. His wind up was distracting to say the least and the ball actually disappeared from view when his long arms and legs came towards the plate, but despite his wind up, his speed was not overpowering. I took a couple of additional practice swings before stepping up to the plate.

Off!

It was the cue daddy taught me to center my focus. Upon thinking it, the world around me blurred and grew silent, until the only thing I heard was the sound of my own breathing, and the only thing I saw was the ball. As the world faded around me, I pointed my bat at Jeremy and dug my back toe into the batter's box.

See the ball.

Jeremy started that arms and legs wind up and released the ball. I tracked it and realized immediately that the jerk had decided to give me a Texas-sized welcome by throwing at my head. I had no choice but to bail out and hit the dirt, but I jumped up quickly. Vaguely, I heard laughs and snickers behind me and shook my head at him.

"Sorry, that slipped," he apologized rather insincerely.

I ignored him and stepped back into the box and pointed my bat directly at him again.

His next pitch dove down and away at the last second, but I had plenty of time to adjust my hands and drove the ball down the right field line. He tried the same slider again; and this time, I lined it right back up the middle, a screaming line drive that whizzed by his ear before he could even lift his glove. The next two pitches, he came back inside, and although I mishit the first one, catching it a little close to the handle of the bat, I drove it with enough power that it landed in deep right center.

Halfway through, I was feeling more and more comfortable with his timing and with each pitch, I drove the ball deeper into the outfield. Then, on my last pitch, I felt it all come together—that sweet, smooth feeling of absolutely crushing a baseball. My hands extended to meet the ball at just the right spot. My hips turned, thrusting my weight behind the swing. The timing couldn't have been more perfect. The screwball he had delivered sailed 325 feet over the left field wall.

Satisfied, I shouldered my bat and took off my helmet. Without a word, I headed back to where the others were standing and glanced back in time to see Jeremy tip his hat.

"Nice swing," Coach Haywood commented. "All right, who's next?"

Finally, we moved to catcher tryouts, and I knew this was where I would shine. Daddy never understood why I enjoyed playing catcher. He thought it was the dirtiest and most difficult position on the field, but I loved catching and there was no one better than me. Cade's stocky friend, Bobby Ray, was the only other player trying out for catcher, and I doubted he could move as quickly as I could. Last year, my opponents dubbed me the human backstop.

I steadied myself into a squat as Jeremy delivered brutally difficult pitches. Dropping down to my knees, diving to my left only to get back up and dive to my right, he threw wilder than any pitcher I had ever caught. After four or five of these wild pitches, I stood and shook the dirt out of my mask and called him out. "So I take it your pitcher can't hit the broad side of a barn, Coach Mac?"

He glanced at me, but didn't respond to my question. "All right, let's see your arm," he said. "And Jeremy, just throw straight!"

Diamonds in the Dirt

Coach Haywood was timing my throws to second base, and this time I would only get three attempts. This was something I had diligently worked on over the last three weeks. I had the best pop time for softball, but with the longer throws in baseball, I really needed to work on my arm strength. It was time to see if all the hard work had paid off.

My first throw was right on target, but I felt sluggish in my release. I held my breath and waited for the next one and got a much better delivery, but my throw was off a little. I took a deep breath and steadied myself for the third delivery. The pitch came in low and I had to drop to the ground to block it as it skipped off the plate. From my knees, I twisted and let loose with a throw that surprised even me. It one-hopped to the short-stop, but still got there pretty fast.

I stood and ripped off my face mask, fixing Jeremy with a glare that could melt ice. Automatically, my mouth opened to give him a piece of my mind, but I just closed it and walked away in frustration.

"That can't be right, Ed," Coach Mac yelled. "She threw from her knees!"

"Then you time it and see for yourself!" he returned coolly. He turned to me and shouted, "Rose, run it again!"

I replaced my helmet and settled into my squat behind the plate.

"Jeremy, no funny stuff this time!" he barked.

Jeremy delivered a perfect strike, and in one swift motion, I slung the ball to second, grunting with the effort. It was a line drive strike right to the short-stop about a foot off the ground. Perfect! I couldn't have thrown it any better.

I smiled now, more than satisfied with my delivery and looked expectantly at Coach Mac. He was shaking his head and staring at the stopwatch in his hand.

"That OK, Coach?" I asked.

His lips were set in a thin line and without looking up he said, "That's fine, Scout. You can take off your gear."

I laid it all on the line today. Without a doubt, I did more than just show I could play baseball; I was stellar and everyone there knew it. It was exactly what I needed to do if I was going to make this team.

As I took off my gear and packed it away, a T-shirt in the stands caught my eye. It said: *Got Blessings? Start Counting Them!* Suddenly, my dad's voice sang in my head, "Do not forget to count your blessings every day. Write them down if you must, but always take time to see what God has..." I squeezed my eyes shut and shook my head. *No! No, God stuff!* I shoved the rest of my things in my bag and hurried off the field.

It was a relief to have tryouts over, but it was not without reservation. I found myself cautiously optimistic. I left everything I had to give on that field Friday and I impressed more than just the coaches, but I still couldn't help wondering. What if, despite all that I had done, they still rejected me? What would I do if I couldn't play ball again?

The sun rose above the roofline of Mary and Brian's Victorian-style home as my feet pounded up the long driveway and slowed to a walk. I glanced at my stopwatch and let out a long breath. I was still off my normal time, but better than yesterday.

Pacing up and down the driveway hands on my head, I took deep relaxing breaths and tried to cool down as my tryout performance replayed in my head like it had my entire run this morning. I really looked good out there; I know I did, but would Coach Mac see me as a ball player or just a talented girl?

My pacing led me to the steps of the wraparound front porch. I removed my tennis shoes and T-shirt, wiping my face, before walking around the porch to the side door. Quietly, I turned the handle and let myself back into the house through the kitchen door.

Diamonds in the Dirt

The early morning runs I so thoroughly enjoyed were just one more thing on the list of Mary's disapprovals. She said she was concerned for my own safety, but I figured it had more to do with waking her from her beauty sleep going in and out of the front door. So I had resigned myself to sneaking in and out of the side door off the kitchen. It was on the opposite side of the house from her highness's bedchamber, and so far I had avoided any early morning chats.

That is until today.

"Enjoy your run?" Brian smirked at me over the top of his paper. I jumped. "Don't worry, I won't tell," he assured me.

"Yeah, right," I mumbled, cutting my eyes at him in skepticism.

"I promise," he said. "I didn't say anything to her yesterday?"

I sighed. "You knew about yesterday?"

He nodded. "Heard you sneaking down the stairs when I got up to visit the restroom. Figured there were a lot worse things you could be sneaking out of this house to do, so I won't complain about your choice of time for exercise. This neighborhood is safe and it's light outside. I think it's okay. Just don't tell your sister I said that!"

I made a motion with my fingers, indicating the zipping of my lips and smiled before pulling a cup from the cabinet. My brother-in-law was so different than Mary. He actually had a good sense of humor, and when it came to conflict, he was the ultimate negotiator. It's probably why he was such a good lawyer. Dressed in khakis and a dark green polo, he sat at the breakfast table, chewing on toast and sipping coffee. His thick blonde hair was parted to the side. I noticed his navy sports coat slung over the opposite chair.

"What are you doing up this early? Are you going into the office?" I asked.

He finished his toast before replying, "It's Sunday, kid. We go to church on Sunday. Didn't Mary tell you last night that your two week hiatus from church was over?"

Angela Geurin

I tucked a stray curl inside my backwards ball cap and reached into the freezer to fill my cup with ice. "Yeah," I said as I filled it with water. "I told her I wasn't going."

"Think that's going to work, huh?" he asked, folding his paper and laying it on the table.

"She can't make me go." I stated between drinks. He shook his head in disagreement. "What? Is she going to drag me there? 'Cause that's the only way, I'm going."

"She might! Do you want to take that chance?" he replied with a chuckle. "Besides I agree with her. This is something that has been a part of your life and you need to get back to where you came from. You've had a month to settle in."

He was right. It was church and I had grown up, going to church every Sunday. Daddy would never stand for us to miss it. He even found a church for us to visit when we were out of town for softball road trips. I just didn't feel like going to church in Booneville. People seemed so stuck up, and stuck-up people always acted fake at church.

I loved our church back home. We were like a family. I couldn't imagine any church in Booneville being like a family. Self-righteous, judgmental, yes, but a loving, active, moving body-of-Christ followers? Doubtful. I wouldn't find that at *The River Nondenominational Church* in Booneville. Besides, I wasn't ready to start worshiping and praising the God who chose to leave my life in such upheaval.

Brian must have read my face. "You know, not everyone in this small town is snooty. There are very real Christians in Booneville that you would love to get to know, but you won't find them, lying up in your room."

I didn't reply and stared out the windows into the gorgeous pink and white rose garden Mary had planted. It was another impressive fact I learned this last month about my sister: she was an incredibly talented gardener. Here I always thought she was afraid of dirt.

The contrasting colors were beautifully laid out and full against the white picket fence. The sun reflected the morning dew and the petals sparkled as if they had been sprinkled with glitter. It was a beauty that pointed directly to a Creator beyond human abilities. Immediately, I felt that tug in my heart that I recognized as my heavenly Father's gentle touch, urging me to spend time with Him, my Creator, my Healer. Almost simultaneously, the bitterness welled up inside too. *You took my only parent away! You took my life away! You did this!* The tears started burning in my eyes and I took a deep breath and blew it all away.

"What if I am sick today?" I asked.

"Think that's going to work for you?" he asked.

"I guess not. It didn't work for you!" I laughed. "Hey, toss me an apple."

"Go long," he said and tossed an apple off to the side and slightly over my head. I reached back and made a one-handed grab in front of the doorway leading to the formal dining room just as Mary walked in. Quickly, I scooted out of the way as she headed for the cabinet to retrieve her pink coffee mug.

She wore a short pink linen dress with matching high heels. Her strawberry blonde hair was piled on top of her head in a perfectly twisted knot adorned with a stunning silver and crystal clip that rested just to the left of her top knot.

Mary growled. "No baseball in the house, you two!"

"Yes, dear," Brian answered in submission. Mary poured herself a cup of coffee and sent a sarcastic smile his way.

"Whipped," I teased, making the motion of a whip with my hand and plopped down in the chair next to him.

"Yes, ma'am, I am."

"You're pathetic."

Mary shot him a look of annoyance in which he responded by blowing her a kiss and returned to his paper. She opened the refrigerator and pulled out a carton of cream, then carried both cream and coffee to the table and sat down on the other side of Brian. He leaned over and kissed her cheek.

"You look beautiful, my love," he gushed as she patted his cheek and kissed his nose.

I almost gagged on my apple.

Simultaneously pouring cream and sugar into her coffee and then daintily stirring it, Mary turned her attention to me. She looked me up and down and then blew out an exasperated breath. "Why are you walking around this house in nothing but a bra and shorts?"

I shook my head in annoyance, held the apple firmly in my teeth, and pulled the T-shirt over my head. "There, that better for you?" Brian, I noticed, was conveniently hiding behind his newspaper.

"Seriously," she returned, "who walks around wearing nothing but a bra?"

"This coming from the lingerie model," I muttered. Brian stifled a laugh and Mary slapped his paper out of his face.

"Besides, this is a *sports* bra! It is practically a shirt!"

"A bra is a bra and besides, you don't have time to go running this morning. We are leaving in half an hour for church."

Brian and I exchanged looks, and I hid a smile. Obviously, the princess didn't recognize my sweat-stained face. "Right," I answered slowly.

"What?" Mary questioned. "You are going to church with us this morning. It's not an option."

"You can't make..." I started and stopped when Brian cleared his throat and shook his head. Exasperated, I huffed. "Oh, fine, but I am not wearing panty hose. It's too hot in this hole of a town for hose!"

I left the table and stormed off to my room. At least I didn't have to hear another lecture about my early morning run. In frustration, I slammed my door shut and banged my shoulder into my dresser. My mother's journal landed at my feet.

"Not now!" I shouted and tossed it onto my desk.

Church was more tolerable than I had expected. We were late and had to sit in one of the back rows, which meant we didn't have to mingle. Just like Brian had said, I only recognized a few people from around town and all of them had treated me very kind from the moment I met them, but I still didn't let my guard down. I stayed to myself, only speaking when spoken to first.

Unfortunately though, on the way out to the parking lot, Brian had stopped to chat with one of his friends about a golf match and Mary was cackling with a group of her hen friends. I sat down on one of the benches outside of the church to wait. Next Sunday if I couldn't get out of going to church, then I would definitely have my own ride.

"Good sermon today, huh?"

I looked over and was shocked to find Coach Mac, sitting next to me on the bench.

"It was all right."

It was strange to see him without his ball cap and mesh jersey. His thinning salt-and-pepper hair was cut short to his scalp and his loose-fitting blue button up was pressed smooth and straight. He really seemed to clean up nice for a grumpy old man.

He nodded. "You know your performance Friday has really made my job hard. It'd been a heck of a lot easier if you'd have just been mediocre, or not even shown up at all."

"Probably," I agreed and then added, "but you know I couldn't do that. I want to keep playing ball."

"At what cost?" he asked. I immediately recognized the seriousness in his eyes. "Have you really thought about everything that you're going to come up against to play here? I mean, really thought about it? You will have a target on your back all season long. Everywhere you go, people are going to go out of their way to try to make you fail, or at the very least, look bad. The stuff that happened at the tryouts is

72

nothing compared to what will happen every time you step onto that field. Is it really worth it?"

I thought about what he was saying for a moment. Cade and Jeremy were really just the beginning. It was a safe bet that every high school we competed against would have a problem playing on the same field as a girl. The media would have a field day with my successes and failures. It was a tremendous amount of pressure, but I had gone through worse things. I was in a pressure cooker all last year between keeping up with school, practice, and Daddy's care. It had made me stronger, and this would too. Plus, I would get to keep playing ball, and with everything else in my life that I had given up since Daddy died, it would be worth it if I could keep something that was special to both of us.

"Yes," I answered confidently, looking him straight in the eye. "Worth every ball thrown at my head, every bruise earned from someone trying to take me out, all the name calling, ridicule, and harassment. It's all worth it, if I can still play."

He looked down and sighed heavily. "Well, we'll see if you are singing the same tune at the end of the season." He stood and started to walk away and called over his shoulder, "See you at practice tomorrow, 2:30 sharp."

For a moment, I was stunned. Did he just say what I thought he did? Did I actually make the team? I had to be sure. "Two-thirty tomorrow?" I repeated.

"Right after sixth period," he replied. "And if you expect to make the starting lineup, don't be late! That's one of my biggest pet peeves."

"You got it, Coach!" I said as the excitement at last bubbled out through my voice. "See you tomorrow! Thanks, Coach! You won't regret this!"

He waved his hand over his shoulder at my last comment and kept walking.

I felt like doing back flips! I did it!

Diamonds in the Dirt

I watched Coach Mac stroll all the way across the parking lot before I couldn't contain my excitement any longer. "Woo-hoo!" I yelled at the top of my lungs.

An elderly couple had just stepped out of the door of the church and I began apologizing profusely as I caught sight of their startled faces. "I am so sorry! It's just…wow! It's a great day, huh?"

The woman politely smiled as they started walking across the parking lot. Her husband furrowed his brow, tugging at his wife's elbow in an attempt to hustle her to the car. He was mumbling something about "crazy people at church today." I apologized again.

Soon Mary and Brian made their way out into the parking lot and I thought I would burst.

"I made it!" I shouted running over to them as soon as the doors shut behind them. "Can you believe it? I really didn't know for sure if they would be able to get past, but they did and…"

"What are you talking about, Es…I mean, Scout?" Mary asked, her irritation coming across in both her tone and the exasperation on her face.

"The baseball team, Mary! I just talked to Coach Mac! I made the team! I get to keep playing ball!"

"That's great news, Scout!" Brian returned excitedly. "Come here!" He wrapped me in a ferocious hug. "I knew you could do it, kid! I am so proud of you!"

"Thanks, Brian!" I bubbled and returned his hug. "Thank you! Thank you! Thank you so much!" I stepped back and looked at him. "I wouldn't have even gotten the chance to try out if you hadn't made it happen."

"It was nothing, Scout; you did all the work. I am so proud of you! This is such great news! We need to celebrate! Let's go to Floyd and June's for lunch!" He turned to look at Mary. "What do you think, honey?"

74

Angela Geurin

I followed his gaze, and for the first time, realized Mary was standing away from the two of us, her body language conveying her annoyance, head held high looking down over the top of her nose, her arms folded across her chest.

"Congratulations," Mary said smugly. "Sorry, but you two can go to Floyd and June's without me. I am meeting Maggie Schroeder to work on the care packages for the nursing center."

I felt completely deflated. Tears welled up in my eyes and the anger and bitterness that I had been working so hard to keep suppressed towards Mary boiled up and finally spilled over. "Is that all you can say?" I asked, the hurt coming out in my voice as I choked back a sob.

"I said congratulations; what else do you expect me to say?" she replied calmly.

"Would it kill you to pretend that you are the least bit happy for me?"

"Congratulations, Scout," she tried again, but her voice rang with sarcasm. "You got exactly what you wanted; you are just one of the guys now."

"Babe," Brian chided.

"Oh, shut up, Brian," she bit out. "You know I am right. She has no idea what she has truly gotten herself into and the fact that you helped her do this…"

"I'm not stupid! I know what I'm doing!" I screamed.

"Really!" she replied. "You weren't in the stands during the tryouts. You didn't hear the things people were saying about you. You didn't see the way the boys looked at you. It's just a silly game, for crying out loud!"

There were a million other names I could have chosen to call my sister at that moment, but I ignored them all and the word that flew out of my mouth without so much as a second thought was ugly, hurtful, and completely unladylike. For a second, I thought that maybe I had just thought it instead of really saying it out loud, but the shock that

75

registered on her face confirmed that I indeed used such a foul word to describe my sister at that moment.

"Now wait a sec, you two. This is way overboard," Brian spoke gently. "We need to just calm down. You are both too emotional right now." He reached out and stroked her shoulder and reached for my hand. "Let's take this down a notch and discuss this together in a more civilized manner."

"Forget it!" I yelled pulling my fingers out of his grasp. "I'm not talking about this with her anymore. I'm done!"

I spun on my heel and took off in a brisk walk across the parking lot towards the road.

"Scout, wait! The car is over here!" Brian was yelling and I just kept walking. "Where do you think you are going?" he shouted after me.

"Away from her!" I screamed over my shoulder.

"Come back here, Scout, don't do this!"

"No!" I returned. "I am not going anywhere near her!"

"Well, I am not chasing after you this time!"

"Good! I can find my way back to the house!"

Angrily, I swiped the tears off my cheek. At that moment, I hated Mary. I really hated her. I hated how easily she could hurt me, how with a single phrase she could turn me into a blubbering fool! How Brian could stand being married to that self-righteous monster I would never know! I listened as my short heels clicked along the sidewalk, which made me angrier because I sounded just like Mary. *Click, Clack! Click, Clack!* I groaned and started to kick off the disgusting shoes, but they were strapped to my feet.

In anger, I ripped at the straps, trying to tug my foot free from their prison, oblivious to the fact that I was being followed by a shiny black rag top. The driver called my name and I turned to peer through the windshield. Recognition hit me like a slap in the face. The driver was one of the cheerleaders from the locker room incident on Friday. This was just great! She waved as her car pulled up next to me. I rolled my eyes and started walking again.

"You need a ride somewhere?" she asked. Her blonde hair was down and loosely pinned back at the crown of her head.

"No, thank you." I closed my eyes and continued walking. Silently, I willed her to drive on, but she didn't.

"So what are you doing then?" she continued slowly.

"Walking," I seethed.

She continued creeping along next to me leaning across the passenger seat. "You know, your fixing to run out of sidewalk and Thompson Road is not the safest place to walk."

I rolled my eyes. "Thanks for your concern, but I am a big girl. I think I can handle it."

"I'm sure you can, but why don't you just let me give you a ride anyway?"

Stopping dead in my tracks, I turned to face her and yelled, "Can you not take a hint? I. Don't. Need. A. Ride!" I spoke the last sentence word by word, hoping to make my point crystal clear.

Abruptly, she put her car in park and stepped out. Leaving her door open, she stormed around the front of it. Standing at the edge of the curb, she stared up at me. "No, what you need is a friend *and* a ride. I am willing to do both." She pointed her finger at me and growled, "So get in!"

I glared at her for another minute and crossed my arms over my chest, contemplating what to do and say. I never really had a lot of friends in KC and I definitely didn't have people lining up to be my friend in Booneville. So why was she trying so hard to be my friend? Was it out of pity? At the moment, did I really care *why* when all I wanted was to put as much distance as I could between myself and Mary?

"OK," I finally said and opened the passenger door.

She didn't say anything in reply, just smiled, got in and we took off.

Her car was fully loaded with black leather seats and it still had that brand new smell. From her rearview mirror hung a crystal angel pendant that painted flickering rainbows across the gray dashboard as it reflected the sun. A circular rainbow reflected just above her head and shown like a halo. Light seemed to surround her, making her glow like an angel. *A guardian angel,* I thought. How strange!

Her hand shifted gears smoothly as we turned onto the main road, headed away from town. The quiet hum of the engine filled the car as we sat in silence. I could feel the tension drain from me the further away we drove and I leaned my head back against the headrest and closed my eyes.

At last she broke the silence. "I don't know if you remember me specifically, but we kind of met Friday. I'm Bonnie." She slid me a sideways glance and rolled her eyes. I didn't say anything. "Yes, I know I am a cheerleader, but I really try hard not to act like it."

I grinned.

"Anyway, don't worry about your sister or brother-in-law coming after you," she continued. "I told Mr. and Mrs. Z. I would get you back home before dark."

"They sent you after me?" I questioned.

"No, but I couldn't help but overhear the argument, and uh, since I figured you needed some breathing room and the last thing you wanted was to be chased down and dragged to their car; I volunteered to give you a ride."

"How noble of you," I responded sarcastically and immediately regretted the remark. Hoping she wouldn't be offended, I quickly asked, "How do you know Brian and Mary anyway?"

"Well, my dad is Mr. Z's golfing buddy and Ms. Z plays Bunco with my mom. I know it might be hard for you to believe, but they are the nicest people in town. They are both so kind and would do absolutely anything to help out a friend. They have done a great deal to help my family." She paused for a moment and then added, "I imagine, though, it's hard to see them that way given your circumstances." She sat there quiet for a moment, seeming to gauge whether or not I would continue this line of conversation, but when I didn't, she changed the subject. "Congratulations, by the way. Maybe with you, they can finally have a winning season. I just loved watching you show up all of those little boys at the tryouts."

"You watched the tryouts?" I asked.

"Well, in between toe touches and heel stretches, yeah," she responded with a smile. "I saw your homerun! That was such a bomb! Oh and the way you took Jeremy's slider right back up the middle, priceless! Coach Mac would have had to fire himself if he passed up on you. There is no one on the team that can hit like that."

"Thanks." I looked at her curiously. "For a cheerleader, you sure know a lot about baseball."

"It's an American pastime, baby! I bet you're a KC fan."

"Heck no! St Louis!"

She slapped the steering wheel. "That really stinks, because I was just starting to like you."

"So you're a Houston fan, huh?"

"Huge! My whole family has followed them for generations. We even have a skybox at the dome!"

"That does stink, because we are *so* winning the division this year."

"Yeah, we'll see about that." We both laughed.

Chapter Five: Searching for Diamonds

There are some people who see a need and walk away, assuming someone else will take care of it; others will write a check; and still others will talk and think about all the ways to fix it. But there are those rare people who see a need and just meet it. Bonnie was one of those people.

She recognized the pain I tried so hard to hide. She also recognized the bitterness that blinded me from goodness. Most importantly, she recognized my loneliness, and the pride that kept me isolated. She knew I needed a friend and chose to be my friend.

We drove out to Frosty's and ate lunch. She didn't ask me a lot of questions or try to get me to talk about my feelings or say things that would dredge up a lot of pain. She talked and told me about the town, about school, about her friends. We even met some of those friends, who were surprisingly fun to be with.

Then we drove around town. She highlighted the hangouts as well as the places to avoid. I learned that Frosty's was the weekend hangout, and on Friday nights you could get free refills on soda with a student ID. She told me that Floyd and June's was world famous for their fried chicken, and that the governor of Texas made a stop every time his travels led him to the Houston area. Neighboring Crescent had a drive-in movie theater, but there were only two screens, so most of the box office hits never showed on their opening day. I learned the beach was just an hour south, and at least every other weekend a big group would make a trip. After a while, Booneville didn't seem so bad.

Bonnie was just a good *friend.* When she finally pulled up to Brian and Mary's, it was 6:00 and I couldn't believe how fast the afternoon had passed.

"There, just as promised. Back before dark," she announced as she pulled to a stop in front of the driveway.

I looked up at the house, dreading the lecture I was sure to receive upon walking through the door. As if she recognized my distress, Bonnie reached over and laid her hand on my shoulder. "Don't worry about it, Scout. I am sure she is over it by now."

"I seriously doubt that."

"You want me to come in with you?" she offered.

I turned and looked at her, stunned and grateful at the same time. "I wouldn't wish Mary's wrath on anyone, but thanks. You know, and thanks for giving me a ride."

"Sure, any time," she replied squeezing my shoulder before dropping her hand. "Say, do you need a ride to school tomorrow?"

Since Mary wouldn't let me ride my motorcycle to school, I was stuck with her taking me or trying to catch the bus. Neither option was very appealing. "Yeah, that'd be great," I replied. "I mean, if you don't mind."

"No, I don't mind at all," she answered. "I will pick you up around 7:30."

"Great! Oh, wait! I have baseball practice afterschool."

"Don't worry about it," she replied. "I have cheerleading practice and I can wait until you're finished and take you home."

"Perfect."

"I'll see you tomorrow."

"See you!"

Diamonds in the Dirt

I opened the door and stepped onto the driveway. She drove off and waved good-bye. Bonnie was such a thoughtful person, being around her almost made me feel guilty. She had gone out of her way today to distract me from my problems, not trying to make me talk about my family, my dad, or anything. Yet at the same time, when I did share some of my frustrations with her, she didn't lecture me or counsel me—she just listened. More than anything, she showed me how to start living this new life in Booneville. She was a friend and at this time in my life, I really needed one.

I returned her wave and sighed. The house loomed before me and the weight that had been lifted from our afternoon getaway returned. I was sure that Mary and Brian would both lecture me. They would probably sell my motorcycle or, at the very least, take away my keys for the next month. Maybe if I went in through the back door off the living room, I could sneak into my room before they realized I was home.

I crept along the porch until I reached the back patio door. The hot tub was bubbling and the top was off, but I looked around and didn't see anyone. By the looks of it, Brian or Mary were about to take a soak, so I quickened my steps toward the door and turned the handle with hopes of avoiding them all together. Quietly, I tiptoed inside and gently closed the door behind me. The lights were off with only the end table lamp casting a soft glow across the sofa and the bare shoulders of...Oh, my stars!

My face flushed in embarrassment as a small gasp escaped my lips. I closed my eyes tight against the sight of Brian and Mary enjoying each other's company on the brown leather sofa that I had watched cartoons on yesterday. *Ugh!* I wanted to poke out my eyes! In a panic, I tried to scoot out the room undetected, but as I passed the back of the couch, I glimpsed a blonde head pop up and then locked eyes with Brian. His eyes were wide at first, but then he flashed a smirk in amusement as he smoothed out his hair.

"You're back early," he chuckled. I heard Mary gasp and then the subsequent rustle against the leather couch as she tried desperately to straighten her bikini top.

Still unable to speak, I backed out of the room. It was a little unnerving the way Brian just grinned and reached for his swim trunks. For the life of me, I couldn't figure out what he found so amusing about this. It was absolutely the most embarrassing moment of my life. I whispered an apology.

"Wait a second, Scout," he said.

Mary's head finally popped up from behind the sofa and she shifted her weight around to face me, trying to fasten the back of her bikini top. Brian reached around her and snapped the clasp in place as she swatted at his hands.

I don't think I'll be able to sit on that sofa ever again.

"No, no, that's ok," I stammered. "I'll go upstairs so that you can, uh, uh…"

"Jump in the hot tub," he said, still wearing his silly grin.

Mary looked horrified and slapped his shoulder as he let out a yelp, but continued to laugh. "This is not funny!" she growled and then looked at me. Her cheeks were flushed and her lips swollen. "Scout, I am so sorry you walked in on this, but when two people are married…"

Seeing where this conversation was headed, I threw my hands up for her to stop and pleaded, "No need to explain! It was my mistake!"

She didn't stop. "When two people are married and love each other, they will express their love…"

"Mary!" I screamed in desperation. "Please if you have any decency left in you, please, I beg you to stop. Daddy beat you to the sex talk years ago and I don't need a refresher course from you! This is bad enough as it is!"

"See, what did I tell you, babe?" Brian reassured her and nuzzled her neck, "She is more mature than you think."

I averted my eyes and let out a groan. "Look, I am really sorry, but I am going to go upstairs. Don't worry about dinner, I have completely lost my appetite after this and…"

Mary nudged Brian in the ribs and he suddenly stood. "Wait a second Scout. We want to talk to you. About some other things, not about this." He laughed softly. "Come on, sit."

I groaned. This was exactly what I hoped to avoid. Another dreaded lecture about what I should and should not say or do. I tried one more time. "Wow, you know, I think I will take a rain check. You know, you guys are busy, and look at the time! I probably should be headed to bed anyway," I reasoned. "I got a big day ahead of me with school starting and all. Maybe we could do this another day."

I turned to leave, but stopped dead in my tracks when I heard him call me back with more force and authority than I think I had ever heard from him. I met his eyes, debating whether or not to head upstairs anyway or run back out the door. He motioned me into the chair adjacent to the sofa. I hesitated and then slowly walked to the chair and sat down, wrapping my legs in a tight hug.

He sat down and draped an arm across Mary's shoulders. Her swimsuit completely restored to its appropriate place, she snuggled into his side and drew her legs under the afghan that was lying on the arm of the sofa.

"Your sister and I have been talking about the way we have handled this whole situation; and even though we have tried to give you the things you need and make this as comfortable a transition as we could, we never took the time to talk to you and find out what you really needed. We are really sorry about that." Mary nodded in agreement and he hugged her a little closer. "Neither of us knows anything about raising kids, let alone a teenager, and so we are going to screw up…a lot. But we just want you to know that we are not your enemy. We love you and we want you to be happy, given what this past year has been like for you."

Mary spoke after a moment. "Scout, honey, I want you to be able to talk to me without it blowing up into a huge fight, but at the same time please understand that I don't know you as well as daddy and most of what I know about you was from what daddy told me, because you don't talk to me."

"I don't talk to you because..." then I stopped as I recognized my defensiveness.

"I don't listen," she finished. "I'm listening now. Would you talk to me now?" She looked at Brian and then back at me. "Would you talk to us?"

I stared at the ceiling. I was a firm believer that talking was completely overrated as a means of problem solving. But I realized after spending the day with Bonnie, I had at least three years left in this town and I could look at it as a prison sentence and just get by, or I could actually make the most of my time. I could have the best life I could while I was stuck in this place.

"OK," I sighed. "Where do you think we should start?"

After my heart-to-heart with Brian and Mary last night, which lasted until nearly a quarter to midnight, I discovered, among many other things, that anger and bitterness fueled my attitude, not Mary. I also discovered I spent a lot of wasted energy keeping tabs on all the wrongs in my life. If I was ever going to be happy again, I had to change my attitude. So I resigned myself to finding the positive in every negative thought that crossed my mind, the blessings hidden among the strife. Mary said that Momma called it looking for the diamonds in the dirt, and that's what I found on my first day at my new school, diamonds everywhere.

The first diamond was Bonnie. I didn't have any classes with her, but she showed up outside of every one of mine and walked with me to my next period. Bonnie seemed to know everybody in the school and everyone seemed to love her. She made sure that she introduced me to

Diamonds in the Dirt

someone in all of my classes and when anyone tried to say something about baseball or my dad, she would swoop in and change the subject without missing a beat.

I was disappointed when I found out we had different lunch periods, but Bonnie had that taken care of too. She hooked me up with Rachel, whom I had met the day before at Frosty's. Rachel and I ate lunch with her boyfriend, Jose Medrano, who at long last had made the baseball team, which meant I had at least one ally this season. So I had a teammate that actually respected me: diamond number two.

Diamond number three was that I only had crossed paths with Cade and his goon squad once today. It was just after fifth period. He knocked my books out of my hand and as I bent down to pick them up, he not only enjoyed the view, but pinched my backside, which made me jump and drop my books again. Everyone, of course, had a laugh at my expense, including, to my dismay, Kiley and two of her friends. It was hard to find anything positive to say about Cade except that, at least, we didn't have any classes together. He was definitely going to be a thorn in my side and it would take every ounce of will power to keep from causing him great physical harm.

It was humid and the sun blazed down upon my back as I ran from the athletic building to the baseball stadium. It felt like July, not January, but I guess that was the KC in me. In KC we wouldn't have an outdoor practice for another two months because of the snowy cold weather. Looking up at the brilliant blue sky above me, I made a check mark in my head. There's another diamond. Year round baseball was definitely better here than in Kansas City.

With my bag slung over my shoulder, I quickly braided my hair and pulled it through my cap as I jogged through the gate and then over to the third base dugout. I looked at my watch: 2:25 just barely on time. My sixth period geometry class lasted right up to the bell at 2:05, which meant I had a long trek from the high school to the athletic building to change for practice and not a minute to spare. Bonnie had warned me that Mr. Tate would not allow anyone to leave early. So I got all of my things from my locker before sixth period. Otherwise I would've started out the season on the wrong foot for sure.

I spotted Jose in left field with some of the other players. Coach Mac was talking to a man in a black suit that looked like an older version of Cade, so I could only assume that Mr. Suit was in fact Mayor Traylor. As typical of assistants, Coach Haywood was doing all the grunt work—moving screens into place on the infield, setting out buckets of balls. Bet he chalked the field too.

Grabbing my glove, I headed out to join my team. They were sizing me up as I approached. I could feel it. Everyone who hadn't made it to the tryouts was checking me out to see if I was legit. I couldn't blame them; I was doing the same thing to them. This was my team after all.

They were a mix of sizes and shapes, but for the most part they were all big and athletic. One was rail thin and looked like I could snap his arm like a chicken wing. Then, of course, stocky Bobby Ray, Cade's fellow goon, looked like he needed to lay off the doughnuts. Their faces were all filled with the same expression, a mixture of resentment and anger. Everyone but Cade, that is—that little sleaze leered at me as I approached, elbowing Bobby Ray as he made some disgusting comment, I am sure. I took a deep breath and blew it all away as I met up with Jose.

"Scout!" Jose slapped my shoulder as I jogged up. "Glad you got here on time! When you said you had geometry with Old Man Tate sixth period, I was afraid you would be late."

"No kidding!" I replied. "Bonnie warned me. That man does not shut up!"

"You nervous?" he asked.

"Are you?"

"Maybe a little," he laughed. "You didn't answer my question."

"I know." I smiled and started stretching.

Diamonds in the Dirt

Right at 2:30, Coach Mac whistled and our team captains, Kevin, a tall dark-haired boy with a barrel chest, and Bull, a giant thick boy with a shaved head, gathered the team together for stretches. Jose and I had decided at lunch that we should stick together since we were in the same boat. So we paired up on everything we could. I trusted him to treat me like any other ball player, and he trusted me to treat him like one of the guys and not some "poor dumb immigrant," which had been his experience since moving here four years ago.

As we finished warming up and headed for water, Coach Haywood caught me half way to the table. "Scout," he called. "You are coming with me. Grab your gear."

"Sure thing, Coach," I answered.

"Good luck," Jose whispered as I moved passed him to get my gear. I nodded my thanks and he handed me a cup of water.

Coach Haywood set out in a jog and I downed my drink and followed, matching him stride for stride. We reached the outfield wall and he grabbed a handle that was completely hidden behind the padding. He pulled and the camouflaged gate leading to the bull pen opened as he ushered me inside. I walked in and dropped my bag by the fence.

Amazing! Playing for the boys definitely had its advantages. In KC, our bull pen was rocky, full of divots, and so uneven that it was hard to keep balanced in a squat. This was nicer than anything I had ever played on before. There were two pitching lanes spaced about ten feet apart. The mounds and home plate were made up of smooth dirt with perfectly cut grass in between. Benches lined the back fence. Beyond the two home plates, just on the other side of the fence, stood two batting cages that I was noticing for the first time today. Protective screens, the same Bearcat green as everything else in the stadium, lined all four sides of the bull pen, slightly obscuring the views beyond the fences. I had to hand it to Cade. His daddy sure knew how to build a ball park. I made another mental check mark under Booneville: diamond number five.

I realized the bull pen was void of other players, but I assumed I was about to meet one of the team's pitchers. I looked expectantly at Coach Haywood. He was looking back at the field with a scowl.

"That knucklehead!" He muttered and then turned back to me. "Go ahead and get your gear on," he said. "I'll be right back." With that he let the gate shut behind him.

I started to put on my gear. Strapping my shin guards on my legs, I reached for my chest protector and pulled it over my head, when I heard Coach Haywood yelling on the other side of the fence.

"Let me explain something to you, Benjamin Acer," he was saying. "You may be the best pitcher in this division, but you play for me and you will throw to whoever I put behind that plate!"

"Coach, you can't be serious! That girl can't hang with my fastball! I'll break her hand!" Benjamin Acer argued.

Well, I'll show him! Who does he think he is anyway?

"That girl is your new catcher and she is the best that I have seen in over a decade," Coach Haywood returned.

I swelled with pride at the compliment. Suddenly, the gate flew open and Coach Haywood leaned on it, holding it in place.

"But coach…" the boy started.

"Remember even the best can be replaced!" Coach Haywood cut him off. "Get in there and start pitching!"

I watched as a boy about my height, with sandy blonde hair that stuck out the sides of his ball cap in small little wisps of curls, stepped through the opening. He had long, lean, well-defined arms, broad shoulders that angled down into a narrow waist, and even longer and more defined legs. He had a round face and as he finally looked at me, I was momentarily taken aback by the intense color of his eyes. They were like blue ice. Although, they were filled with fire and anger at the moment, I found it difficult to pull my gaze away.

"Scout Rose, meet Benjamin Acer," Coach Haywood said as I directed my eyes back to him.

Shaking my head clear, I offered my free hand. "Nice to meet you," I responded. Benjamin Acer ignored my outstretched hand and looked away in disgust. So I pretended to shake his hand. "Nice to meet you too!"

"Shut up!" He mumbled. Coach Haywood glowered in his direction.

"Scout, Acer here is…well, our ace. You are going to be catching him all season," Coach Haywood explained.

"You got it, Coach," I replied. "What are we working on, anyway?"

"Everything," he replied.

I wasn't sure I liked the sound of that, but Coach did say he was the team ace. He couldn't be that bad, but in my experience, when a pitcher needed to work on everything, it usually meant I was in for a rough practice.

"He has a complete arsenal: fastball, curveball, slider, and changeup. You name it, he throws it," he continued. "Get to know his pitches. Then, maybe you can start helping him with his mental game."

"Mental game?" we asked in unison.

Coach Haywood laughed. "See you two are on the same page already! I told Mac this would be a great battery." He turned and headed to the gate. "I will be with the outfield. Scout, you can hit when you two finish."

When we were alone, I turned and headed to the plate, putting my helmet and facemask on as I crouched down. I waited for him to step up onto the mound, but he just stood there, staring at the ground. "Hey!" I hollered. "You want to get started, or are we just gonna watch the grass grow?" He stomped his way up to the mound and kicked the dirt around, but didn't speak a word. "What do you want to work on first?" I asked.

No response.

He just continued sulking, digging his cleats into the ground in front of the pitching rubber. I waited another moment and repeated the question.

Still no response. More digging in the dirt.

Exasperated, I threw my hands up and yelled, "You know what, meat, just give me your best shot!"

Without any warning, he leaped off the mound and threw the ball. It was lightening fast, but completely wild. His mechanics forgotten and his body out of control, he fell off the mound and caught himself before he hit the ground, a contortion of legs and arms. I watched the ball sail higher and higher, so high in fact that I didn't even bother jumping for it. I leaned my head back and watched as it cleared not only the bull pen fence, but the batting cage, and then heard a loud "ping" as it hit the light pole and bounced back onto the roof.

"Wow," I said. "Now I see what Coach Haywood meant about your mental game. You got another ball?"

"Yeah, I've got two!" he yelled. "How many do you have?"

It took a moment to realize what he was implying and I shook my head in frustration. Enough with the verbal sparring! This was getting old, and I was trying hard not to be negative. I bit back the retort that I wanted to make and instead looked around for another ball. I spotted a pile against the fence and nonchalantly tossed one to him.

In one quick motion, he caught it and threw it back at me. He was hoping to catch me off guard, but reflexively, I reached up with my bare hand and caught the ball before it could hit my right temple. I spun the ball and examined it. "Something wrong with this one?"

His azure eyes were wide with shock and his jaw hung open. Casually, I whipped the ball toward his groin and he barely had enough time to get his glove in position to catch it. "You know, if I didn't know any better, I would think you were trying to knock me out," I said. He raised an eyebrow and I couldn't stop my alligator mouth this time. I gestured to his groin. "You and your two balls had best remember that unlike you, I am deadly accurate and can hit any target, at any distance, at any speed, anytime I want to. Throw at my head again and you'll be choking on those balls of yours!"

I walked to the plate and crouched again, sliding my mask down over my face. I punched my glove a couple of times. "Now that introductions are over, why don't we start practicing?"

"Two more and then get out of here, Scout," Coach Mac instructed behind the pitching fence as he stretched his arm.

I nodded and tightened the grip on my bat as I waited on his next delivery. It was a screwball and I got fooled as the ball dove low. I tried to get my hands through the ball, but wasn't quick enough to get a good piece. My follow through made up the difference and I muscled it down the third baseline.

"Nice screwball, Coach," I complimented.

"Flattery will get you nowhere, Scout," he said seriously as he threw his final offering.

He was right; the next ball he threw was high and tight and I couldn't get my hands completely inside of the pitch, but sent it screaming back up the middle. It ricocheted off of the protective net and rolled back towards home plate. Reflexively, Coach Mac jumped back, but tried to play it off as he strolled off of the field.

"You're done!" he yelled. "Bring 'em in, Ed!"

The team met in front of the third base dugout and took a knee as the coaches reviewed the first practice of the season. Benjamin Acer was kneeling directly in front of me, his eyes focused on the coaches, but still luring me into their depths. There was something familiar about him, but as I went over in my mind all the people I had met at school today, I knew he wasn't one of them. I just couldn't figure out what was so familiar.

I shut my eyes, but couldn't shut him out of my mind. He was a jerk, but Acer was a phenomenal pitcher. His movement on the ball was deadly and his fastball was like a bullet shooting out of his hand, but he was easily frustrated. When he got distracted and lost his focus, his pitches were all over the place. I had taken two off my left bicep after they hit the front of the plate and my legs were sore from lunging out to snag pitches that would have been behind a batter.

He was still not happy with me as his battery mate, and made it clear every time he opened his mouth. Apparently, he had an alligator mouth too. He started referring to me as "Amazon" halfway through practice, so I started calling him "Postal" when he lost his temper. No, he was definitely not happy with me as his catcher, but I was pretty sure that I showed him I could hang with his fastball.

As the circle dispersed, I turned to see Bonnie, sitting in the stands. She waved and I walked over to the backstop. She was wearing green shorts and a tank top with her curly blonde hair pulled into a high pony tail. Her smile was big and bright as she stood up from the bench and met me at the fence.

"Hey girl!" she said. "Good practice today."

"Thanks," I answered.

"You ought to open up your stance if you're going to crowd the plate," she said. "Coach Mac was eating you up on the inside corner."

"Thanks, I'll have to try that tomorrow," I replied. "Hey, I left my backpack in the locker room. I need to go get it, before we go."

"Just meet me at the car. I parked by the athletic building." She stood and waved. "See you in a few!"

I walked into the dugout, pulled out my bag and started repacking all of my gear. Out of the corner of my eye, I spotted Postal, taking off his cleats just down the bench from me. He looked up and our eyes met for a brief awkward moment before I quickly averted my gaze. When I looked back in his direction again, Jose stepped into my view, putting a cleat on the bench next to me. Postal got up and headed out of the dugout as Jose whispered, "So, how'd it go with Acer?"

"Who?" I asked as I followed Postal out of the dugout with my eyes.

"Benjamin Acer, the ace pitcher. Everyone calls him by his last name: Acer, or Ace," he explained. "Ace is the perfect baseball name, right?"

"Oh, you mean Postal," I smirked. "You know, same old thing. Tried to take my head off, so I had to show him who was boss. After that, he settled down and actually threw pretty well. He has a wicked curveball. How'd you do?" I unlaced my cleats and slid my feet into my running shoes.

He laughed. "You know, same old thing. Spent most of infield practice playing backup to Cade at second base, had to wipe the grin off his face with my cleats," he mocked my nonchalant tone of voice.

I laughed and gave him a high five. "Sounds like we both had a good day."

"Yeah, can't wait to do it all again tomorrow." He rolled his eyes and followed me out of the dugout and through the gate. "I'll be lucky to get any PT this season, but at least I made the team. You need a ride home? Rach is waiting for me. I know she wouldn't mind."

"Nah, Bonnie's waiting on me. Thanks for the offer."

"OK," he answered. "See you tomorrow at lunch, right?"

"You bring those homemade tortillas you promised and I'll be there."

He laughed. "You got it!"

On my way to the locker room, I thought about Bonnie's advice. Opening my stance would give my hands more room. It made sense. I would definitely try it out tomorrow. If only she could tell me how to deal with Acer. He was such a jerk and unless I could convince him to work with me and not against me, this would be a long season.

I scooped up my backpack and hustled through the winding hallways of the athletic building. Bonnie said to meet her in the parking lot, but I didn't spot her car right away. I scanned in all directions as I walked through the lot, and came up short when I finally spotted her.

To my surprise, Bonnie was not alone. She sat on the hood of her car, and next to her, with his arm draped around her shoulders, snuggling her into his side was a familiar sandy blonde curly-headed boy, Benjamin Acer.

I was momentarily frozen in place.

Bonnie had never mentioned she had a boyfriend. I'm sure of it. Why wouldn't she tell me she was seeing the star pitcher of the team? Surely, she had plenty of opportunities to introduce us. Maybe she knew we would not get along because he didn't think I should play on his team or maybe she thought I might be jealous? Whatever the reason, I really didn't want to deal with Acer anymore today. I'd had all I wanted of him.

Rooted in the same spot, I debated whether or not to run in the opposite direction or just suck it up and deal with the fact that "Postal" was dating my friend. Before I could decide what to do, Bonnie spotted me and waved. Acer looked up and shook his head, disengaging his arm from her shoulders and then slid off the car. Still unsure of how to react, I casually walked over to Bonnie.

"Hey girl!" she called.

"Hey yourself," I returned softly. I looked from her to Acer. "I am sorry; I didn't mean to interrupt you two."

"No, don't worry about it," she waved off my comment. "Bennie was just telling me about his new catcher." She winked.

"Bennie?" I asked with a laugh. "Oh, you mean *Postal*. Did he tell you that he threw at my head when I wasn't looking?"

She smacked the back of his head with her hand and glared at him. "No, he left that part out!"

"Ow!" he hollered. "Ask Amazon here, where she tried to hit me!"

"You probably deserved it, you big bully!" she scolded and then playfully patted his cheek. He hugged her and tugged on her pony tail.

After a moment, I decided to ask, "How long have you two been together?"

They both looked at me curiously, their heads tilting in the same manner. I noticed for the first time other similarities. They had the same curly sandy blonde hair and matching azure eyes.

"Together?" they both said and looked at each other quizzically. There was a moment of silence before they both burst into laughter.

"Wait, you think we are like *together,* together? " Bonnie asked, holding her sides as her shoulders shook with laughter.

"Gross!" Acer feigned disgust. They looked at each other again and laughed some more.

"He's not my boyfriend, Scout!" Bonnie held her sides and slapped Acer on the back. "He's my brother!" She laughed again.

"Twin brother actually," he added.

I slapped my forehead. Acer was Bonnie's twin brother! Wow! This was just great! My friend's twin brother was the cocky, hot-tempered, ace pitcher who I would catch for all season long.

Where is the diamond in this pile of dirt?

Chapter Six: Opening Day

The following weeks flew by and before I could blink it was the end of February. It had been nearly two months since I moved to Booneville and as much as I hated to admit, my life was pretty routine now. School was getting easier; Mary and I were getting along; baseball was tough, but not any worse than expected. So why couldn't I sleep? I couldn't remember the last time I had a decent night's sleep.

My mind raced for hours all night long and to make matters worse, it was the day of our first game. I needed to be refreshed and ready to go, but sleep never came. My eyes were wide open at 4:30 in the morning, and after staring at the dark ceiling above my bed for half an hour, I gave up and went for a run.

With nothing to listen to but the rhythmic pounding of my shoes hitting the pavement, I turned my attention to my inner voice and reflected on the past few weeks. Bonnie's advice on opening my stance worked, making me the most consistent hitter on the team. Surely Coach Mac would put me in the starting lineup today, but it was hard to tell. Some days I felt like he really saw me as a ball player, and other days he treated me like a nuisance. Cade's constant harassment and Acer's temper tantrums didn't really help with that. One thing about Coach Mac, though, was he wanted to win, especially this year with all his eggs in *my* basket.

The last couple of practices, the team had really come together. The infield was looking strong. The offense was showing improvements, and the pitchers well, they were getting there. Acer and I continued to butt heads, but at least he hadn't *thrown* at my head in over a week. So I had some hope. It didn't happen as often as it should, but when he focused, he was almost untouchable. I think he could take on any team in the state and shut them down, but most of the time, he was still battling his temper.

During yesterday's inner squad scrimmage, he went postal over his curveball. It was flat and getting crushed. At first he blamed the ball, so we changed balls, but then he blamed the mound and said there was a hole he kept stepping in that threw off his timing, and after we filled in the *imaginary* hole, he blamed me and said that I was giving it away by my position behind the plate.

Yeah right!

"It's fat!" I told him. "You might as well put a big sign on it that says 'Express Airmail!'" He needed to throw a different pitch because it wasn't working, but he wouldn't listen.

"Just waddle on back behind the plate, Amazon!" he shouted and then threw his rosin bag at me. I caught it in my glove, bit back the retort that came to mind, and tossed it back behind the mound.

"Fine, throw what you want! What do I know anyway?"

I called every pitch in his arsenal, except the curveball and he had refused every one. He wouldn't give it up and so finally, I called what he wanted, shook my head and watched another ball blast off into the outfield for a double. As the next batter stepped up to the plate, I tried to call another pitch and he shook me off again. This time he threw his curve and overcorrected. The ball ended up so far outside I had to dive and knock it down.

I went out to the mound, fuming and wondering if Coach Haywood would do anything, but when I glanced at him, he was in deep conversation with Coach Mac. If they were aware of the situation taking place at the pitcher's mound, they didn't let on. I was on my own.

Halfway there, Acer turned and yelled, "Not you again! I thought I told you to stay behind the plate, Amazon!"

I kept coming, dropping my helmet to the ground. "Throw what I tell you, Postal!"

"Get off my mound!" He shouted and then showered me in dirt with his left foot before he spit on my shoe.

That had done it! Enough was enough!

Much like at my daddy's funeral, I snapped, and before he could blink, I threw down my glove and charged. He didn't get a chance to comprehend what was happening. I tackled him to the ground and straddled his chest. He pushed against my chest protector, but I clearly had the upper hand as I picked up his rosin bag and shoved it into his face.

"You spit on my shoe, you disgusting pig!" I shouted.

Acer grabbed at my wrists but I broke his hold every time. His eyes were open wide in shock at my outburst. The drama lasted only a matter of seconds though, before Kevin, the first baseman, grabbed me by the back of my chest protector and jerked me to my feet. He stood between the two of us, and I held my hands up in innocence. The coaches ran to the mound and I knew it was over. They were going to kick me off the team. Hanging my head down, I stopped struggling and fought back the tears in the back of my throat. In frustration, I threw the rosin bag next to Acer's head and backed away.

Bull, our third baseman, a smile playing at the corner of his lips, pulled Acer to his feet and handed him his glove.

"Can you believe this *Amazon*?" Acer said sarcastically.

Then to my chagrin, Kevin turned on Acer. "Shut your mouth and throw what your catcher tells you to throw, Ace!" he returned. "And her name is Scout!"

I couldn't believe he stood up for me. My face must have shown my appreciation because Acer turned an icy glare my way, and then started towards me, but Bull pushed him back. Kevin placed a hand on my shoulder and nodded.

Finally, Acer jerked his arm away from Bull and walked away. The coaches stepped in at that point and assigned Acer and I extra running after practice. Thank goodness, they didn't kick me off the team, though.

"Show's over!" Coach Mac shouted. "Let's get back to work! Next batter!"

Kevin bent down and picked up my glove. He handed it to me, but didn't say a word. Bull handed me my helmet and patted my shoulder. It was clear. Our team captains had my back, even when it came down to our own pitching staff. I was really a part of the team now.

The world started to wake up and the moon faded, giving way to early dawn as the first rays of sunlight stretched across the horizon. I rounded the corner and sprinted towards the house. I had to figure out a way to convince Ace to trust me, but nothing I said seemed to work. His temper was bad and I seemed to bring it out of him without even trying. Bonnie was such a good friend, I didn't want to put her in the middle of our problems, but after that scrimmage yesterday, I had to talk to her about his temper, see if there was anything she could do or say to help us get along.

Finished with my run, I showered, dressed, and ate breakfast before heading to the porch to wait for Bonnie. It was 7:20, and Brian and Mary both had left the house early. I was about to open the front door, when the phone rang. Sprinting back into the kitchen, I picked it up on the third ring.

"Hello."

"Hello, Scout?" a woman asked.

I didn't recognize her voice, but she spoke in a thick west Texas drawl. It was so stereotypical Texas that I felt like I was in a western movie.

"This is she," I stifled a giggle.

"Oh, good, this is Beverly Acer, Bonnie's mom," she said, her voice as sweet as sugar. "I'm glad I was able to get a hold of you, hon. Bonnie is ill and won't make it to school today."

"I'm sorry to hear that, Ms. Acer. Does she have the flu or something?"

"No, no, nothing like that, hon; don't you worry about catching what she's got," her tone was strange. I started to tell her that I wasn't concerned about her being contagious, but she cut me off. "Bonnie told me that Mary is taking classes now, so I'm sending Benjamin to pick you up and get you to school."

I didn't want to ride to school with Postal! Especially on a morning like this when my nerves and lack of sleep would get in the way. It wasn't so much riding to school with him that bothered me as it was the *alone* part. Being around him was an emotional drain and we still needed a referee most of the time. With our first game this afternoon, I didn't want to risk a blow up. The less opportunity we had to get on each other's nerves before the game, the better off we would be.

"That's okay, Ms. Acer; Mary hasn't left yet," I lied. "I'll just catch a ride with her."

"Good. Tell her I appreciate her understanding."

"I will. Tell Bonnie I hope she feels better."

"I will. Take care now. Bye, hon."

"Bye."

I slammed the receiver down in frustration. Why did I just lie like that? It was too late to catch the bus and I couldn't just skip school today or else I couldn't play in this afternoon's game. I paced back and forth thinking of my options, cursing Postal and the emotional roller coaster ride he sent me on every time we were together.

I guess I was walking the five miles to school, unless...I did have my motorcycle parked in the garage. Mary took my keys the last time I got caught sneaking out for a ride, but I bet Brian would help me, given the circumstances. Growing up with a single parent I never had the opportunity to play one over the other, and even though I felt a twinge of guilt, I went ahead and tried my hand at parent manipulation.

I picked up the receiver and dialed Brian's office, crossing my fingers that he would pick up. As luck would have it, he answered on the second ring. Quickly, I explained the situation and he told me where to find the keys.

"Don't worry about Mary. I will call her and smooth it over," he said. "We can't have you walking to school and you can't stay home and miss opening day. I think this qualifies as an emergency, right? Wasn't that one of her conditions?"

"Yes, most definitely an emergency," I chuckled.

"Good, it should be an open-and-shut case then."

"I love it! You can argue anything!"

"That's why I do what I do," he said, the smirk coming through clearly in his voice. "Good luck this afternoon, and please don't do anything that will make me regret this, Scout."

I thanked him one last time and retrieved my keys. Hustling through the house, I locked things up and then sprinted to the detached garage where my hog awaited. With sweet anticipation I watched the garage door lift inch by inch, slowly revealing my 1971 classic motorcycle. I loved my hog and it was absolute torture that Mary wouldn't let me ride it.

Besides God, Daddy had two passions in his life: baseball and classic motorcycles. Although Danny Joe was Daddy's usual partner in crime when it came to restorations, at the time he found these two gems, a 1971 special and a 1950 classic, Danny Joe was too busy cleaning up his life to help. So he recruited me.

We spent two years working on those beauties. By the time we were finished, both were restored to about eighty-five percent original. It was a huge accomplishment, and when he tossed me the keys and told me the bike was mine as soon as I got a license, I was shocked.

Angela Geurin

Looking back, I realized it was a once-in-a-lifetime experience that I probably would never attempt again. I still don't know the first thing about engines, carburetors, or transmissions. I couldn't tell you how to rebuild an engine or attach a fork and suspension like Danny Joe, but I knew every inch of this baby by heart. I don't think I could ever let it go.

I smiled and felt a tear slide down my cheek remembering our time together in daddy's workshop. He was the patient teacher and I was the willing student. It was his last project before his cancer came back. I wiped away another tear, but smiled as I gazed upon my baby, Angelfire.

My fingers trailed down the chrome handles, grazing over the red-orange script that exploded across the side of the purple gas tank. Daddy had a habit of naming all of his hogs and Angelfire was the name he chose for mine. I caressed the black leather seat and reached for my helmet.

"Hello, baby," I said seductively. "Miss me?" Shouldering my backpack, I shook my hair back and donned my purple helmet.

Grinning like a Cheshire cat, I straddled the seat, balancing my weight, and in one quick motion, popped the clutch and turned the engine over. Gently, I tiptoed the bike out of the garage and punched the opener before shoving it in the left saddlebag. I gave Angelfire the gas, felt the deep rumble all the way into my chest, and heard the low drumming sound of an engine that could only be a classic. Reveling in the feel of power beneath me, I adjusted the mirrors and, with a rebel yell, took off hard and fast.

As I pulled into the parking lot at school, my fellow students gathered in the front entrance before first bell. I headed to the back lot and turned down the last row when I was nearly sideswiped by my favorite team mate, Cade, in his silver sports car. He smirked and whipped into a spot. Just one time I would love to wipe that look off of his face! I had my visor down, so there was no way he knew it was me, but when he did realize, I was sure he would go out of his way to rub it in.

I slid to a stop in the space furthest away from the crowd, but hesitated to take off my helmet. None of the students rode motorcycles to school and my entrance was already gaining curious looks. The moment I took off my helmet they'd all know it was me. I took a deep breath, kicked the stand down, and swung my leg off the seat.

"Can't avoid them forever," I said out loud. "Better get this over with."

I pulled off my helmet, shook out my tangled hair, and examined my reflection in one of the chrome mirrors. It was only a matter of seconds until curiosity finally won over a few students and they headed in my direction.

"Woo!" I heard, and looked up to see two boys whom I recognized from English class, walking towards me. Kiley had her arm around the one that spoke and two of her friends followed behind them. "Nice ride!" he stated.

"Thanks!" I replied nonchalantly. I tucked my helmet under my arm. Kiley scowled at me as did the two girls with her.

"Check out the custom paint," the other boy was saying. "Angelfire! Cool!"

The three girls' patience waned, and soon they tried unsuccessfully to regain the boys' attention. "Come on, Darren, we're going to be late," Kiley pouted and pulled on his arm.

He ignored her and turned his attention over my shoulder. "Hey, Acer!" he hollered, "Get a look at Scout's hog!"

I turned and saw Acer, striding nonchalantly in our direction. He glared at me and I had to wonder what I had done this time. The boys continued their examination as Acer stood silently beside me.

Kiley huffed again. "Darren, come on!"

"In a minute, babe!" he blew her off, which sent her fuming.

"What year is it?" he asked.

"I bet it's a smooth ride," the other commented.

Enjoying her annoyance, I rubbed it in her face that I had stolen everyone's attention. "It's a '71, restored to about eighty-five percent. It's got the original 1200cc engine with four stroke and 45 V-Twin. Definitely a smooth ride."

"Wow!" he was saying. "You rebuilt it yourself?"

"Yeah, my dad and I rebuilt this and a 1950 classic two years ago."

"Sweet!" Darren said. Kiley rolled her eyes.

"Darren, let's go," she seethed.

"All right!" he turned to me and shrugged. "See you in English, Scout."

"Yeah, see you!" I replied and then couldn't stop myself. In a singsong voice, I taunted, "Bye, Kiley!"

She scowled and made a big show of wrapping her arms around Darren as they walked across the parking lot and disappeared into the crowd.

"I thought you were riding to school with your sister?" Acer asked angrily.

He had been so quiet that I had forgotten he was standing next to me. I shifted my helmet on my hip and defiantly stared into his face.

"Change of plans," I answered. "Why do you care?"

"I don't," he returned obviously flustered. He looked me up and down and then looked at my bike. "You really think riding that crotch rocket to school on game day is a good idea?"

"Crotch rocket?" I huffed and headed across the parking lot. "Again, why do you care? You don't want me playing on the team anyway."

"I *don't* care," he bristled. "But I am sure that Coach Mac wouldn't be happy to see you showing off on your motorcycle on opening day."

"Showing off? I just drove up and parked. How is that showing off?" I asked him. "If I didn't know any better, Ace, I would think you were jealous."

We got to the door of the school and he hustled ahead to open it for me. I had already stepped inside before it registered what he had done. "Uh, thanks."

"Jealous of you and your little bike?" he asked in disbelief. "No way."

"I could take you for a spin later if you want," I teased. "You've never lived until you straddled the back of a motorcycle."

"No thanks."

I started to turn left at the main hall when I realized he was headed in the opposite direction. Turning around, I called out to his back, "Acer!"

He spun around. I closed the distance between us and looked at him seriously. "What's wrong with Bonnie? Your mom seemed kind of weird on the phone."

Something passed just below the surface of his eyes. My question struck some kind of emotion with him. He looked away from me and stared over my shoulder when he answered. "She's just sick…again."

He wasn't going to elaborate even if I asked him to, so I nodded my head, softly punched him in the shoulder, and said, "Well, I hope she gets better. See you at the field."

"See you," was all he said.

"Boys," Coach Mac started, then quickly added, "and girl." I tried not to roll my eyes. "I don't need to remind you the importance of opening day." He paced back and forth in front of us along the left field line. "Now, I know we open our season with last year's state champs. They are bigger than we are, and stronger than we are, but we

106

can win this game because we have more heart. That team over there is cocky. They're riding the coattails of their championship, and last time I checked, that year was over. This is a new season. This is our year! This is our field! This is our team! Now, let's go out there and remind them who they are playing today!"

We erupted into a series of whistles and cheers as we circled around Coach Mac.

"Let 'em hear ya, boys…and girl!" Coach Haywood yelled. I did roll my eyes that time.

"Bearcats!" We yelled and dispersed into the dugout.

After a few minutes, the announcer called out the starting lineup and we ran to our positions. The national anthem concluded and I glanced up into the crowd. The stands were pretty full. Mary perched herself about five rows up, wearing a white off the shoulder cowl neck dress and spike-heeled boots. Her hair was long and flowing, and her sunglasses rested perfectly across the bridge of her nose while ridiculously big thick gold hoop earrings hung from her earlobes to her bare shoulders.

What was she thinking?

I shook my head. She was dressed for a runway not a baseball game. Brian sat down next to her, still in his black three piece suit. He'd come straight from work so he had an excuse, but I could guarantee Mary had taken the time to plan and coordinate her outfit just for this occasion. I was willing to bet she deemed this outfit worthy of an afternoon baseball game.

This was the first game in a long time that I would play without Daddy there to watch. I looked up at the bright blue sky and thought about him.

"I wish you were here," I whispered. "I miss you so much."

I crouched into position behind the plate, waiting on Acer to get ready for our warm-up pitches and brushed my fingers in the dirt. Before it even registered what I was doing, I glanced down and realized that I had written the word *Dad*. Shocked, I stared at it for a moment and then heard Daddy's words echo in my head. *"Scout, I'm not leaving you. I am going to live on with you forever in your heart, in your mind, just like your momma."*

He was right here.

Satisfied and at peace, I turned my attention to the pitcher's mound. Acer and I completed warm-ups, and the infield threw the ball around the horn. From behind me I heard those infamous words that signaled the start of every baseball game in the country and pounded my glove in anticipation.

"Play ball!"

The first batter stepped up to the right side of the plate. Everyone was in position, ready for the first pitch of the season. Acer was standing at the back of the mound, staring out into the outfield and I looked up at the hitter. He looked down at me and sneered, knocking dirt off of his cleats with his bat. When Acer turned back around, his face looked determined, focused, just what his team needed.

We were ready to go.

I flashed Acer the signal for fastball and he obliged, the ball hugging the black line of the plate. The batter didn't swing and as the ball popped my glove. I framed it perfectly.

"Strike one!" the umpire yelled.

I stood and threw the ball back to Acer and watched the batter take a few practice swings. The holes in his swing jumped out at me as I studied him. The way he threw his whole front side, his open stance, he could never touch a ball on the outside corner with a swing like that.

I crouched and gave Acer the sign for curveball. His curveball really looked good during warm-ups and no one could touch that curve when it was on. Mentally, I crossed my fingers and waited on his delivery.

Angela Geurin

It was beautiful. The ball started down the middle of the plate and just as the batter swung, it dove down and away out of the reach of his bat.

"Strike two!"

We got him. Now he was behind in the count no balls and two strikes, he had to swing at anything close to the plate and we had room to try and get him to chase. I called for slider way off the plate and Acer delivered a perfect pitch that finished just above the white chalk line on the outside part of the plate, but the batter didn't chase it this time. Still ahead in the count, I watched him step up to the plate again, only this time he made an adjustment to his stance and now stood with his toes on the chalk line right next to the plate. He was expecting an outside pitch and so we would surprise him.

He would never catch up to Acer's fastball on the inside corner and with the way his fastball always moved up through the zone, we might just get this batter to pop up.

I settled into position and let Acer know what I wanted. The pitch came in high and tight, right on the batter's hands and just as I had hoped, he barely got a piece of the ball. It popped up toward the opposing team's dugout. I jumped up and ran under the ball, but it was dropping fast. I realized, through my peripheral vision, the on deck batter was rooted in my way. At the last second, I dropped into a figure four slide, my momentum carried me passed the ball and I had to reach back over my head, kicking my feet up in the process. I snagged the ball before it hit the ground, cradling it in my glove as my cleats connected with the on deck batter.

He toppled over on top of me, screaming out in pain, and then everything around me exploded into motion. Something connected with my jaw, whether it was a fist or a knee, I wasn't sure, but for a minute I was seeing stars. The on deck batter pinned me to the ground with his weight and pulled at my glove hand. Reflexively, I slammed my fist into his stomach, trying to throw him off, still cradling the ball protectively against my chest.

109

Diamonds in the Dirt

The next thing I knew, the players at the dugout opening were shouting and leaping towards us. Rolling to the side, I fought myself to the surface of bodies and backed away. The player I had taken out with my slide shouted, calling me all kinds of creative names, and two other players were holding him by the arms.

Someone grabbed my arm and I jerked it free before I realized it was Kevin. He quickly stepped back with his hands up. Wisps of auburn curls were in my eyes and I angrily tucked them behind my ears, turned to the umpire and showed him the ball still in my glove.

He nodded and closed his fist above his shoulder, signaling out number one. "He's out!"

"Get control of your team!" Coach Mac yelled as he raced across the diamond towards us.

"Get control of your catcher!" the opposing coach fired back and then whirled around and faced the umpire. "She should be thrown out of the game, blue! She tried to take him out!"

"She was going for the ball!" Coach Mac argued.

"She cleated him in the groin!"

I started to argue, but realized I really didn't see where my cleats connected. I just assumed that they hit his shins. No wonder everyone was so worked up.

The ump said it looked like a clean play and asked if the batter was wearing a cup. It was my cue to leave so I started toward the mound, working my jaw around. Mary was probably flipping out, but I didn't dare glance into the stands.

Kevin patted me on the back and followed me to the mound. "You all right?"

I nodded. "Sorry, I turned on you. Thought you were someone else."

"No problem. Nice catch!"

"Didn't know it would start World War III," I replied drily.

Cade and the rest of the infield gathered on the mound. He smirked and spit behind him as we approached. "Enjoy your roll around the dirt?" he sneered.

"Why? Are you jealous?" I returned and looked at Acer. "You looked good that series, Ace. That curve you threw broke a foot. Keep it up."

He stared beyond me into the stands without responding. It was fine by me.

Coach Mac arrived at the mound and examined my jaw. "You all right?" he asked.

"Yeah, it's nothing," I returned.

"It'll be something tomorrow," he replied. "Watch your back out there. They'll be after you now." I nodded and he spoke to all of us then. "Let's get back to the game. Acer, keep it up. You got one out. Get the next two so we can come and get some runs for you." He jogged back to the dugout.

I put the ball in Acer's glove. "Strike these jokers out."

He did just that.

For seven innings Acer was stellar, but our bats were cold. We had managed to squeeze one run across the plate in the bottom of the third. Then I scored from second off Kevin's single to right center in the fourth, but that was it.

In the top of the eighth, Acer looked tired. He walked the leadoff batter then hung the next pitch, but it was far enough off the plate, that the ball was just a squib to the shortstop. Routine double play ball, but Chris mishandled it, and had to rush his throw to first, launching it way over Kevin and into the opposing team's dugout. The dead ball put the runners on second and third with no outs.

111

I stepped out in front of the plate. "Shake it off, guys!" I shouted. "Focus! Let's get this next one."

The next batter came up and cranked Acer's fastball to deep center field. Jon raced back to get it and made a spectacular catch on the warning track. Quickly, he shifted his momentum and threw the ball towards the plate. It was a beautiful throw, but I knew it wouldn't be in time to get the runner that had tagged up from third.

"Cut it off!" I yelled to Chris and watched as the runner crossed home plate. Chris held the runner at second and then tossed the ball to Acer. "Time out, ump."

"You got time!" he responded.

I dropped my mask and jogged out to the mound.

Acer turned and glared at me. "What do you want?"

I returned his glare, but didn't take the bait. "You're losing the spin on your curve and your fastball has lost some zip. How you feeling?"

"I'm fine, but that runner never should have made it to third in the first place. Chris needs to get his head on straight! That should have been a double play!"

"You forget that *you* put that runner on base in the first place. So don't go blaming Chris for your mistake." He started to make another excuse and I cut him off. "Look, you've thrown a heck of a game! Would you like to finish it or do we need to go to the bull pen?"

"This is my game. I am going to finish it!"

"Good!" I returned. "Then suck it up and throw!"

I turned and strutted back to my position. "One down! Runner on two!" I shouted as I faced the infield.

The batter stepped up to the plate and I gave Acer the sign for fastball. He shook me off. I gave him the sign for slider and he shook me off again. I groaned and shook my head, knowing what he wanted: curveball. He had forgotten that this guy crowded the plate and had launched the curveball into deep right field last at bat. *What the heck is he doing!* I stood up and yanked off my mask in frustration.

Standing in front of the plate, I shouted. "What? You think you can call your own game now?"

"Yeah! You don't know what you're doing back there! Sit down and catch the ball!" he returned, stepping off the rubber.

"Can you believe this guy? He's given up two hits in eight innings and now he's going to start calling the shots!" I seethed, slamming my mask down on my head.

The umpire and batter chuckled.

I huffed and didn't bother with giving signals. He waited until finally I hollered, "Just bring it! It's your call now!"

The pitch came in flat as a pancake, but outside and I cringed as I heard the ear-piercing crack of the bat. Just like in his last at bat, the ball screamed into deep right center and I prayed that it would stay in the yard. It hit the top of the wall, and Jon played the wall perfectly, holding the batter to a double. I watched in disappointment as our one run lead disappeared when the runner on second crossed home plate. Tie game.

Coach Mac signaled me to join him on the mound and I jogged out to meet him. He waved off the rest of the infield. "What's going on, you two?"

"Ask the boss," I said drily. "He's calling the shots now."

"Don't get your panties in a wad because I shook you off," he seethed. "My curveball is on today."

"Doesn't matter when the guy crowds the plate and swings for the outside pitch, now does it? How far did that ball go? Oh, yeah, 320 feet!"

"Enough!" Coach Mac shouted. "Ace, how're you feeling? You look sluggish and they are starting to get to your pitches."

"I've still got plenty in the tank," he replied.

"You don't have to be a hero. I've got Jason out there fresh and ready to go." Coach Mac looked at me then and asked, "What do you think, Scout? Can he finish it?"

I looked Acer in the face. Those narrowed azure eyes dared me to say anything different. As much as I knew Acer wanted this game, his pitches were weak. He wasn't throwing as well as when he started and if we didn't change it up; this game would go downhill fast. He would be ticked off at me, but I had to think of what was best for the team, not his ego this time. I looked back at Coach Mac and shook my head. "He's throwing beach balls up there, Coach."

He nodded and signaled for the bull pen. Jason appeared and started jogging in from the outfield.

"No!" Acer shouted. "You're just mad because I shook you off! Are you going to listen to her, Coach Mac? This is my game! I'm going to finish it! She doesn't know what she's talking about! I can finish it!"

"Take a seat, son," Coach Mac replied pointing toward the third base dugout. "Jason will finish it. Rest up; we've got at least four more games this week."

Then Postal went postal. He slung the ball at me and I barely had enough time to get my glove up. Then he picked up his rosin bag and slung that in my direction too. Kevin started over and I waved him off. Coach Mac stepped in between us and pointed him to the dugout. Acer spewed all kinds of names and words in my direction as he stormed off the field. As soon as he made it across the chalk line, Coach Haywood ushered him into the dugout and Acer kept going. He threw bats, helmets, balls, anything in reach. Nobody could avoid looking in the dugout watching his three-year-old tantrum. Coach Haywood finally grabbed two cups of water and dumped them over Acer's head.

"Sit there and cool off!" he shouted.

I turned and handed Coach Mac the ball as Jason made it to the mound in relief. He tossed it to him. "Ready to go, son?" he asked.

"Yes, sir," he answered and turned to me. "What's coming up?"

"Heart of the line up," I responded, "but we already have one out."

He took a deep breath. "Let's do this, then."

Jason did well in relief. He struck out the first batter he faced, but the next batter hit a hard ground ball up the middle and they scored the go-ahead run. They tried to steal second base and I nailed the runner for out number three, but the momentum was too much in Coronado's favor, and they shut us down the next two innings. We lost 3-2.

It was a hard pill to swallow. I had never lost the first game in a season ever, but like Daddy always said, *"At the end of the day, the only game that matters is the next one."* I just had to hope I would be lucky enough to see the next game.

Chapter Seven: Handcuffed

A week had passed since our opening game. The team had made a strong comeback after the disappointing loss against Coronado. We took second at the Bradford tournament, winning two games and losing two. Unfortunately, Acer took both of the losses.

He was so much better than his record showed. If he could just learn to trust me and his teammates behind him, he could be a high school All-American. It was frustrating to watch him implode on the mound, but until he was willing to listen and let go of his pride, there was nothing I could do to help him. He just couldn't seem to get over the fact that he had a girl as a catcher and that I might actually know a thing or two about calling pitches.

Everything I did added fuel to the fire. He knew exactly which buttons to push to make me lose my temper, and even though I bit my tongue so many times that teeth marks were permanently etched into its tip, there were times when I just lost it.

Like during the championship game Saturday, when our discussion over their number five hitter turned into a heated argument, which turned into a shoving match, which landed us both on the bench. He didn't let up though, when we were in the dugout. He kept yelling and hurling insults at me even when I sat far away from him on the opposite side of the bench.

I waited for one of the coaches to step in, but they were busy doing their job coaching the game; so whether they had learned to tune him out or just figured he'd eventually grow hoarse, they didn't make a move. But when he insulted my dead mother, I took matters into my own hands. Calmly, I sipped my water, threw the paper cup in the trash can, and walked down to where he was sitting. When he stood up to meet my angry gaze with a scowl of his own, I slapped him as hard as I could in the face.

"Don't you ever say another word about my mother," I warned and walked away just as calmly as before. He shut up then.

I had never been yanked off a field in the middle of a game, especially a championship game. I'd never even gotten into a fist fight with anyone other than Danny Joe. It was humiliating! What was happening to me?

Coach Mac had given us Monday off from practice, but he stopped me outside of fourth period and said he needed me to be at the field at 2:30 sharp. It wouldn't surprise me if Acer was there too. He was probably going to run us until the sun set, or worse, make us clean gum off the bottom of the bleachers.

I deserved it. Whatever punishment he gave out, I deserved it. Acer may be known for his bad temper, but I have always been known for my composure, and it made me sick to think how much disappointment this would have caused daddy.

Before geometry, I tracked down Rachel to let her know I was staying late. Since Mary still refused to let me ride my motorcycle to school and Bonnie was still sick or whatever was really going on with her, Rachel and Jose were my ride.

"You need me to stick around?" Rachel asked.

"No, this is going to be a long afternoon, but thanks for the offer," I answered. "I'm sure Mary will be home on time tonight. I'll just give her a call and have her pick me up when I'm finished."

"OK. Well, call me if you need a ride."

She started to head into her class and I stopped her. "Rachel, wait," I called after her. She turned on her heel. "Have you heard from Bonnie? You know she's been gone for a week now."

Rachel thought about it for a minute. "You know," she started. "I've been so busy with this whole Spring Dance Committee thing, I haven't thought about anything else. Has it really been a week?"

I nodded. "Yeah, it's been a week. That's kind of a long time to be sick."

"What does Ben say?" she asked.

I shook my head. "He doesn't say. He just says she is sick."

"That's weird."

"Yeah, I know. What do you think is going on with her?"

"I don't know; maybe you should give her a call." She glanced at the wall clock. "I got to go, Scout. Let me know what you find out."

Let her know what I find out?

I was beginning to think I was the only one at school concerned about Bonnie. It seemed crazy to me because I had only known Bonnie for a month, and everyone else had known her for years. Was I missing something?

Brrrrrrring!

I groaned. Great! Coach will add another three laps for being tardy.

I got to the field at 2:20 and looked around. There was no sign of either coach or anyone else so I walked to the third base dugout and took a seat on the bench. It was chilly and I hugged my arms around my shoulders, trying to warm up. Five minutes later, I heard the gate open and shut. Just as I expected, Acer rounded the corner and came to an abrupt stop at the foot of the dugout steps.

"What are you doing here?" he spat.

"Coach Mac told me to be here at 2:30," I explained. "You here for the same reason?" He nodded and slumped down on the opposite end of the bench. "Wonder what kind of punishment we're going to get?"

"You know this is your fault!" he accused. "If you wouldn't have slapped me…"

"My fault! You insulted my dead mother! Besides you're the one who started it when you slapped my face mask out of my hand!"

"I guess your throw just accidentally hit me in the knee cap. Come on! You said yourself you don't ever miss your target!"

"It wouldn't have hit you in the knee cap if you were paying attention!"

"How do you expect me to pay attention to you when all you do is nag, nag, nag? Your curve's flat! Your fastball's too slow! You need to hit your target!"

"I wouldn't have to nag you, if you would just throw what I called!"

"Enough!" Coach Mac shouted. His voice echoed off the walls of the dugout, and Acer and I jumped to attention. "I have had enough of this bickering from you two!" He continued. He started to pace in front of us. "Do you have any idea how frustrating this past month has been for me?"

Neither of us spoke as we stared in stunned silence. I heard the opening and closing of the gate followed by footsteps and I slid my eyes sideways to see Coach Haywood step down into the dugout, stopping behind Coach Mac. He slid something into the back pocket of his jeans before resting his hands on his hips.

"Do either of you know why they refer to the pitcher and catcher as the battery?" Coach Mac asked. I was afraid it was a rhetorical question and didn't answer. "Well!?" he yelled.

I jumped and blurted out, "Because they are the ones that make the game go, like a car battery."

"That's right!" Coach Mac clapped his hands together. "Every play in baseball starts with the pitcher and catcher." He pointed at each of us, indicating pitcher and catcher for emphasis. "Just like your car won't run without the battery, you can't play baseball without a battery. You two are the complete package: the perfect battery." He walked in front of Acer and stopped. "Acer, God reached down when you picked up your first baseball and blessed your arm. You have movement and you have speed, and it's all natural." He turned and stood in front of me. "And Scout, you are like a wall behind that plate. You are quick, strong, and God blessed you with an unrivaled mental edge. You are a student of the game. You study hitters. You study your teammates and you see the plays before they happen."

Student of the game, I was momentarily taken aback. Daddy used to tell me that a true ball player didn't just play. A true ball player was a student of the game. They studied its every aspect, much like you would study algebra. I couldn't help, but smile at the compliment.

Coach Mac scowled and my smile dissolved as quickly as it had appeared.

"When you two work together, I would go to battle with you against anyone in the nation! But you spend too much time pushing each other's buttons and getting caught up in your own pride!" He just shook his head. "Neither of you can stand alone. You can't pitch without a catcher and you have nothing to catch if there is no pitcher! You have to work together. You need each other in order to be the best that you can be. Come here."

He motioned us forward and cautiously, I approached. Acer came up next to me, still keeping his distance. "Now stick out your left hand, Scout."

Nervously, I hesitated, but did as I was told, my eyes stayed on his face, unsure of what was about to happen. I half wondered if he was going to slap it with a ruler.

He took my hand in his and turned to Acer. "Now give me your right," he said. Acer stuck out his left. "Your other right, son."

I snickered. Acer shot blue daggers my way and gave him is right hand. Coach Mac held our hands next each other. "Now just stay put a minute."

Acer tilted his head and raised an eyebrow, a look Bonnie had given me a time or two the past month, but coming from her brother made my stomach flutter. Our hands side by side, his right and my left, I glanced down and then back up at Coach Mac and beyond him to Coach Haywood's sly smirk. *What was going on?*

Suddenly, I felt something cold and metal around my wrist and before it registered, I heard the soft click of the lock, too late to pull free. This had to be some kind of joke: Acer and I were handcuffed together.

Acer exploded and jerked his hand free of Coach Mac's grasp, yanking my whole arm in the process. "Come on, Coach! You can't do this!" he shouted.

I jerked my hand back down, with as much force as he had used on me and I had the satisfaction of watching him stumble off balance. "Is this a joke?" I asked.

Acer retaliated and yanked our chained hands back towards him which threw me off balance and my forehead connected with the side of his jaw. We both cried out in pain.

"Stop yanking me around, Postal!" I shouted, straightening up and rubbing my head with my free hand. "What the heck is going on? You can't do this! This has got to be illegal or something!"

Coach Mac and Haywood chuckled. "No, nothing illegal. I cleared it all with the athletic director. You could ask your attorney to find a loophole, Scout, but I think in this case he will agree with me," Coach Mac stated, still grinning at my scowling face. "Here's the deal, kids; for the next two hours, you can do whatever you want, but you're doing it together. At 4:30, get yourselves to Floyd and June's and I will set you free. Maybe even treat you to a piece of pie, if you convince me that you can work together."

"How are we supposed to get there?" Acer asked.

"Oh, no, that's your problem. You two figure it out. Four-thirty sharp," he repeated and then waved to Coach Haywood. "Come on, Ed, let's get some grub and leave these two to resolve their issues."

Coach Haywood grinned and followed Coach Mac out of the dugout and through the gate. I heard him ask as they rounded the corner, "You think this will work, Mac?"

"Yep."

"Before they kill each other?"

I could not believe this! I would have rather scraped gum off the bottom of the bleachers for three hours. I turned to sit back down on the bench, forgetting the situation until I felt my arm jerk to a stop.

"Where do you think you are going?" Acer yelled.

"I'm going to sit on the bench!"

"For two hours?"

"What else are we going to do?"

He plopped down on the bench, tugging me down beside him. "I don't know! Mac has lost his marbles!"

We agreed on that! I felt my hand go up again and I looked over at Acer. He was rubbing his temples and angrily I flicked the knuckles on his hand.

"Hey!" He shouted and then quickly put his hand back down as he realized what he was doing. "Sorry. It's just…this is crazy!"

"Mac is crazy!" I agreed.

We sat there in silent frustration, stewing over the insanity of Coach Mac's attempt at a lesson. Our hands rested on the bench between us and I tried hard to keep my set of cuffs away from his hand, but there was only so much distance we could put between ourselves.

It *was* crazy, and creative and clever. I had to hand it to Coach Mac. This would probably accomplish more than any kind of traditional punishment. Acer and I had been at each other's throats for a month. The only way to get the two of us to work together was to force us into

Angela Geurin

a situation in which we had to completely rely on each other. I just
hoped neither of us had to use the bathroom during the next couple
hours.

I shivered as a chilly gust of wind blew through the dugout. "Can
we get out of here?" I asked.

"Where do you want to go?"

"Anywhere, as long as it is inside. I didn't think I needed my
jacket. I thought I would be running a million foul poles this afternoon.
Not..." I held up my left hand.

"Handcuffed to your enemy," he finished.

"I don't think you're my enemy, Ace," I answered softly. "Maybe
you see me that way, but I don't see you like that."

He glanced at the ground. I could have sworn he was avoiding my
eyes and his cheeks looked flushed. "All right; let's get out of here,"
he decided.

We stood together and then walked in opposite directions.

"This way!" we both shouted at the same time and then huffed in
frustration.

I stared at him angrily and ceded. "Fine!" I grumbled, then
followed him, out of the dugout and through the gate. "Why do you
think you need to call all the shots?" I asked as we walked around
the bleachers. "I mean what makes you think you know more than
everybody?"

"I don't think I know more than *everybody*. I just think I know
more than you."

"Why? Because I'm a girl?"

"Yep."

I stopped and turn to glare at him, anger flaring in my chest, but
soon realized his blue eyes were twinkling with his lopsided grin. He
was joking. I smacked him playfully in the ribs.

"Seriously though, why do you always have to have your way?"

He sighed. "I don't know. I just do. I know I have a bad temper, but you don't help the situation. You're so…cocky!"

I bristled. "I'm not cocky! Just confident."

"Is that what you call it?"

"Don't you realize that from my position on the field, I can see everything? I can see how the batters are adjusting to your pitches. I can see how deep the outfield is playing, and I can see when your arm gets lazy and your curve is going flat."

"So you get ticked off when I shake you off. I get it," he continued. "But I'm not stupid. I know my pitches and I have faced most of these teams before. Besides, you have never even played baseball."

"That's not true. I played baseball until junior high. I only started playing softball in eighth grade because they finally started a girls' softball team at my school and I got picked up by a travel team. So, that's two years of softball compared to nine years of baseball. Which one do you think I know more about?" I asked.

I jerked him to my side of the light pole before he clotheslined us.

"I didn't know that," he answered honestly. "The guys just said that we had some softball chick playing with us this year because Booneville doesn't have a softball team. I just thought you had played softball all your life and thought that you could just jump ship."

"Well, now you know. You shouldn't believe the rumors," I returned smugly. "You probably believed the one that I was really a boy dressed up like a girl just so I could make the team this year, too."

"No. No boy could look as good as you," he blurted.

A shock rippled through my body and I looked away to hide my blushing cheeks. "Oh my, is that a compliment, Mr. Acer?" I said in my best Texas drawl. "I do believe you are calling me pretty."

It was his turn to avert his gaze. "Pretty cocky!" he replied. "You think you're the boss of the diamond?"

"Well, yeah. I run the field because I am the only one in a position to do it. I mean you act like I want you to give up hits and put runners on base, like I am setting you up to fail."

"No I don't," he returned.

"Yes, you do."

"No I don't!"

Yes, you…You know what, forget it. If I have to be handcuffed to you for the next couple of hours, I don't want to fight. So can we just agree to disagree?"

He shrugged his shoulders. "OK."

We headed out the main gate to the parking lot. Our strides were nearly the same length so it was easy to keep up with his brisk pace. "I guess I'm driving since you rode with Rachel today."

"How do you know I rode with Rachel?" I asked incredulously.

"I saw you get out of her car this morning in the parking lot," he responded quickly and then in Bonnie-like fashion changed the subject. "Is that bike really yours?"

"You mean my *crotch rocket*?" I responded sarcastically. "Yep, she's my baby."

"Why don't you ride it to school instead of bumming rides every day?"

"Mary won't let me."

"Your sister won't let you? Why?"

"I guess you're not the only one who thinks they are too dangerous for girls."

Acer drove a shiny red pickup truck, so typically Texan, but not that I stalked him or anything. I'd seen him in the parking lot before school too. As I scanned the lot, his truck was nowhere in sight.

"Where's your truck?" I asked.

"How do you know I drive a truck?" he asked skeptically, imitating my earlier tone.

"I've seen you driving it into the parking lot before school. It's crimson. It's always shiny. It's a nice truck. Who wouldn't notice it?"

"Oh," he said slightly flustered. Then he playfully wiggled his eyebrows. "You like my truck?"

"It's a nice truck," I repeated, nonchalantly.

Suddenly he stopped in his tracks and stared at our handcuffed wrists.

"What?" I asked.

"I drove Bonnie's car today and it's a stick."

I sighed heavily. "Well, I guess this will be our first lesson this afternoon."

We approached her black convertible sports car and I automatically started heading to the passenger side before Acer jerked me over to the driver's side. "You're going to have to get in on my side," he reminded me.

"You *could* get in on my side."

"No way! It's my car and I'm driving, so you are doing the sliding."

"It's Bonnie's car," I corrected. "You could put the top down and we could crawl over the seats."

"Just get in and slide over," he bit out and gestured with his free hand to the open driver's side door. "Ladies first, remember."

I huffed at him and then carefully eased down into the seat and let my arm rise above my head as I climbed over the console and into the passenger seat. Acer followed after me.

"See, that wasn't so bad," he commented. "The tricky part is shifting gears with two hands."

Angela Geurin

"There's not enough chain between our hands to allow for one of us to shift gears," I concluded and laughed. "Guess we have to hold hands."

Acer looked at me with a silly lopsided grin. "Perfect! We get to hold hands, too!"

"It's not that big of a deal."

He gently pulled my hand across the console so that he could start the car. Then, he eased our hands back down to the gear shift. I grabbed the soft leather knob and felt the momentary spark as he covered my hand with his. Our elbows jockeyed for position on the armrest until I finally relented and inched over just enough that his elbow rested flush with mine.

"Compromise at its best," I muttered.

He shifted gears with my hand and maneuvered the car out of the parking lot. We sat in silence for a moment and for the first time since meeting Acer, I felt...peaceful. His fingers slid in between mine and a tingle spread over my hand that ran clear up my arm. I stared at our hands a moment and shook my head.

"What?" he asked.

"Guess Coach Mac knows what he is doing. I think this is the longest we have been around each other without fighting."

He laughed. "Bonnie would get a kick out of this," he said. "You know she has a theory about us."

"No, I didn't know that. What is her theory?"

"She thinks we are like magnets that need to be flipped."

"What does that mean?" I asked in confusion.

"She thinks we are alike, but at the same time polar opposites. So we don't get along because we know each other's weaknesses and we attack them, instead of using our own strengths to complement each other. We repel each other like magnets when you force the same poles together. We just need to flip."

127

"That's an interesting theory," I replied drily. "So how do we flip?"

"Bonnie thinks that if we focus on doing the things that make the other happy, instead of focusing on our own agendas, we could help each other out and get along," he said.

That made sense. We were both egomaniacs and we both insisted on having the last word—to be the one who was right. Neither one of us was willing to feed the other's ego. We just kept trying to force our own way, our own agendas on each other. But if we both consciously fed the other's agenda and ego, we'd both get what we wanted and there would be nothing to fight about.

In reality, our agendas were the same. We wanted to play ball and win, but we just approached them from opposite directions. Acer reacted to things by action, following his gut, and I reacted to things by thinking, planning, and analyzing—setting my emotions to the side.

But I realized even that wasn't so true anymore. Ever since Daddy died, I had been an emotional wreck. I hadn't acted like the strong, young woman he raised me to be. I thought about my very public outbursts: at Daddy's funeral, with Mary at church, the game last Saturday; I was letting my emotions drive my actions. I had changed, and not for the better. I needed to get back to my calm, cool, and collected self. That was truly me, and what Acer needed me to be.

"Smart girl that Bonnie," I said and then shifted in my seat. "Acer, how is she doing?"

His face gave away no emotion, but his eyes seemed to lose a bit of their luster. "She's OK…considering."

"Considering what? Acer, what's really going on with her? I know it's not the flu. There's something more, isn't there? It's like she's fallen off the planet."

"She needs to be the one to tell you. I won't do it."

"Well, can we go and see her?" I asked. "Now?"

128

He waited a second, pondering my question before answering. "I just can't spring this on her without talking to her first. You understand, right?"

I sighed, unable to hide my disappointment.

Acer must have sensed it because he nudged me with his elbow. "Look, how about after coach frees us, I drop you off at your house and go talk to Bonnie. Then if she's ready to talk to you, I'll let you know and you can stop by and see her after dinner."

It was not exactly the solution I was hoping for, but maybe I could finally get a straight answer. I really hoped everything was okay with Bonnie, and I hoped that whatever it was that was so private was something she would feel comfortable sharing with me. After all, she had listened to me drone on about Mary and her brother. I wanted to be there for her too.

"OK."

In complete Bonnie fashion, Acer shifted the topic. "I could use a snack. Let's go to Frosty's. You in? My treat."

"Like I have a choice right now," I snickered, "but yeah, Frosty's is great, especially if you're paying."

We drove to the edge of town and I had a momentary flashback of my first afternoon with Bonnie as I watched her little angel dangle and sparkle from the rearview mirror. The sun wasn't shining as brightly today as it had been when I met Bonnie, but I found my eyes following the refracted light as it danced throughout the car and across Acer's chest.

I leaned my head back and turned casually towards Acer. He looked so much like Bonnie, but unless you had seen them side by side you wouldn't really notice it. He had the same blonde curls, but much shorter and his full lips and button nose were identical, but seemed to sit just a little lower on his round face. The rest of him was very different. Bonnie was petite and her skin ivory like a porcelain doll. Acer, on the other hand, was godlike, as if chiseled from stone. His sun-kissed skin and tall, muscled frame was no comparison. He was really nice to look at when he wasn't arguing with me.

Suddenly, I felt his thumb brush softly over my knuckles as our hands rested on the gear shift. His touch was warm and the warmth spread until it finally settled into my stomach. Sitting this close to him without arguing, it was really nice.

"Magnets," I murmured.

He looked over at me and grinned, wiggling his eyebrows in amusement. "Flip." He squeezed my hand and I realized he must have felt something too.

"Mary, please don't make me beg," I pleaded. I had gotten the call from Acer about 7:15 that evening and he said that I was good to come over for the next hour, but Mary was standing in my way.

"It's a school night, Scout," she returned evenly, "You agreed to the rules."

"I know, but this is important," I whined. "It's sort of an…"

She cut me off. "Don't you dare say it's an emergency!"

I cringed. Mary had not been very pleased when she'd discovered my dishonesty about the emergency motorcycle ride to school. I knew it would come back to haunt me; I just wished it wouldn't be haunting me at this very moment.

"But she's sick," I pleaded. "She hasn't been to school in over a week."

"If she's that sick then she doesn't need any visitors," she returned.

"Please, Mary!" I begged and then I changed tactics. "I'll vacuum the stairs for a whole month."

She rolled her eyes and then I caught sight of Brian behind Mary, pantomiming something that I couldn't make out. I shook my head in confusion. She noticed and whirled around to face him. He quickly ducked his head and focused his attention on the TV. Mary turned back around and faced me.

"Do the dishes," Brian coughed.

"I'll do the dishes!" I offered and nodded my head as Brian winked at me and went back to watching television. "For the rest of the week," I added. "Starting tonight. When I get back home."

Mary sighed and shook her head. "All right," she relented, "you can go. But be home in an hour."

"Yes! I will! Thanks, Mary!" I did a mental fist pump as she walked into the kitchen and returned with the keys to my motorcycle.

I arrived at the Acer's home around 7:45 and stood on the front porch, waiting for someone to open the biggest wooden door I think I had ever seen in my entire life. Nestled on the golf course, their house was a huge monstrosity made of white stucco with an orange-tiled roof and black, wooden shutters. It was incredibly resort-like, with palm trees in the front yard and exotic flowers in the flower beds by the door. The entire front yard was lit up by multicolored spotlights. It was beautiful.

At long last, the door creaked open and Acer stood before me wearing nothing but blue mesh shorts. I inhaled sharply and consciously made sure my mouth was not hanging open as I took in his perfectly muscled chest and abs.

I swallowed hard. "I'm here," I announced.

He grinned. "Yes, you are." He looked at me and then visibly shook himself into motion. "Oh, Bonnie, right." He opened the door wider and waved me inside. "She's on the patio by the pool."

I stepped inside and stared awestruck at the grand entryway of their home. It was like walking into a hotel. The foyer was open to the second floor and a wraparound staircase made of dark, stained wood headed off to the right side of the room, ending at a wooden balcony that stretched across the entryway. There was a large chandelier that hung over a very expensive looking rug covering most of the terra-cotta colored tile.

"Beautiful house," I complimented.

"Thanks," he returned. "It's my mom. Interior decorating is her hobby."

He led me through a small hallway that opened up in to a sunken living room lined with floor-to-ceiling windows that showed a sparkling rectangular pool illuminated by colorful lights. Beyond the pool was nothing but the lush greens of the golf course and the western setting sun. It was a breathtaking view.

We continued through the living room towards a pair of French doors and I automatically reached my hand out to grab the door knob in the same instance that Acer's hand covered mine. We both laughed, remembering the afternoon we spent together with our hands in a similar position. Gently, he used my hand to turn open the door. I stepped through onto the tiled patio and spotted Bonnie, lying back against a plush, burnt orange-colored lounger.

"Bonnie," Acer called. "Company's here."

She was wrapped from head to toe in a blanket and she sat up, smiling as we approached. Her face was pale and sallow with dark circles under her eyes. My heart froze. I knew that look. I had seen it a hundred times over the past year.

Tears sprang to my eyes and I shook my head. A wave of nausea spread through my stomach. "Oh, God," I whispered, "not you too."

Chapter Eight: Open Journal

I'm sorry," I said for the twentieth time, wiping the tears from my eyes with the tissues that Acer had brought me from inside. "I don't know what is wrong with me."

"Shhh," Bonnie consoled, "It's OK. You can cry. You have nothing to be sorry about." Her hand rested on my leg and squeezed soothingly.

The fact that Bonnie was the one with cancer, and yet was consoling *me,* made my tears fall harder. To say that I was in shock was an understatement. Seeing her resembling the way that I had seen Daddy look so much of the time last year, and recognizing what the cause of that look was, was heart wrenching.

She didn't have to tell me how sick she was; I knew. When I saw her, it was like being hurled back through time to last November when I had watched Daddy die. My heart hurt for her, with her. I felt a strong desire to carry this burden for her. I didn't want to watch my friend go through this journey.

I had fallen into a fit of uncontrollable sobs shortly after seeing her, and had it not been for Acer standing so close to me, I would have landed on my knees when they buckled under the weight of my emotions. Without saying a word, he guided me to the lounger next to Bonnie and disappeared inside only to reappear with a box of tissues. After a minute or two of watching me work through my grief, he left us alone.

Finally, I gained some of my composure and took a deep breath. "How long have you known that you have cancer?"

She leaned back against the lounger again and cleared her throat. "It's been there all my life. As long as I can remember at least," she spoke softly. "I have a rare form of a very aggressive leukemia. I think they first discovered it when I was two or three years old. It's not very common in children. It's more common in adults. Anyway, I don't remember much about the treatment back then, but I know that I had to have several blood and platelet transfusions. I went into complete remission around age five, but then at eleven, they found it again. That time they did a bone marrow transplant and they thought it was successful, but two weeks ago my annual scan showed more blast cells. So here we are again."

I tried to maintain my composure, but it reminded me so much of what I went through with Daddy that fresh tears stung my eyes. When I was eight, Daddy found out he had colon cancer. I didn't understand very much back then, and my Aunt Charis was still alive and stayed with us while he was going through treatment, so I wasn't as involved in his care at that time. All I remembered was that the medicine made his hair fall out, made him tired, but made him better. He was in remission for six years.

Then, a year and a half ago, daddy found out that he had cancer again. I think we tried every treatment, but nothing seemed to work. I remember the doctors using that same term—"aggressive" cancer—when they explained that there was nothing left that they could do but make him comfortable.

I hated cancer.

A lone tear fell down my cheek. "So what kind of treatments are you doing this time?" I asked.

"Radiation and chemotherapy for the next six weeks," she answered, "Then sometime after spring break, they will do a splenectomy. They are trying to convince me to allow another bone marrow transplant."

"They shouldn't have to *convince* you to get another transplant," Acer nearly shouted.

Bonnie and I both turned toward the doors to the house in surprise. His face registered anger, but carefully he carried three mugs of steamy liquid towards us. Glaring at Bonnie, he handed her a cup, then handed one to me, before settling himself on the foot of Bonnie's lounger. It was hot chocolate—a welcome comfort, and surprisingly thoughtful considering who provided it.

Eagerly I took a sip and thanked him.

Bonnie rolled her eyes in annoyance. "Bennie, not now."

"You are fortunate enough to have a perfect match. Most leukemia patients wait for months to find a donor. It shouldn't be a difficult decision."

"What are we talking about now?" I asked her. "Who's your match?"

"Bennie," she answered, but the look of annoyance didn't leave her face. "He's been giving me parts of his body since we were toddlers."

He covered her hand with his. "And I will do it a hundred times more, if it makes you better," he said, the desperation bleeding through his voice.

She stared into his face and her gaze softened. "I know you would, but it's not making me better. Nothing you have given me has made this cancer go away and I am tired of putting you through all that pain for nothing. When we were little we didn't have a say in any of this, we were just stuck with whatever decisions mom and dad made, but now, I have a say. It's my decision, not yours."

"It's *our* decision, Bonnie!" he shouted, pulled his hand away, and abruptly stood. "I won't sit here and watch you die when I can give you what you need!"

"It's my body!" she returned vehemently. "It's my cancer! It's my treatment! My decision!" She tried to stand and lost her balance, Acer and I both lunged for her at the same time and bumped heads.

"Ow!" we said in unison, rubbing our heads. Bonnie sat back and laughed, the sound delightful, full of happiness. Soon we joined her and the tension of the previous argument dissipated.

"So I guess you won't be going to school for the rest of the year," I commented after our laughter died down.

"Actually, I am released to go now half a day. I tried to go last Friday, but the treatment makes me so tired I can't keep my eyes open for very long, but it would be better than lying around here." She adjusted the blanket around her shoulders.

"Good luck convincing mom of that," Acer said.

Bonnie stuck her tongue out at him. "You could help me with that, little brother."

"What if I agree with Mom?" he returned.

"Then I will just have to change your mind too."

I remembered how tired Daddy was all the time and how much effort it took for him just to get up and go to the bathroom sometimes. "You don't want to rush back, Bonnie. Surely, they can make other arrangements for you," I added.

"They can, but if I am going to die anyway I might as well get the most out of this life while I can, and I won't get it sitting around this house." She answered. "Besides, I go into the cancer center in Mason for my treatments on Tuesday, Wednesday, and Thursday afternoons. I figured I could at least go to school in the mornings. That shouldn't wear me out that much and I am pretty sure I can convince Mom and Dad that I would be OK for two or three hours."

It dawned on me that their parents were not here and that Acer had insisted that I come over at this time. I was curious about all of the secrecy given the conversation we were having. "Are your parents going to be mad that I am here? I mean, is that why no one at school knew about this?"

"Oh, no!" Bonnie answered. "It's just less annoying when my parents are out of the house. They mean well, but they meddle too much and we wouldn't have any privacy. They would have had to put in their two cents worth."

I snickered. "Kind of like Acer here?"

He furrowed his brow as Bonnie jumped in, "No they would be ten times worse! And to answer your other question, honestly, you are the first person who has asked about me. It's not like we are keeping this a secret or anything. My teachers know, the cheerleading sponsor, she knows, but I don't know if she has made a big announcement to the squad or anything. So, it could be that most people just think I've got the flu or something."

"Why does that surprise me?" I asked seriously. "Walking around with you at school, I would have thought everyone would be concerned that you were gone this long."

"That is so sweet, but really, I don't have a lot of close friends. You know, not anyone that I ever wanted to open up to anyway. Bennie's been the closest thing I have ever had to a best friend." She reached out and squeezed my hand. "Until I met you."

I squeezed back and felt tears spring to my eyes again. Bonnie was my best friend, I just didn't think she would consider me hers. It really warmed my heart to know that she felt as close to me as I did her.

"Do you remember the story of David and Jonathan in the Bible?" she asked.

I nodded my head and she continued. "Remember how they were like kindred spirits? You know how Jonathan's soul was knit to David's and Jonathan loved him as his own soul. That's what I felt when I overheard your argument at church. I felt a connection with you that I've never felt with anyone else. I hurt so deeply for you and what you have gone through losing your mom, your dad, having to completely uproot your life and move to a place that really didn't welcome you with open arms. I wanted to carry that burden not just with you, but for you."

Hadn't I just had that same thought when I first saw her tonight? I wanted to carry this cancer for her. I felt overwhelmed. As much as I wanted to deny it, I couldn't. This was a God thing. I had been running from God for the last few months and that whole time I was running, He was waiting for me to stop. As angry as God could have been with me and the way I had chosen to act, He was right here anyway—right here, right now on this patio, loving me and giving me exactly what I needed, a true friend.

"Wow!" was all I could say. I threw my arms around Bonnie's neck, felt her arms encircle me, and we embraced each other tightly. "I know exactly what you are talking about, Bonnie. I felt that same way when I saw you tonight."

"God is so good!" she whispered. "All the time, God is so good."

"My daddy used to say that." I squeezed again.

My heart warmed inside me and the wall I had built up around my heart crumbled to pieces. I didn't just feel Bonnie's arms comforting me. I felt my heavenly Father holding me, reassuring me that I was not alone. I was exactly where I needed to be and He had a plan.

"Thanks for checking up on me," she continued. "Thanks for being my friend."

Still holding her, I said, "No, thank you, Bonnie. Thanks for coming after me that day. I never thought I would find a friend, especially here in Booneville."

"And now you have two," Acer piped in and encircled us both with his long arms.

I looked over their shoulders and shook my head. What a difference a couple of hours could make. Just like that, my world had changed again, but this time for the better.

When we finally separated I asked, "So if you can have visitors, you think I can come over some time?"

"You can come over anytime," she responded. "I would love the company."

"Good. I will talk to Mary and see if I can come over after our game tomorrow." I caught a glimpse of the clock hanging on the wall by the pool. It was almost 9:00. "Speaking of which, I better head home before Mary sends out the National Guard."

I stood to go and leaned over and hugged Bonnie one last time. "You take care."

"I will." She looked at Acer sitting by her feet. "Would you walk her out for me, Bennie? I barely have the energy to make it back into the house."

"I can walk myself out," I said.

"I can do it," he returned, a little too quickly. "Bonnie, just stay there; I'll come back and help you into the house after I walk Scout to her ride."

Acer rested his hand on the small of my back and we left Bonnie sitting on the lounger, looking at the stars. Instead of going back through the house, he led me along a winding stone path that was lit by small blue-colored lights. The path followed the outside of the house, passed through a large wooden gate and ended at the edge of the driveway. Neither of us spoke until we arrived at my motorcycle and I grabbed my helmet.

"Thanks for coming over," he said at last. "I know she really needed that."

"Well, Bonnie was there for me when I needed a friend and I want to be there for her now." I started to put my helmet on and he put his hand on it and held it in place. His lips started to form words, but stopped, only to restart again and stop again.

"What?" I asked.

He visibly swallowed before he squeaked, "Scout, I..." He stopped again the next word forming on his lips, but refusing to come out.

"Just spit it out!" I groaned impatiently.

"I'm sorry," he spoke the words slowly. "I haven't treated you the way you deserve to be treated. I've been rude and pigheaded and I'm sorry. Especially about the championship game, I shouldn't have said those things about your mother."

"Wow! How did that taste?" I teased.

He flashed his lopsided grin and my stomach fluttered. "Like vinegar, but I mean it. I'm really sorry and I am really going to work on controlling my temper." He reached up and tucked a stray curl behind my ear. "You really are the best catcher I've ever had."

"Thanks," I answered sincerely. Then, feeling the weight of my own guilt, I added my own apology. "I'm sorry for slapping you, tackling you, and throwing at your knee cap."

He pointed his finger at me playfully. "I knew it! I knew that was on purpose."

I shrugged. "Well, at least, you were able to get your glove on it and slow it down a little bit."

He reached up and squeezed my shoulder. "Flip!" he said.

"Flip!" I echoed, laughing at his reference to Bonnie's magnet theory. I shoved my helmet on my head, straddled my bike, and started the engine. Acer patted the top of my helmet before I rode away.

When I arrived home, Mary was sitting in the recliner in the living room, reading one of her nursing textbooks. Every so often she would highlight something with the pink marker she was twirling between her fingers. I slipped into the kitchen, depositing my keys in the small pink polka-dotted cookie jar on the counter as I headed to the sink to do the dishes just as I had promised.

Shockingly, the sink was empty and when I opened the dishwasher, it was completely empty as well. There was a note on the whiteboard that hung on the refrigerator. It read:

This one is on me! I know you had a tough day.
Try not to get handcuffed tomorrow. Brian

Angela Geurin

So he knew about Coach Mac's plan! I had wondered what coach meant when he said my attorney would agree with him. He must have talked to Brian, or at the very least given him a heads up. He would have had to, for Brian to know about it.

I opened the refrigerator and grabbed an orange and my water bottle, then headed to my room. On the way, I stopped by the living room and said good night to Mary.

"Hey," she stopped me. "How's Bonnie?"

I turned, walked back into the living room, and plopped down on to the sofa before answering. "She's got cancer."

She sat up in her chair and closed her book, using her highlighter as a place holder. "You're kidding me."

"No, I'm not. Some kind of aggressive form of leukemia," I said flatly. "Apparently it's her second relapse."

"Harold and Beverly must be devastated! Did they just find out? I haven't heard a word about this from anyone."

I took a long slow drink. "Bonnie didn't say exactly, but it sounds like maybe two or three weeks. She started treatment last week." I took another drink as we sat there in silence. "Mary, I'm scared of losing my friend. I can't take any more losses this year."

Mary stood and made her way to the couch next to me. Without saying a word, she sat down and wrapped me in a warm hug. I leaned my head on her shoulder and she smoothed my hair. I'm sure she thought I would cry, but I was all tapped out of tears.

"This sucks!" she said, a remark out of character for her. I raised my head.

"Yeah, it does," I agreed with a laugh. "And I can't believe you just said that word!"

"There's no other way to describe it," she explained. "Things like this, they just suck the life right out of you!" Then, in what had become a common question between us since our heart-to-heart so many weeks ago, she asked, "What can I do to help?"

141

I didn't hesitate. I knew exactly what she could do. "I want to be there for Bonnie, like she was there for me. She needs a friend," I responded and Mary waited patiently for me to finish. "I need you to make an exception to our rules and let me go to her house during the week. I can be sure and come home before ten every night, but I want to be with her when I can. She needs me and I need her."

"Sure, no problem."

I pulled away and eyed her curiously. "That was easy. What's the catch?"

"There's no catch, Scout." She ran a hand through her strawberry blonde hair. "I understand what you need and you showed me tonight that I can trust you. You didn't try to sneak out of the house or lie and go behind my back to Brian. You came home when I asked you to and you came straight in to do the dishes just like you promised."

I started to tell her that Brian did the dishes, but she raised a hand and stopped me. "Don't worry. I know Brian did the dishes for you. I also know that when you could have snuck off to your room and hid the keys to your motorcycle, you didn't. You put them back."

"Thanks, Mary."

"You're welcome." She kissed my forehead. "Now you better get to bed since you have a game tomorrow."

I smiled, impressed that she remembered my game. We stood and I headed upstairs again, but stopped at the door. With everything that happened today, I had forgotten to let Rachel know that I needed a ride to school. It was too late to call. "Hey, Mary, you think you can take me to school tomorrow? I forgot to call Rachel."

"Sure. I was going to go in early and get some practice in on the SIM dummies, but I can do that on Thursday instead."

"You sure?" I asked again. "I don't want to cause you any problems."

"No, it's no problem," she answered. "Good night."

"Thanks, Mary. Good night."

Sleep evaded me. I was exhausted, but there was too much that happened for me to settle down my mind and sleep. After tossing and turning for an hour, I turned on my bedside lamp and looked around the room. Lying on top of my dresser, I spotted daddy's Bible. Curious as to why that of all things would catch my eye, I chalked it up to another God thing, and retrieved it from the dresser.

I padded out into the sitting area that connected my room to the rest of the second floor and sat down in the large chair and a half. It was the one that used to be in Daddy's study at our home in Kansas City. I inhaled the familiar leather smell that reminded me of Daddy and started thumbing through his Bible.

When Mary had offered me Daddy's Bible, I didn't really want it, but I was so angry that I took it anyway because I didn't think Mary or anyone else deserved it. I hadn't opened it until now, and as I thumbed through the worn pages, I realized just how treasured this book was— not only because it was God's Word, but because it was full of Daddy's memories. There were verses underlined and highlighted throughout and even comments written in Daddy's own hand in the margins. This Bible was like a journey through my daddy's heart.

I skimmed over and stopped at the book of Psalms, heading over to the 23rd chapter, one of Daddy's favorite passages, but stopped short as a folded, yellowed piece of paper fell out. I noticed an underlined passage with the name of my mother, Mariah, written next to it.

The underlined verse was Psalm 22:24, *"For he has not ignored or belittled the suffering of the needy. He has not turned his back on them, but has listened to their cries for help."*

Slowly, I reached down and picked up the yellow paper and inhaled sharply as I discovered, it was a letter to my dad from my mom.

My Darling Daniel,

I have loved you with an everlasting love that transcends time and space. Hand in hand, we walked this journey together, not knowing how it would all unfold, but knowing that as long as we were together the outcome was irrelevant. Today, we know that our journey together here on earth is near its end and that you will continue on without me, your helpmate. I know you are angry and I know you are scared, but remember that God will be, and always has been, your helpmate. When you are uncertain of what you should do, cry to Him and He will hear you. When you feel alone and lost, cry to Him and He will hear you. Cling to your faith, my love, because your faith is what will carry you to your journey's end.

With all my love,

Mariah (Psalm 22:24)

I held the letter close to my heart as my mind absorbed every word. God had sent me yet another message, showing me once again that He was right here, waiting to help me and all I had to do was ask. I started to cry as I realized that He sent this message across time through the mother that I hardly knew.

For the first time in my life, I really truly thought about my mom. I thought about the strength she had. I thought about the incredible faith she must have had to be so strong when her life was so sad. I wished I could remember her, like the rest of my family. I didn't know her, but I could get to know her. She had left me a journal, filled with her thoughts.

Trying to remember where I put it, I frantically searched through my room until I spotted the leather bound book on my desk, buried beneath a pile of my school work. I unsnapped it carefully and padded out to my sitting room with my quilt wrapped around my shoulders. My fingers flipped to the front page and I read once again her words to me.

For Esther Aileen, God's beautiful miracle,

144

Angela Geurin

God opened my heart the day you were born and showed me that all things are possible for those who love the Lord. May you find comfort and assurance all the days of your life in the arms of your heavenly Father.

Love, Momma

August 16, 1978

I turned to the first entry, January 1, 1978.

"This means that anyone who belongs to Christ has become a new person. The old life is gone; a new life has begun!" (2 Corinthians 5:17).

Thank You, heavenly Father, for giving me this word today. It's a new day and a new year and I can't wait to see what You have in store for me. For You already know the plans You have for me and they will be so good. I praise You for the good work You will do in me this year. Lead on, Lord. I'm ready to follow.

I skimmed through the pages. Every page was filled with Scripture and Momma's prayers. As I reread the first entry, I got the message loud and clear: God was in control of my future. This was my new day, my new beginning.

"God is so good!" I breathed. I reread the letter she had written Daddy, and felt fresh tears sting my eyes. *Cry out to Him...*

The floodgates opened then and I cried out to my heavenly Father. I prayed and prayed and prayed to Him. Verses that I had memorized as a young child poured out from the depths of my heart. I thanked Him for waiting on me. I thanked Him for my momma, for Mary and Brian, for Bonnie, and everyone else that He had placed in my life. I begged His forgiveness for my bitterness and all the terrible things I had done to those around me. I asked Him to forgive me for running

145

away and turning my back on Him. I prayed for Bonnie and Acer. I even prayed for Cade and Kiley.

When I had finally released everything to Him, I felt a peace settle over me that I had never felt before. I was full of peace and happiness despite all the problems that were surrounding me. I leaned back against the chair and my mind started racing again. I needed to talk to Bonnie and Acer. I needed to talk to Mary and Brian. I needed to fix everything that I had messed up. I needed to get some sleep.

Momma's journal was opened to June 15, 1978 and the verse at the top read: *"Be still and know that I am God!" (Psalm 46:10).*

If only this little gift you have given me could understand this verse right now, I might get some sleep. It's so hard right now with this stomach and back pain and I am so weak and tired, but I know You are in control and I know that You are God. Help me be still. Help this little baby be still and give us both some much needed rest tonight. What an unexpected blessing You have given me. Here I thought Danny Joe would be the last child I would have the privilege of raising, but as always, You know the plans You have for me, plans for good and not for evil, to give me a future and a hope. I hope this little one will make a big difference in the world, and as you knit this baby together in my womb, help us be still and rest in Your loving arms and wait for the fulfillment of Your promises.

An audible voice in my head said: *Scout, it's 2:30 in the morning. Get up and go back to bed.*

And so I did, and it was the best night's sleep I ever had.

The next morning over breakfast, Mary and I talked about what I found in Daddy's Bible and I shared with her what had happened after I read the letter from mom and the journal entries. I asked for her forgiveness and we shed some tears together. Then, she shared stories that I never knew about mom and her incredible faith, and before we knew it we were both running late.

I rushed to the bathroom, finished getting ready for school, and then headed out the side kitchen door. Mary was trailing behind me, so I leaned against the passenger side door waiting for her to unlock the car so I could get in. As I waited, I caught a glimpse of a red truck pull in front of the house. When it didn't immediately drive off, I walked down the driveway to investigate.

Leaning against the front fender of his truck, dressed in his typical collared shirt, jeans, and loafers, Acer smiled and waved.

"Good morning!" he greeted me.

"Good morning," I returned. "What brings you here?"

"You," he answered. "I thought maybe we could ride to school together. You know, since Bonnie can't take you."

"Oh," I responded, momentarily surprised. "O-OK. Let me tell Mary."

I headed back up the driveway with quick steps and a racing heart. Acer had said he was going to try to be nicer to me, but I wasn't expecting him to show up at my house unannounced, offering to give me a ride to school. It was shocking to say the least.

Mary was locking the door behind her when I sprinted up the steps. She jumped when she saw me. "Good heavens! What is it, Scout? You scared me to death!"

I panted, "I guess I have a ride after all."

"Oh, so Rachel showed up anyway?"

"No, Benjamin Acer, actually," I said slowly.

Mary raised an eyebrow. "Really? He just showed up?"

"Yeah, he said that he thought we could ride together this morning."

"I thought you two hated each other."

"Well, Coach Mac sort of made us work together yesterday and so we came to an agreement to try and be nice." I really had no idea how much Mary knew about the handcuffing thing so I decided to leave that part up to her imagination. "I guess this is his way of being nice."

"Really?" she asked skeptically.

"W-well," I stuttered and swallowed, gaining my confidence back. "Well, yes! He's just trying to be nice. His sister's got cancer and she was my ride to school and he's trying to make up for it."

At least I hoped that was all there was to it.

"All right, Scout," she threw her hands up in mock innocence, "if you say so."

"It's just a ride to school, Mary," I muttered.

"OK. No need to get defensive! It's just a ride to school," She glanced at his truck and back at me with a smirk. "Just stay on your side of the truck." She patted my shoulder and winked. "Now go on. I got to go."

I headed back down the driveway and Acer opened the passenger door for me as I climbed inside. Mary backed out of the driveway and wiggled her fingers in a delicate princess wave and headed to her class.

It's just a ride to school! I thought, but I knew that the moment we pulled into the parking lot together, the rumor mill would start up. Acer obviously thought the same thing, but didn't seem to care as much. He flashed me his little lopsided grin and said, "Don't you know, we'll be the talk of school this morning!"

"Probably," I agreed drily. *Maybe this wasn't such a good idea after all.*

Chapter Nine: Worry, Worry, Worry

Acer chattered the whole way to school. I'm not even sure he ever stopped to take a breath, but that was fine with me. I was already feeling a little flustered about him showing up at the house this morning. Booneville High School loomed in the windshield and I resisted the urge to duck out of view. My knee was bouncing uncontrollably the closer we got to the parking lot and it must have caught his attention.

"You want me to park on the back row so no one sees you get out of my truck?" he asked.

"I'll be fine," I said, coolly glancing around as he turned into the parking lot. "I'm just excited about the game this afternoon."

"Right," he answered and turned down the last row anyway.

When we pulled into a spot, I reached down, hoisted my backpack onto my lap, and watched as its entire contents crashed to the floor board. Everything, and I mean everything, even the tampons that I kept in the front zipper pocket, spilled onto the floorboard of his truck. My cheeks flushed in embarrassment and I spared a glance towards Acer, but thankfully he had already stepped out, shutting his door behind him. Hastily, I grabbed and stuffed fistfuls back into the bag, hoping to get everything returned before he came around to check on me, but I wasn't quick enough.

Diamonds in the Dirt

I had a handful of tampons when he opened the passenger door for me. His eyes darted to my hand and my cheeks flushed again. Frozen in place, I tried to cover my embarrassment with a chuckle but it came out high pitched and squeaky. I expected him to make some sarcastic remark, but he didn't. Instead, he leaned in, picked up my mom's leather bound journal that had slid under the seat, and placed it on my lap.

He grinned his little lopsided grin. "I do have a twin sister, remember?" he said quietly.

"It's still embarrassing," I returned.

Unfrozen, I finished packing my bag and zipped it up. Acer took it from my hand and waited for me to step out of the truck before handing it back to me. Unfortunately, Cade was there to witness the whole thing, and in typical Cade fashion, he ribbed us both.

"Well, look what we have here!" he taunted. "It's our girl-power catcher making it with her all-star pitcher. You get around pretty fast, Red! Is that the reason you tried out, so you could hook up with somebody? You could have saved time and taken me up on my offer at tryouts!"

I refused to acknowledge him and walked off. Acer said something, but I didn't even hear it. As always, Cade was a thorn in my side. Acer caught up and put his arm at the small of my back, much like he did last night. I lowered my backpack on my shoulders, which knocked his hand away. He got my not-so-subtle message because he walked the rest of the way with his hands in the pockets of his jeans.

This was all just too weird for me right now.

I avoided Cade the rest of the day, changing all of my normal paths around the school, but I didn't think about Acer. Every new path I took, he was there. I must have passed him a dozen times in the hallway, which was strange because up until today, I had never seen Acer during school hours. I felt like a stalker, and probably looked like one to anyone who paid attention. Each time he saw me, he waved or gave me a high five, nothing more, but it was still weird.

Angela Geurin

By sixth period, I was totally exasperated and unable to focus on anything that Mr. Tate was saying, so I asked to use the restroom, explained that it was a girl thing and skipped the last half of class. There are no gym classes during sixth period, so the girls' locker room was deserted. Sitting on the floor leaning against my locker, I pulled out my mom's journal, and flipped pages until I found today's date written across the top.

February 23, 1978

"Don't worry about anything; instead, pray about everything. Tell God what you need, and thank him for all he has done. Then you will experience God's peace, which exceeds anything we can understand. His peace will guard your hearts and minds as you live in Christ" (Philippians 4:6-7).

Lord, I need Your guidance today. I know I have made the right decision, but I am faced with the judgment of my closest friends and family, and they just make me doubt. You put this little life inside me, knowing all the while that the lump I found was cancerous. I can't risk any treatments that could harm this baby. I know I am not being selfish, despite what Evelyn thinks. I know that I have four other children and a husband, but I can't knowingly harm the little life that is inside me now just because it might save my own. Is this cancer really going to take my life? Are you really ready to take me home before my children are even grown? How will Daniel cope on his own? How will he raise five kids without me? I know, Lord. I'm at it again. Worry, worry, worry. I am reminded that Your Word tells me to leave all my worries with You because You care for me. So I give this all to You. I trust You to bring this new life safely into my waiting arms and work on Evelyn's heart in Your own time. Thank You for this precious gift. Thank You for Christ Jesus. Thanks for listening.

That's just what I needed this morning, wasn't it? What would have happened to me if momma had listened to Evelyn? I can't believe

151

my mom had to make such a difficult choice: my life, for hers. How sad! Daddy had told me that she waited until after I was born before starting any cancer treatments. He told me she just wanted to give me the best shot at life. But he never said anything about what people thought about her decision.

Don't worry about anything.

Her worry seemed a little more justified than mine. Worrying was all I had done today, and compared to what my mother had worried about, it seemed pretty silly. I worried about being harassed by Cade. I worried about what people would say about Acer and me riding to school together. I worried about what people would think about me crossing paths with him all day. Worry, worry, worry. Not once had I thought about Bonnie, and she was fighting cancer.

I repeated the verse in my head. What a waste of a day.

The locker room door opened, followed by a group of voices, and I knew my solitude was over. Reluctantly, I closed momma's journal and slipped it back into my bag. In the distance, I heard the bell, signaling the end of school.

Worry was such a waste of time.

I stood against the railing watching our team take the field for our afternoon game. Jason and Blake had drawn the start for our home game this afternoon and Kyle was penciled for relief, so essentially, Acer and I had the day off. It was probably a good thing. My head was still distracted by the events of the last twenty-four hours.

Don't worry about anything, I heard softly in my head and kept my eyes on the field.

"Hey, school's over for the day, so why the pencil and paper?" Acer asked.

He nudged my elbow down the padded rail, squeezing himself in between me and the dugout steps. Consciously, I took a step away from him and glanced at Cade on second base. I was relieved to see that the little weasel was facing the outfield and couldn't see us.

"I'm scouting Bowie's hitters in case we have to throw against them later in the season," I responded, watching the second batter taking his practice swings. "Since I haven't got a photographic memory, I use pencil and paper. Besides, it keeps me from getting bored on the bench." *And thinking about the craziness in my life right now.*

I made a note next to the first batter indicating that he had ground out to the second baseman and took Jason to a full count. As I finished, Acer snatched my notebook out of my hand and started flipping through the pages.

"Hey! Give it back!" I protested and tried to grab it from him. He jerked it away and turned his body, blocking my reach.

"This is really detailed," he commented." You have notes on all the hitters and teams we have played so far this year." I reached again, and again he yanked it just out of my reach. "OS, CS, SIB, CH, DSH, DB what is all that mean?"

"It's just my short hand," I returned. Exasperated, I poked him in the ribs and he bent to the side, crouching away, laughing like a little girl.

"No, no don't do that!" he laughed. "Here you can have it back." He held it out for me, but did not let go when I tried to pull it out of his grasp. "Tell me what all of that stuff means."

"Why?"

"Just tell me."

"Not until you tell me why you want to know," I stated meeting his gaze.

"Well, maybe if I understood why you were calling the pitches that you called we would be on the same page when we were out there."

It was a logical reason, but I was still skeptical and raised my eyebrows before responding. "You really want to learn how to study hitters?"

"When I grow up, I want to be smart, just like you," he mocked. I narrowed my eyes and he quickly added with more sincerity. "No seriously, Scout, teach me. Help me become a 'student of the game.'"

"Ok," I said after a moment. I pointed to the hitter that was walking up to the right side of the plate. "Look at his stance. What do you see?"

He tilted his head slightly as he stared at the next batter. It was something he did frequently when he was in deep concentration. "Well, he's short and he makes himself shorter by how much he is bending his knees."

"Yes," I agreed with him. "What do you notice about his bat?"

"It's on his shoulder," he answered. "So what does all of that tell you?"

"Typically, your two-hole hitters are not going to hit for power. They may get lucky every once in a while, but they're table setters. Their job is to either move the lead off runner or get themselves on a base," I watched the hitter look at Jason's first offering which was practically down the middle of the plate and wrote FPL.

He leaned in close to me until he was looking over my shoulder. The heat between us made me feel a momentary flutter in my stomach and my face flushed. I ducked my head down, praying that no one noticed.

"What's FPL?" he asked.

"First Pitch Looker," I answered. "He didn't even take the bat off of his shoulder. He was never going to swing at the first pitch and it was so fat, he probably could have gotten lucky if he had swung." I took a tiny sideways step down the rail, trying to put a little more distance between us again before continuing. "See how far he's bent at the waist. I bet he is a really weak hitter, but gets a free ride most of the time. That's probably why he leans over the plate and crouches low in his stance. If Jason comes inside too much, he'll probably lean into it and try to take one for the team."

Before the words were out of my mouth, Jason's next offering came in high and inside. The batter turned his back to the pitch and it struck him just below his shoulder.

"He's hanging over the plate!" Jason threw his hands in the air and yelled in protest.

Coach Mac hustled out of the dugout to conference with the umpire.

"Wow!" Acer exclaimed. "You're good. You called that perfectly."

I looked at Acer and playfully brushed the pretend dirt off of my shoulders before taking a bow. "Thank you very much."

"So tell me what you would have done?" he asked, scooting in close to me again.

I stepped down a little bit more and answered, "I probably would have started him the same way, fastball right down the middle because he is not going to swing. Then, I would have gone with either a curve or slider on the outside corner because I am guessing he doesn't swing until he is behind in the count. If its strike two, I would go high and outside off the plate and then if he still didn't swing, bust him knee high and inside for strike three."

"What if he turns into the pitch like he did with Jason?" he asked.

"He wouldn't."

"How do you know?"

"There's no meat on your knee. You turn into that pitch and you're done for the day."

He nodded his head and turned back to look at Coach Mac who was headed back to the dugout. "You going to tell me what all of your shorthand means?" he asked leaning in over my shoulder again.

I sighed. "OS is Open Stance. CS is Closed Stance. BS is a Bucket Stepper," I explained further when he looked confused, "You know they step away from the pitch more like down the third baseline. Daddy always called it "stepping in the bucket." Anyway, CH is Casts Hands, you know like a fisherman casts his line, and DSH is Dinky Stinky Hit; those are the hits that are weak, but drop between the infield and outfield because they are just far enough in no man's land that no one can catch them. My pitcher in Kansas City coined that one."

"So what about DB?"

I was hoping he would forget about that one because I came up with it after my first practice with the team and it originally referenced him. I hesitated until at last, I relented and explained. "Dirt Bag."

"Dirt Bag?" he laughed. "What exactly does a DB do that is so important to make notes?" He kept laughing.

"Well, these are the dirty players. They try to intimidate and distract their opponents by annoying them. They're the ones who make sexist jokes, kick my mask or helmet around, kick dirt in my face, spit on my shoe, or throw at my head. You know, they act like dirtbags, and they are the ones that I have to watch out for because they don't want to outplay me, they want to take me out."

"I bet you think I'm a DB," he said, quietly studying his cleats.

"Yep, you're a DB," I agreed and then nudged him with my elbow. "But you're starting to change my mind."

He tilted his chin up. "Flip."

I laughed in agreement and went back to watching hitters.

The game continued on in much the same fashion. I taught him how to break down a hitter's swing and he taught me the finer techniques of overhand pitching, pointing out some of the flaws of the opposing pitcher. It was like we were in our own world, but completely involved in the game at the same time.

It was a great game too! We couldn't push enough runs across to take the lead as Bowie matched us run for run every inning, but the defense was spectacular. Jose looked like a vacuum cleaner, sucking up every ball that came to that side of the infield. Nothing got past him and he turned a double play that looked like a pro. He caught Cade's quick flip from second base barehanded, jumped over the diving runner, and nailed the throw to first.

Now, in the bottom of the ninth, things were starting to look up. We were down by one run. Jon had reached first base on an error. Jose sacrificed bunted him to second. Cade drew a walk and Kevin hit a DSH that loaded the bases. It didn't get any better than this. This is what baseball was all about.

I watched eagerly as our catcher, Blake, strode to the plate. He had struck out his first two at bats and we needed him to get a piece of the ball. With one out and bases loaded, we only needed him to put the ball in play.

Suddenly, Coach Mac turned and looked at me. "Scout! Grab a bat!" He headed to the umpire and patted Blake on the shoulder, nodding him toward the dugout.

Acer got my helmet and tossed it to me. "Remember what I told you about his arm. You'll know what's coming," he instructed. I slid my helmet in place and saluted him.

As I headed up the dugout steps, Blake bumped me in disgust, but surprised me by turning around, catching my arm in the process. "He has stayed with his slider early in the count, but it's never a strike. Be patient; he can't afford to mess around with you too much."

I acknowledged him with a nod and strutted out towards the plate. I took a couple of practice swings, while Coach Mac finished with the umpire. He stopped by me and looked me in the eye. "Sit back and wait on the fastball," he instructed his voice low and deep. "I want you to show everyone here, why I put you on this team."

I nodded. "You got it, Coach."

Striding forward, I looked at all the holes in the outfield, all the places where there was nothing but green grass, and then I looked at the scoreboard and the outfield walls.

"So desperate they got to send a chick to the plate," the catcher taunted. Then he shouted to the infield, "Watch out! They're bringing in their secret weapon! Better be ready, she might get this past the pitcher's mound."

"Don't break a nail, sweetheart!" someone from the stands hollered.

I stepped into the batter's box and set my hands and feet.

Off!

The noise faded to silence and my vision field closed in on the pitcher. I saw the back of his glove as he presented the ball. He wiggled his fingers inside the web, getting his grip and let loose with his first pitch. It looked like it was coming right down the middle, and I was tempted to swing, but like Acer had explained earlier, the angle of his arm was sliding around the ball as he released it. It was his slider and I knew I had to lay off, so I did. The ball finished low and off the plate. The next pitch was yet another slider and this one looked inside, but dove down and hooked the inside corner for strike one. He wasted his third pitch, throwing his third straight slider and it was off the plate for ball two.

"Just like a girl to window shop!" the catcher yelled as I backed out of the box.

I took another practice swing and then breathed in and out slowly. This was my shot. It was time to shut everyone up. As I dug into the batter's box, waiting for his next offering, he snapped a throw over to the third baseman and Jon dove back under the tag.

He couldn't afford to take me 3-1 with bases loaded, so I was willing to bet this next one would be the fastball I wanted, probably inside corner since the last pitch was out and they got me to hesitate on the inside slider.

Off!

Angela Geurin

My focus on the pitcher, I noticed that his glove was slightly turned, facing his right hand as he gripped the ball. No wiggling fingers this time, no hesitation, just grip and go. It had to be a fastball.

Come on! Throw me that big fat beach ball!

He did. The ball was hard and about thigh high on the inside part of the plate, but not far enough inside for me to mishit. I exploded into motion, my hands extending inside the ball in perfect timing with my hips and when the ball connected with my bat, I felt that wonderful powerful feeling of perfection, known as the sweet spot. The ball launched off the bat like a rocket.

Crush!

I didn't watch it go. I ducked my head and took off in a run and it wasn't until I was half way to second that I realized the ball went yard. It was a walk-off grand slam! I slowed to a trot, touching second base and then third. Coach Mac high fived me as I headed home and said something about "that's why you're on my team."

Our team gathered around home plate, cheering, and the umpire stood next to the catcher, watching me as I touched home plate. In a gesture of sportsmanship, the catcher patted my shoulder and nodded towards the fence.

"Nice hit," he said and walked away.

"Thanks," I replied to his back.

My team swallowed me up as they patted my helmet and cheered. The stands were roaring. I was the hero for the day and I couldn't have felt better. It was the first home run for the team this season. If I didn't have the respect of my teammates before, I definitely had it now.

Or so I thought.

We shook our opponent's hands and headed into the dugout. That's when I felt someone slap my backside. Now I know that in all sports, a slap in the backside means encouragement, congratulations, better luck next time. But as the only girl on a team of teenage boys, it was way out of line. I whirled around and caught sight of Cade. He winked at me and lifted his chin.

Making like I was going to high five him, I grabbed his hand and twisted it around to the middle of his back. "You got your freebie in the hallway at school," I growled in his ear. "Consider yourself warned, Cade. Touch me again and I will break your arm off and beat you with it."

He winced, but chuckled. "You know you enjoyed it."

I shoved him forward and he stumbled into Acer. He steadied himself and then gave me one more wicked grin before heading into the dugout.

"What was that all about?" Acer asked.

"Nothing worth talking about," I muttered.

Leave it to Cade to turn an exciting moment into trash! Acer playfully punched me in the shoulder. "Nice hit!"

"Thanks! Nice call on the fastball," I returned. "He completely gave it away, just like you said." He took a bow. "I guess Coach Mac was right. We can make a good team when we work together."

"Yep. Just needed a little flip!" He winked and jogged over to the dugout.

Acer took me home after the game since Bonnie hadn't made it back from her treatment. We rode in silence most of the way. My mind kept replaying the events of the afternoon. Acer and I had finally clicked, but when I thought about Cade, I cringed. He was one guy I wished would fall off the planet. I don't think I would ever have his respect. He didn't respect anyone.

"Here you are." I heard through my thoughts. Acer's truck rolled to a slow stop in front of my house and he put it in park.

"Thanks for the ride." I started to open the door, but he grabbed my arm.

"I can give you a ride in the morning," he stated. His voice cracked on the last syllable. "I mean if you need one. I could give you a ride to school any day. Just let me know."

He acted nervous, kind of like he did last night trying to apologize. It was cute actually and I grinned. "You know I have not given up on convincing Mary to let me ride my motorcycle to school, but that is still a work in progress." He laughed. "So I could definitely use a ride tomorrow."

"All right, then, I will see you in the morning," he almost looked excited. "Same time as today?"

"Sure. See you tomorrow."

"See you."

I walked up the long driveway to the kitchen door. Acer and I were definitely headed in the right direction. I couldn't wait for our next game. Coach Mac was so right. With Acer and I both working together we could turn this season around. Our team could really make a run for the championship. We just had to avoid anything that would throw us back into a standoff again. I opened the door and stepped inside, closing it behind me and feeling better than I had in a while.

"Hey, kid," Brian said, startling me out of my thoughts. "We've got some news. Have a seat." He gestured to the chair across from him and next to Mary. I noticed immediately that her eyes and nose were red from crying.

"Oh, now what?" I spoke the thought out loud and slumped in my chair.

Chapter Ten: Surprise

I gripped the table in anticipation of the terrible news that was surely to come. My imagination was running wild. For those few seconds I felt panic stricken, unable to conceal the fear of the arrival of yet more bad news. I mean, why else would Mary be in tears?

I looked at Mary, waiting as she tried to compose herself. "Scout, you are going to be an aunt again," she said quietly.

Relief flooded me when I realized that no one had cancer or died or anything else bad. Then I wondered: If it was happy news, why was Mary crying? "Who's pregnant?" I asked.

Mary didn't look up and started sobbing again.

Brian rubbed her shoulder and laughed. "Who do you think?"

I stared dumbfounded at the two of them. If Mary was the one pregnant, she would be ecstatic, not a sobbing, emotional train wreck. So it had to be one of my other siblings. David and Emily had been married forever with no children and no desire to ever have them. So it wouldn't be them. Maybe it was Ruth. Julio had just been cut from his minor league team and he was back on the market again, but Ruth always talked about having a family some day. A baby could make it hard for them, but it would definitely be happy news. Danny Joe on the other hand, was out of work again and Sadie was threatening to move back in with her parents if he didn't get off the couch and find a job. It would be a real headache to add another baby into that mix.

"Is Sadie pregnant again?"

"Nope, Mary's got a bun in the oven," Brian spouted off with a laugh. Mary looked horrified and slapped him hard in the shoulder. "Ow! Take it easy, Mama."

My jaw hit the floor. This was definitely not what I was expecting to hear from the two of them today. but after the initial shock wore off, I felt elated! Mary was going to have a baby! So, if I felt happy, and Brian felt happy, why was Mary angry and crying?

"Mary, this is great news!" I nearly shouted. "Why are you crying?"

She started sobbing again and Brian reached across the table and took her hand. "I'm not ready for this!" she wailed. "I mean, I just started back at college! I was going to finish my degree and work a couple of years and then think about having a family. You would be out of the house by then. The timing of this is just awful! It made sense my way. This doesn't make any sense at all!"

"But it's so much more exciting and fun this way," Brian said. "You will be so busy with school you won't have any time to think about being pregnant and with Scout here, we have a built-in babysitter for the next three years."

"Hey, I didn't volunteer for that," I protested.

He grinned and continued. "Face it, babe, you are not in control of as much as you think, and this is God's way of showing you that." She glared at him. "Think about it! We are going to have a baby! Me and you! And with our genes, you know this baby will be the most beautiful baby in the world. We are talking beauty queen, our little princess."

"Or prince," she added quietly.

That's what I loved about my brother-in-law. No matter how serious things were, he never failed to lighten the mood and put things back into perspective, but I could understand Mary's fear. She went back to school for Daddy. It was the same kind of drive that made me determined to play on the boy's baseball team, and I am sure that her fear of not being able to do something that meant so much to her and Daddy was the same as well.

I reached out and grabbed her hand. "He's right, Mary," I said gently, "There are plenty of diamonds in the dirt, if you'll take a minute to look down and find them." She smiled then, recognizing her own words. "You can still finish school. You don't have that many credits left. You'll have most of them done before the baby even arrives, especially if you go during the summer like you were talking about last week. We can all help and make it work. You just tell us what you need us to do."

Brian nodded in agreement.

"Thanks," she said after a moment.

"So when is this little booger supposed to arrive?"

Mary and Brian exchanged a look before she answered. "August 16th."

"August 16th!" I exclaimed, and then playfully patted Mary's tummy. "Sorry, kid, that day belongs to Aunt Scout, but if you are nice to momma and let her get through nursing school, I'll think about sharing my birthday with you."

During the month of March, our baseball schedule picked up. Every other day we had a game. It was exhausting, but when I thought about how exhausted Bonnie was from her treatments and Mary was from feeding the little peanut in her tummy, it didn't seem all that bad.

Our team had hit a rough patch with our hitting and had dropped back-to-back losses at the Sinclair tournament, but turned around the following week to beat Clements at home. We came in second place at the Marshall tournament, but broke even, winning two and losing two. Then the following week we dropped three straight losses on the road, giving us an overall record of 8-9 heading into spring break. All of our losses were close—within a couple of runs—which was frustrating because our defense was solid, especially at pitcher.

Acer was looking better each time he threw, but he still hadn't finished a game. The good thing though, was that he wasn't going postal when he was yanked, and he didn't get as worked up when I went out to the mound to get him on track. We actually seemed to get along like you would expect of any battery.

"Ball four, take your base," the umpire called behind me.

It was the bottom of the seventh and we were down by two runs on the road yet again, this time against Southwest Houston. I stood and waited until the batter had reached first base and then called time out.

"Time!" I heard from behind me.

I lifted my mask, resting it on the top of my helmet, not daring to leave it on the ground at the plate. I learned quickly that this team was full of DBs. Real class acts. They played dirty, talked dirty, and did disgusting things—like spit loogies in the catcher's mask. Deliberately, I walked out to the mound and tried to block out what was coming.

"Oh-oh, here she goes, boys. Work it, work it, work it, oh yeah, sugar!"

I rolled my eyes. I didn't have to turn around to see who it was. It had been the same jerk for seven innings. I had finally asked the umpire in the top of the third how long he was going to let that nonsense go on, and he had said he didn't know what I was talking about. Coach Mac had asked a similar question in the bottom of the fifth when the pervert had shouted something about my anatomy that was very PG-13. Whatever excuses the umpire had given Coach Mac, they weren't good enough because the conversation quickly escalated to a lot of yelling and dirt kicking, until at last the umpire had all he wanted and tossed him from the game.

"I want to punch that redneck in the teeth!" Acer said when I made it out to the mound.

"Somebody's already beat you to it, Ace," I joked. "You'd have to punch the one tooth he has left and one tooth is not worth the effort."

That got the lopsided grin I was hoping for. "How can you just ignore it? I mean he's been at it the whole game."

165

"You forget I've been listening to this kind of stuff all season. It starts to sound like static after a while."

He blew out a breath and changed the subject. "So what do we have coming up now."

"Lead off CS BS," I answered.

He glanced at the batter coming up to the left side of the plate. "Oh, yeah, the DB that spit in your mask back in the fourth."

"Yep, that's the one."

"What's the plan, boss? Sliders on the outside?"

"We've got two outs with runners on the corners. He was pretty freaked when you lost that curve and buzzed his ear last at bat. Let's get into his head. Time for some payback. Bust him high and inside first pitch. Fastball as hard as you can right below his chin."

"Chin music?" he responded, "He's a BS. What if he turns on it? Isn't that kinda pitching to his strength?"

"I'll take care of that on my end." He furrowed his brow in confusion. "Trust me, Ace. It'll work."

Reluctantly, he stared me straight in the eyes. "All right, let's do it."

He turned around and I grabbed his arm. I could sense the umpire heading towards the mound. "Oh, and Acer, don't listen to anything I say during this at bat. You have pitched a great game and you are the best in the state."

"Okay," he said slowly, confusion written all over his face.

"Let's play ball!" the umpire said impatiently.

I turned and smiled sweetly at him. "Thanks, sir, I think we got it figured out."

We walked back to the plate side by side. He was a dark-skinned man about my height, with dark brown serious eyes. I didn't envy his choice of occupation. Officiating any sport is a thankless job. No one ever compliments an umpire on a call he made or when he hustles to get into position to make the right call. Most of the time when they are recognized,

Angela Geurin

it is for their mistakes, so I try to cut them some slack. But listening to my fan club for the last seven innings and the lack of response from the man beside me, I felt he just might be partial to our opponents.

"Did you kiss it and make it all better or is that for later?" my number one fan yelled from the stands.

I looked sideways at the umpire as we continued walking. "You really didn't hear that."

"No, ma'am," he responded curtly, not even so much as glancing my way.

I shook my head and slid my mask down over my face. "Neither did I."

"Play ball!" he yelled as the leadoff DB stepped up to the plate.

"All right, guys, two down! Runner's at the corners; we just need an out!" I crouched into position and flashed the signals to Acer and the infield. "Come on, Acer! We just need strikes."

The ball was perfectly placed and with the upward tail of Acer's fastball, DB was ducking for cover. His bat clattered to the ground, and he lay, momentarily stunned, with his back in the dirt.

I snagged the ball at the last second in mock surprise. Grinning as I saw the runner on third take the bait and jump towards home plate, I immediately snapped a throw down that was just a half second shy of his reaching hand as he dove back toward the base. I glanced at the runner on first base. Good, he was staying put.

Bending over, I picked up the bat and knocked it against my shin guards before handing it to the batter. "You all right, man?" I asked as he finished brushing himself off and reached for the bat. "I'm sorry about that. I swear sometimes this joker can't hit a broad side of a barn!" Then turning my attention back to Acer, I slid my mask up and yelled, "Come on, Acer! You got to hit your targets!" Then for the hitter's benefit, I added, "Please just throw strikes. We don't need you to be a hero!"

I continued to rattle on about Acer's pitching as I crouched into my squat and gave him the sign for a slider. The batter didn't dig into

167

the box as much as he had his previous at bats, and by the look on his face, I could see that my chatter towards Acer was getting on his nerves. Acer delivered the pitch in just the right spot and the batter mishit it just as I had hoped, popping the ball straight up in the air.

I jumped up and threw my mask off, tracking the ball just in front of home plate. "I got it!" I yelled.

Kevin and Bull called my name in response. Settling under the ball, I waited for it to fall into my glove and heard the soft pop as leather contacted leather. Then, I felt a wrecking ball punch into my stomach, sending air rushing out of my lungs. Simultaneously, my body flew through the air as I covered the ball with my bare hand and squeezed my glove shut tight. All too quickly, the ground rushed towards me and I winced in pain as I landed hard on my back. My head slammed into the ground and my vision exploded into stars.

Dazed and trying to catch my breath, I lay there, looking up at the umpire hovering over me. My ears were ringing from the impact and I couldn't make out what he was saying and had to guess. I opened my glove and showed him the ball. He gave the signal for an out before gesturing with his other hand at the player that was hovering around my peripheral vision. It was the runner who tried to take me out from third base!

"You're out of here!" the umpire said, jerking his finger toward the stands.

Immediately, the opposing coach ran from the coaching box at third. "That was a clean play. You can't toss him because she's not tough enough to handle a little contact!"

"He was out of the base path and made no attempt to slide, coach," he explained.

The batter joined in the argument and I heard Bull throw in his own choice words. This was escalating too fast. Yes, it was a cheap shot, but I was more than capable of handling a little contact and decided to show everyone there that this girl was just fine.

In one swift motion, I rocked my legs back towards my head and hurled my body into a standing position just as Kevin had reached

Angela Geurin

down offering assistance. The movement made me dizzy, but I willfully steadied my legs and stood tall and strong, refusing the help. Nonchalantly, I tossed the ball to the umpire and had the pleasure of seeing the startled expressions of Southwest Houston's players and coaches. The umpire caught it and touched a finger to his backwards hat in salute. I saluted back.

I strutted past the gathering crowd and stepped into our dugout. Acer was two steps behind me, but didn't speak a word, nor did he attempt to help me down the stairs. He just trailed behind and plopped down next to me at the end of the bench.

The trainer had an ice pack for me and I refused to take it. Acer took it instead and laid it across the top of my head. "Don't argue," he said. "You flew ten feet and slammed your head really hard. We've got two more innings and I need you to help me finish this game."

Reluctantly, I slid the icepack down just above the base of my neck and leaned back against the wall, holding it there.

"How do you feel?" the trainer asked and flashed a pen light in front of my eyes.

"Like I've been run over by an eighteen wheeler," I said sarcastically. "But I'm fine. I've been knocked down a lot harder than that."

"How old are you?"

"Sixteen," I spat.

"Where are you right now?" she asked.

I rolled my eyes in annoyance. *Didn't I just say I was fine?* "Look, we are at Southwest Houston, top of the eighth inning, down by two runs. I've got some jerk in the stands, sexually harassing me. Coach Mac got tossed in the fifth. Acer is throwing his best game so far this season, and some cyclops just ran over me at the plate." She stared at me in stunned silence so I added, "I'm batting fourth this inning and only have three hitters to shake my head clear so I can deliver some major payback. Would you mind leaving me alone?"

Diamonds in the Dirt

Coach Haywood leaned into the dugout just then and looked expectantly at our team trainer. "Well, she OK?"

"Oh, yeah, she's just fine. Feisty and rude as ever," she returned and walked to the other side of the dugout.

Guilt stricken, I hollered before she got too far. "I'm sorry. I don't mean to be rude. I'm just mad."

She turned and fixed me with an amused grin. "Don't worry about it, sweetie. I've dealt with much feistier players before and they don't even apologize. Let me know if you get dizzy."

Just as I had hoped, I got my chance at the plate. With my head still fuzzy, I strode confidently into the batter's box with runners at second and third and only one out. I smashed the first pitch I was given. It was a line drive that whizzed by the pitcher before he even saw it. Both runners scored and as they tried to throw out the runner at home, I took off for second and dove toward the outside part of the base. Clutching it with my fingers, my body jerked to an abrupt halt.

I raised my hand to signal the umpire for time out and cringed as the shortstop purposely stepped on my thumb and pointer finger, resting on the top of the bag. His cleats crushed my hand and he started twisting his foot. He wouldn't get off my hand so I punched at his foot with my right, my balled fist connecting hard just above his ankle. He reared back to kick me and I grabbed his foot and stood with it still in my hand.

"Get off me, punk!" I yelled and threw him to the ground, which was easy to do with him standing on one foot.

He jumped up ready to fight. The umpire stepped in between us. "Easy, you two!" he yelled. He started to walk the shortstop back to his position.

The short-statured boy hollered, "You better watch it, girl! This ain't cow town! You're on our field."

I stood as tall as I could, glowering down at him, until he made it to his position.

Angela Geurin

Bull popped up to the first baseman after the commotion, and even though I tagged, there was no way I could make it to third. Now with the game tied, Jose was our last chance this inning to take the lead. I shouted encouragement to him and watched Coach Haywood give the signs. A ripple of surprise coursed through me as I realized he was calling a hit-and-run with two outs with the weakest hitter in the lineup. Talk about guts!

I took my lead, readying my feet to go on the pitch. The pitcher was throwing from a stretch and as I watched his front toe, it turned quickly towards me. I immediately got back to the bag. The second baseman slapped me hard with his glove.

I took an even bigger lead this time. My weight was centered on the balls of my feet, poised and ready to run on the pitch. The pitcher's front toe started heading to the plate and without hesitation, I took off. A second later, I heard the crack of Jose's bat as he connected with the ball and glanced back towards the plate. It was a perfect execution, grounder sneaking by the diving first and second basemen.

Ducking my head, I saw Coach Haywood signaling me home and I hit the inside corner of the base and dug hard. I could feel that it was going to be a close play at the plate and I watched as the catcher played up the baseline, waiting for the throw home. The ball bounced into his glove and he started heading up the line towards me. Like a running back, dodging a tackle, I jerked my head toward the baseline and watched as he followed my motion, and then headed in the opposite direction towards home plate.

Realizing his error, he dove back towards me and I slung my legs and arms towards the plate, sliding just out of his reach. I landed on my stomach, my head facing third base and slapped the plate with my right hand.

"Safe!"

I jumped up and pumped my fists in the air as my teammates circled me in congratulations. We finally had the lead and so help me, we were not letting this one go!

Diamonds in the Dirt

When the bottom of the ninth came around, the score remained the same. Southwest Houston threatened in the bottom of the eighth, but Acer kept it together and popped up the last batter with runners at second and third. Unfortunately, our offense went three up, three down in the top of the ninth giving our opponents the momentum they needed to mount a comeback.

The first batter hit a line drive right at Bull on third base. He snagged it, but it was a really hard hit and Acer knew he had missed the pitch. The next batter was a looker, and it was a good thing because Acer just didn't have the same zip on the ball and his first two strikes were flat as a pancake. With the count 0-2, Acer threw three straight balls off the plate before running the ball inside and freezing his hands for strike three.

Just when I started to think Acer could complete his first game, he walked the next two batters after taking them to a full count. Now with runners at first and second, we were facing their best hitter with the tying run in scoring position.

"Time out, Blue," I requested.

Waiting until my request was granted, I took off my face mask and tucked it under my arm, then headed out to chat with Acer.

"Uh-oh, Look out, boys, there she goes! Show him whose boss out there, honey!" I heard from my biggest fan. He whistled and whooped.

"Hey, Deliverance! Why don't you shut up!" Someone yelled.

I hesitated in my step as it hit me. I knew that voice. We had maybe half a dozen fans that showed up for the game, none of which would have stood up for me and none of them would have sounded like that.

My fan continued taunting. When I made it to the mound, I spared a glance into the stands just in time to see an auburn-haired young man lean down to the second row where my fan sat and dump the contents of his drink on his head. He jumped up and whirled around. As the younger man stepped down the bleachers to meet him, I saw the familiar face, realized it matched the voice I had heard, and shook my head with a mixture of surprise and irritation.

Like the parting of the Red Sea, the people between the two men slid to either side of the bleachers, creating a large path. The verbal jabs continued for a minute or two and then my tormenter lunged and the fists began to fly. As happy as I was to see the guy that had harassed me for nine innings get pummeled, it was causing a distraction at a very crucial moment in this game.

"You have got to be kidding me!" I groaned, and felt a dull throb in the back of my head.

"Who is that?" Acer asked as we watched security escort the two men out of the stands.

"That, Acer, is my hot-headed brother, Danny Joe," I stated flatly. "I hope he's smart enough to stop before he gets thrown in jail."

"You didn't tell me that your brother was here."

"I didn't know my brother was here until now. My brother is supposed to be with his wife and kid looking for work in Olathe, Kansas." I shook my head again. "None of that matters." I slapped the ball into the web of his glove. "Are you going to finish this game or is Coach Haywood going to have to go to the bull pen?"

I saw irritation surface on his face again: Postal threatening to rear his ugly head. "I could have finished it two batters ago if you would have just stuck with the fastball."

"All right then, if it's fastballs you want then we will stick with fastballs, besides this guy has crushed all your breaking stuff all day long," I patted his shoulder. "Nothing over the middle of the plate, keep it on the black."

"Whatever you say boss," he answered.

I grinned and said, "Flip!"

The lopsided grin reappeared and he returned, "Flip!"

"Dig deep in the tank and blow it by him so we can win this game and finally head home." *And hopefully not have to bail my brother out of jail on the way.*

He nodded as I headed back to my position. En route, I looked at Coach Haywood who was standing outside the dugout and waved him off. "He's good, Coach!" I hollered. "We got this!" Then, before crouching in position, I yelled, "Touch any base out there guys! We've got two outs!"

I slid my mask in place as the batter dug in and gave the signal. Acer nailed the first pitch on the outside corner for strike one. I called the next pitch low and inside, and the batter's swing was too late. Acer delivered the next pitch inside like I wanted, but too much over the plate and I held my breath as the ball sailed over the left field wall, but foul.

"Long strike, Ace!" I said. "Come on; you got this!"

His next fastball hugged the black line of the plate and the hitter barely reached it as he threw his bat out and fouled it off. I called for another fastball and indicated to Acer that I wanted it off the plate. His final pitch screamed just out of reach of the batter's swing for strike three. As I caught the ball, I blew out the breath I had been holding and flipped the ball to the umpire.

I stuck out my hand and he shook it. "You called a good game back there, sir."

Shock registered in his stern face. "Thanks. You are one tough cookie."

I shrugged. "Have to be since I'm playing with a bunch of boys."

As I headed to join my team and congratulate Acer on his first complete game of the season, my injuries and fatigue started to hit me. My head hurt, my legs hurt, and for some reason my brother had driven over 700 miles to watch me play a high school baseball game.

I was relieved to learn that Danny Joe had not been arrested after the game. He followed the bus back to Booneville, stopping with us along the way for dinner. Acer and I were seated in a booth across from each other, when he showed up and slid in next to him.

"Danny Joe," he introduced himself, offering Acer his hand.

Acer wiped his fingers with his napkin and shook his hand. "Ben Acer."

"Nice name!" he commented. "Acer, like Ace," he tested it out and nodded his head in approval. "That's a strong name."

I rolled my eyes. Danny Joe had a thing for names. He always said strong names are remembered and if he had a son, he was giving him a strong first name, since his last name would be Rose. Somehow I didn't think Sadie would let him name any son of theirs Ace though.

"What brings you to Houston?" I asked.

"Hey, Sis!" he greeted me as if just now realizing I was across from him. "That was some game! The way you faked that guy out and slid home for the winning run...awesome!"

"Danny Joe! Answer me! Why are you in Houston? How did you even know I was playing? I haven't heard from you since the funeral," I asked exasperated. He slid a sideways glance to Acer and I added, "Ace is just fine. He's my friend. Now answer me."

"You know, Sis, same old story. I got laid off and Sadie took Adalie and moved back in with her parents...again," he explained. "I'm down here because I couldn't find a job and Brian got me one doing maintenance at a golf course in town. I called Mary from a truck stop about ten miles from your game and she mentioned you were playing in Houston. I haven't seen you play since you were like ten, so I thought I would drop by and catch an inning or two."

"And beat up a teenager while you were at it," I added smugly.

"That was no teenager. He was a twenty-six-year old redneck and he had it coming! Sister or not, no one deserves to be talked to that way, especially a teenage girl!" he argued.

"Thank you," Acer agreed. "I've been arguing that since we left the field."

"Heckling is just part of the game. You can't go beating up everyone that tries to razz me," I argued and took a sip of my drink.

"That was not razzing!" They both said and then chuckled.

175

Danny Joe turned to Acer. "I like you, man! You can date my little sister any time!"

Acer and I both sputtered and choked. He recovered quickly, but my eyes burned from the soda that spewed through my nose and I continued to cough.

"You okay, sis?" Danny Joe asked.

I nodded. "Yes," I coughed. "Just went down the wrong pipe. Go on."

"That guy took it too far. He made it personal and he deserved every bit of what he got," he explained. "I'm sorry if I embarrassed you."

"You didn't embarrass me. You scared me. I was afraid you would get thrown in jail and I didn't know how I could possibly explain that to Mary, especially since I wasn't entirely sure she knew you were in town," I said and then added, "Thanks for standing up for me though."

"Anytime," he answered and stole one of my french fries with a wicked grin.

I wondered when he had last eaten. With him out of work and Sadie back with her parents, he probably didn't have a lot of money for food. I handed him my box of fries. "Here, you can take the rest. I'm finished." He graciously accepted them and started talking to Acer.

I smiled to myself. We were closer than any of my other siblings. He stuck around KC when the rest of them hit the road as fast as they could. Probably because he couldn't get too far away from daddy's wallet, but he was always there for me when I needed him, and I was glad he was there today.

Chapter Eleven: Playing Beauty Shop

For the next several days, I slept well at night and I tried not to worry so much. I finally felt better about my life in Booneville. Yes, Bonnie still had cancer and Mary was going to have a baby, and Danny Joe had moved to Booneville, but I felt happy, at peace for the first time in a long time.

Acer picked me up for school nearly every day. Cade still harassed us every chance he got, but at least he kept his hands to himself. Acer and I would meet up again at baseball, head over to see Bonnie afterwards, and he'd take me home again.

When I'd get home, I would help Mary with dinner and then she and I would settle at the dining room table to study. One of the things Mary said we could do to help was cleaning the bathrooms and floors, something I hated to do. Apparently, Brian hated it too because the next day, he hired a cleaning service to come in once a week and clean the entire house. I just loved the way that man thinks.

Bonnie finally convinced her parents to let her return to school, though just in the mornings. She would ride to school with Acer and me, but he would take her back home during their lunch period. I didn't see her much at school, which made me even more grateful for Mary's understanding; otherwise, I would only see her in the morning on the way to school.

Diamonds in the Dirt

Word got around that Bonnie had cancer and so when she was at school she was bombarded by people asking her millions of questions and giving all kinds of unwanted advice. She never acted like any of it bothered her, but one particular afternoon, she vented her frustrations to me.

We were lying in her gigantic canopy bed, channel surfing. Acer was down the hall, playing video games and somewhere out of left field, she just went off.

"People say the dumbest things to cancer patients!" she yelled and threw her remote across the room.

I stared at her, eyes wide for a minute, before responding. "Okay, people say dumb things to non-cancer patients too," I replied. "What is this about?"

"Kiley had the nerve to ask me if I was wearing a wig," she growled. "Can you believe that girl? This is my hair! It's attached to my head!" She gave it a tug to make her point. "It's a little bit coarser, and thinning a little bit on the top, but my hair is still attached to my head. See look. Isn't it?"

I examined her hair closely. "Yes, Bonnie, still attached, a little thinner at the top, but no patches or bald spots and you still have your eyebrows and eyelashes. I wouldn't give her a second thought." I hugged her neck.

"I know, but if she thinks that, how many others think that too?"

"Wise people treasure knowledge, but the babbling of a fool invites disaster. I read that in momma's journal today."

"Proverbs 10:14," she said quietly.

"Kiley is just a babbling fool, Bonnie. She only knows how to be cruel, and one day she will have to account for every hurtful word she has ever said. Don't give her another thought. She's not worth it."

She hugged me back. "Thanks, girl. I needed to hear that."

We didn't talk about the incident again for the next couple of days and I really didn't think it bothered her until I got a call from Acer.

Angela Geurin

It was a Sunday afternoon. Mary and Brian were having lunch with their Bible fellowship class at church and I was working on my physics project for school. The solitude was such a welcome change that I nearly didn't hear the phone when it rang, but when I picked it up and realized it was Acer, I was a little surprised. We had seen each other at church just an hour or so earlier. He had told me that Bonnie was tired and sleeping in and that he was going to go home and do the same. When I heard his voice on the line, I knew that there was something wrong.

"Scout!" he said his voice full of panic. "She's locked herself in the bathroom and I can't get a hold of my parents. She won't come out and I've been trying to get her to open the door for the last thirty minutes. I'm about to kick it in!"

"No, don't do that," I returned as calmly as I could. "I'm on my way. Just tell her I'm on my way."

Hastily, I scribbled a note on the fridge whiteboard, telling Mary I had to go to Bonnie's and would explain later, then headed to the garage as fast as I could. I arrived at the Acer home in record time and rang the doorbell. Within minutes the door flew opened and Acer grabbed my hand and yanked me inside. He led me up the winding staircase to the door to the bathroom that adjoined his and Bonnie's rooms.

"I've tried all three doors, they are all locked, and she won't open any of them," he was explaining things so fast I had a hard time processing everything. "I don't know what she is doing in there, but I keep hearing something turning on and off and she's crying hysterically, and I just hope she doesn't try anything stupid!"

I furrowed my eyebrows, "You don't really think she is going to kill herself, do you? Come on, Ace; you know her better than that." I rested my hand on his shoulder as I looked at his panic-stricken face and ran my hand the length of his arm to his fingers and squeezed. "It'll be OK. We'll help her through whatever it is."

He laced our fingers and squeezed back as I knocked on the door with my free hand. "I said leave me alone, Benjamin!" I heard her shout from deep within the bathroom. "I'm not opening the door and if you kick it in, mom's going to make you pay for the replacement!"

"Bonnie, it's me," I said softly. "I know you won't let in Acer, but will you let me in? He's really worried about you and just wants to make sure you are all right. I don't even have to stay long. I'll just check on you so he knows you are okay."

I waited and there was no response for a minute or two and then, at last, I heard the lock click. Turning, I looked at Acer and smiled. A wave of relief flowed over his face and shoulders, a sigh escaped his lips. "Go play your video games or something," I instructed. "I'll come and get you if we need you."

He lifted my hand to his lips and gently pressed them in a soft kiss. "Thanks, Scout. I owe you one." He wrapped me in a quick hug before he headed to his room as I silently crept inside.

Like everything else in their house, the bathroom was huge. There was a water closet immediately to the left, and across from that was a small porcelain water basin nestled on top of a mahogany antique dresser. Beyond was a narrow hallway that held two individual sinks to the left and right. They were perpendicular to the doors leading to both bedrooms. I looked to the right at Acer's sink and noticed how immaculate it was, especially for a boy. Everything was neat and organized and the marble-tiled countertop was so spotless it shined. To the left, I noticed Bonnie's was cluttered with toiletries and the cabinets stood wide open, almost as if she had emptied their contents in search of something.

In between the two sinks was another door that stood wide open and I stepped inside. The large square room held a huge walk-in shower and another water closet. The walls were taupe and as I turned back to the right, I noticed a gorgeous porcelain whirlpool tub.

On the floor in front of the tub, with her head in her hands, I spotted Bonnie. She was in her pink terry cloth robe, sitting with her knees drawn up to her chest. "I am so disgusted with myself," she said through her hands. I walked over to her and gently eased down next to her, leaning my back against the tub. "It's not like I haven't gone through this before. It shouldn't be such a shock."

I realized for the first time since walking in the room, the floor was covered in clumps of blonde hair. "Bonnie, I'm so sorry." was all I could say.

She looked up, and her eyes were red and swollen. Large patches of her hair were missing and the other parts looked like they'd been hacked at with a weedwhacker. Lying next to her was what looked to be long pointy scissors with blunt ends, more than likely Acer's nose hair clippers and his electric shaver.

"I look hideous, don't I?" she said smugly.

"Hideous is pretty strong, but it is a very interesting look for you," I joked. "Kind of psychotic actually." She didn't laugh, but a smirk crossed her lips. I hugged her neck and rested my head against hers. "What can I do to help?"

She shrugged then picked up a long strand of her hair. "Can you style this so it looks like I still have hair?"

I pulled out my ponytail and draped my long hair over the top of her head. "Here, we can share mine."

She did laugh then. "Now all we have to do is walk around attached at the hip and we are good to go."

"I bet I can arrange that," I added, thinking of Coach Mac's handcuffs. After a minute, I asked, "What did you do the last time your hair fell out?"

"My mom bought me all kinds of little blonde wigs that matched my hair. I hated them; they were itchy and uncomfortable, but I spent most of my time at the hospital then, so I didn't really have to wear them much because all the kids at the hospital looked like me."

I remembered the day that dad's hair fell out. He had thick white hair cut close to his head, but it would curl in little wisps when he was

181

sweaty. It didn't seem as devastating to him as it was to Bonnie, but it solidified for him that his cancer was real and although he didn't show it, losing his hair did bother him a little. Daddy decided to shave his head clean and had come into the kitchen while I was making dinner and asked me to shave the back of his head for him. I did, and I remember thinking that he was more handsome without his hair because his eyes stood out. He had beautiful eyes.

Then I remembered a picture I had noticed a couple of days ago of Acer and Bonnie as toddlers. It was sitting on the hallway table displayed in a gorgeous crystal frame. Immediately, I jumped up and dashed to the hallway and snatched it. They were beautiful little squatty-bodied toddlers. Both were completely bald and their piercing blue eyes seemed to smile along with their chubby-faced grins. They were nearly identical except for the clothes and the little stud earrings in Bonnie's tiny ears, but they were absolutely gorgeous, bald and beautiful.

I walked into the bathroom, locking the door behind me, still holding the picture and sat back down next to Bonnie. She leaned over and studied the picture and then looked at me curiously.

"You know the first thing I notice about you and Acer is always your eyes," I said. "I don't notice your hair; I notice your eyes. Your eyes are beautiful. They are like the brightest blue sky. And when you smile, they sparkle and shine like a beautiful sunny day."

"Are you talking about mine or Bennie's?" she joked.

"Both," I answered seriously. "Why don't you just shave your head and get rid of all of your hair? Don't worry about itchy wigs. You really don't need them to be beautiful."

She took the picture from my hand and stared at it for a minute before picking the razor up off the floor and handing it to me. She nodded slowly. "Let's do it. Will you help me?"

"Sure."

She led me to Acer's sink and I went to work with the electric shaver. When I had shaved off the last patch of hair, we heard a knock at the door. I looked at Bonnie through the mirror and she nodded. "Let him in."

I reached over to unlock the door and let Acer enter. He stared at our reflections and then reached up and rubbed the top of Bonnie's head. "You know," he said, "the electric razor won't cut it close enough. It's going to be itchy until the rest of it falls out." He reached across Bonnie and grabbed his razor and shaving cream. "You really need to use this."

"Okay," Bonnie said and met my eyes, nodding towards the shaving cream.

Bonnie shivered as I slathered it along her head. Acer filled the sink with water and helped spread it around so I could start. After the first two strokes across the top of her head, Acer reached out and took my hand. "No, do it this way, Scout," Acer instructed. "You need to go against the grain." He guided my hand in a long upward stroke from the base of her neck to her forehead.

Slow moving warmth slid up my arm from his touch and started to turn my cheeks pink. After the fourth stroke, I removed my hand from Acer's and handed him the razor. "Here finish this up; I'm going to get a towel," I said.

I scooted out of the room and headed to the towel rack next to the shower. My heart was jumping in my chest after the jolt of energy that coursed up my arm from Acer's touch and I had to catch my breath. It reminded me of Bonnie's car when we were forced to hold hands and warmth had spread throughout my body. My skin still tingled and I tried to gain my composure. I whispered, "There is nothing to get excited about, girl. We're just trying to help Bonnie."

When I was confident that I could breathe easier again, I rejoined my two friends in the makeshift beauty shop. Acer had finished and was draining the water from the sink. I put the towel over Bonnie's head and started wiping off the excess shaving cream. As I pulled off the towel, Acer and I held our breath, waiting for her reaction.

"I really do have pretty eyes," she commented quietly, rubbing her hand across her bald head. "It's so smooth."

"Beautiful," I agreed. "You are beautiful."

Then her eyes filled with tears. "Bald and beautiful." The tears began to fall then. "I'm the only bald teenager in Booneville!"

I felt tears sting my eyes. This was my fault. I just wanted to help, but I'd made it ten times worse! I wiped the corner of my eyes with my thumbs and said, "You don't have to be. I'll shave my head too. We can be bald together."

"No!" Acer and Bonnie said in unison.

I stared at them dumbfounded. "Why not?" I asked. "It's just hair. It will grow back."

Bonnie turned around and faced me. "I can't let you do that. It's too much, Scout. Besides, there really wasn't anything spectacular about my hair before it started falling out, but yours..." she paused and grabbed a handful of my thick auburn locks and brushed it gently with her fingers.

"...is gorgeous." Acer finished quietly and locked eyes with mine in the mirror. His gaze was intense and serious. Immediately my cheeks colored and I quickly averted my gaze.

"Exactly!" Bonnie said oblivious to the short exchange in the mirror. "It's gorgeous and I can't let you ruin it for me. Please don't shave it...ever!"

Acer nodded in agreement and ran his hand down the back of my head to the tip of my hair at the middle of my back and rested it there. "Don't shave it off. Just think of the ammo it would give Cade."

I grabbed my hair and pulled it up to a pony tail and secured it with the tie that had been around my wrist. "I don't care about Cade," I spat, "but I do care about Bonnie. I won't shave it off if you don't want me to. I just don't want you to feel alone."

"She won't," Acer said. "I'll shave my head and we can be bald and beautiful together."

Bonnie glanced at the crystal framed picture of them as toddlers and nodded. "Okay, but let Scout and me do it. I've seen your face after you shave in the morning. You would probably hack up your head."

An hour later, after all remnants of the beauty shop had been removed from the bathroom, the three of us sat on the living room sectional looking through old photo albums. Mrs. Acer apparently took pictures of everything and had several albums crammed full of memories. It was like watching Acer and Bonnie grow up in still frame.

That was exactly how we were when she and Mr. Acer returned from their afternoon church social. Mrs. Acer greeted me and then immediately her expression fell. "Oh, Bonnie," she cried, "Your hair! Sweetie, what did you do?" She rushed in, leaning over the sofa embracing her warmly and kissing her cheek. "You should have called the Spencer's. We would have come home."

"It's OK, Mom. Scout and Bennie were here."

"Well, don't worry; we will go out tomorrow afternoon and get you some nice wigs, and pretty scarves," she was saying.

Bonnie cut her off. "No, I don't want any of that. I don't need hair to be beautiful."

Acer threw his arm around her. "*We* don't need hair to be beautiful." He leaned back and kissed his mother's cheek.

As if just realizing that Acer's head was shaved clean, she slowly reached up and rubbed her hand along the top of his head and burst into tears. "Oh, you silly kids!" She stood up and yelled. "Harold! Get in here and look at what your children did while we were out." She looked down at me and sighed in relief. "Thank goodness, you had more sense than these two. I don't know if Mary would have ever forgiven me if I'd sent you home without hair."

"You can thank your kids for that," I replied. "They talked me out of it. I guess they figured that unlike the two of them, I *do* need hair to be beautiful."

"No, you don't," Acer said, next to my ear. The look in his eyes revealed more than just friendship. My face grew hot again and I couldn't hide a grin.

"We like your hair too much!" Bonnie added. "We would miss it if it was all gone."

Just then, Mr. Acer walked in the room and shook his head. "What happened? Did the three of you get bored and decide to play beauty shop?" He walked over and rubbed the top of Acer's head and then bent down and kissed the top of Bonnie's. "Or are *you* to blame for this?" He slid his glance towards me.

"Guilty, sir," I replied sheepishly. "But they were both willing customers."

His hard gaze softened. "Well, thanks, I guess. How much do a shave and a haircut run these days?"

Chapter Twelve: Riding the Waves

Slowly I opened my eyes and blinked through the haze of my sleep. Sunlight was pouring in through my window from across the room, blinding me, and I threw my hand up in response. I am not one to waste a day sleeping, but after six weeks straight of baseball, I was exhausted.

It was the first Saturday of spring break. Coach Mac had to give us the next four days off because of school policies, which was a shame because we were really starting to come together as a team, but it was nice to have some free time. I arched my back and rolled over trying to focus on the alarm clock next to my bed. It was 9:00 a.m. and faintly I smelled bacon. My stomach growled. So I decided to check it out before heading out for my morning run.

I threw on the first things I pulled out of my drawer and headed downstairs. Finding a hair tie wrapped around my wrist from the day before, I shook my hair out and twisted it into a messy bun while my nose followed the scent of bacon and eggs down the stairs into the kitchen. My journey, however, came to an abrupt halt as I rounded the corner to find a cozy family breakfast and one stray.

Danny Joe was at the stove wearing an apron, spatula in one hand, cracking eggs with the other, and sitting at the kitchen table, laughing with Mary and Brian, was Acer. I tried to retreat without anyone noticing. Even though, my eyes hadn't viewed a mirror yet,

I was pretty sure I wasn't presentable. I hadn't even put on a bra yet! Quietly, I backed out of the room until I heard Danny Joe blow my cover.

"She's alive!" he shouted. "Get in here, Scout! Your friend is here."

Too late to change into something decent, I turned around and faced my surprise guest. "Good morning, everyone," I said nonchalantly. Then I met Acer's ice blue eyes. They seemed to sparkle in the light from the windows. I noticed the big plate of bacon and eggs in front of him too and he shoveled a fork full into his mouth. "Geez, save some for the rest of us," I teased.

He visibly swallowed and then flashed me his lopsided grin. My stomach fluttered in response. "Can't help it! Your brother is a great cook!" he exclaimed, taking another bite.

Danny Joe set a plate down in front of the empty seat at the table. "Not to fear! Your bacon and eggs are here! Order up, Sis!"

"Are you a short order cook now? I thought your new job was in maintenance," I said.

He gave my bun a tug and my hair loosened. "I thought I could be nice and make breakfast for my sisters and the man of the house this morning since I am crashing your humble abode. Then my new buddy, Ace" he nodded to Acer, "showed up and, well, can't turn away a growling stomach."

Mary eyed me quietly and took a bite of her food. She casually scanned me up and down, probably noticed I wasn't wearing a bra, and wished I looked better with all these men in the house. She herself looked picture perfect. Her hair fell loosely about her shoulders and her pink satin robe completely hid her pajamas. I avoided her gaze and looked at Acer instead.

"What brings you here this morning?" I questioned and scooped some eggs onto my fork. "Or did your nose follow the scent of bacon like mine?"

"Bonnie wants to go to the beach," he stated in between bites. "So we are going to the beach today."

"*Can* she go to the beach?"

Two weeks ago she was put on house arrest, as she called it. Her white cell count was way down again and the doctors were afraid that she would catch a virus which could be disastrous. Visitation was not allowed, so we had resigned to talking on the phone. Ms. Acer let me visit this past week, but only if I washed up as soon as I walked in the door. So far she hadn't so much as coughed, but I was surprised that her mom would let her go to the beach.

"Not really," Acer answered. "But her whites are almost normal again and the doctor said that she could leave the house, but if mom had her way she wouldn't be going anywhere today and definitely not the beach. Dad and I ganged up on her and won this round. With her surgery next week, she needs to get out of the house. The fresh air would do her some good," he explained. "You want to come with us? There may be a couple others joining us later."

I didn't answer right away. In all my travels, I had never been to a real beach. I had gone to Branson a time or to and spent time on the beach at the lake, but never at the ocean with all those waves and jellyfish. Acer's eyes met mine, searching for the reason behind my hesitation. He looked like he was sitting on pins and needles, waiting for my reply.

"I don't know, Acer, I've never been to a real beach," I answered.

Brian interrupted my thoughts. "You ought to go, Scout. You've been focused on nothing but school and ball for a while. It would be nice for you to take a break. You should do something fun. You'll have a good time. The beaches are nice this side of Houston."

"You don't have to worry about anything. I'll keep you safe," Acer added.

I still hesitated. Seeing Acer's eager face made me uncomfortable. It was silly, but hanging out with him at a ballpark or with Bonnie at his house was one thing, but sitting on a beach in a swimsuit with him felt a little more intimate. How did things change so fast? This day was about Bonnie though. Not me, and definitely not Acer.

"Sure," I resigned. "I'll go with you two."

Acer's face lit up. "Great!" He stood and carried his plate to the sink and rinsed it. "I'll be back in an hour to pick you up. Thanks for breakfast, D-man." He turned to Danny Joe and they engaged in one of those complicated handshakes. He walked back to the table and retrieved his ball cap.

"Anytime, dude!" my brother replied.

In turn, he gently hugged Mary and shook Brian's hand. "Mrs. Z., Mr. Z. I'll take care of Scout and make sure she has some fun today." He slid his cap on backwards, covering his still bald head.

"I trust you, bub," Brian said. Mary was stoic, but smiled politely.

"See you in an hour, Scout." He playfully pulled my loose bun and my curls spilled down my back as my hair tie fell out. He laughed. "Oops! Sorry."

My swiping hand just missed him as he scurried out the kitchen door. I returned my attention back to my breakfast. Danny Joe joined us at the small table and after a moment, I realized that the room had grown silent. All eyes were on me. Mary's eyebrows were raised over the rim of her coffee cup, Brian's brow furrowed quizzically across from me, and Danny Joe smirked while he chewed his food on my left.

"What?" I asked when no one would speak.

"Is this a date?" Brian asked.

"What? No!"

"I completely approve if it is," Brian continued. "I think Benjamin is a nice young man. He was raised right. He comes from a good family. I'm just surprised you didn't mention anything to me before that's all."

My cheeks grew hot. "Why would you think this is a date? Is that what Acer said it was?"

Brian and Danny Joe exchanged grins. Then Brian answered, "Not in so many words, but he did ask my permission to take you to the beach with him and his sister and some other students. I assumed that was because this was some kind of group date thing."

Acer had asked permission to take me out? What a very gentlemanly thing to do. In fact, since our afternoon punishment from Coach Mac, Acer had done a lot of very gentlemanly things. He was probably just being polite. Sure, there were moments when the looks he gave me made my stomach do flip-flops, but that wasn't on purpose, was it?

"Scout, what is really going on here?" Mary asked.

"I don't know, Mary," I said quietly. "I'll let you know when I figure it out."

An hour later I was dressed and waiting on the porch with a beach bag that Mary had packed for me. She tried to talk me out of my backwards baseball cap, but I wasn't going to get sand stuck in my hair, so I won that argument. I didn't own a swimsuit, and reluctantly had to borrow one of Mary's. Apparently, she only wore bikinis, so I decided to wear a pair of my running shorts and a mesh tank top over the skimpy suit.

Acer arrived right on time. I climbed in next to Bonnie and we headed to the beach. Bonnie slept most of the hour drive, leaning on her brother's shoulder, which left Acer and I to our own conversations. Most of the ride we played Twenty Questions.

"OK, favorite food," Acer said.

"Bean burritos with cheese and sour cream," I replied. "What about you?"

"Hot dogs," he replied and adjusted his arm around Bonnie.

"Really?" I asked with a smirk. "If you were on death row, your last meal request would be hot dogs?"

"Not just hot dogs," he said. "Hot dogs loaded with chili, cheese, onions, relish, and tons of mustard."

"Sounds like a gut bomb to me."

"Bean burritos aren't any better."

I feigned shock. "Shut your mouth! Perfectly handmade flour tortillas, slathered in spicy refried beans, covered with shredded cheese, sour cream, and hot sauce. It is so good."

"I have never seen anyone get so excited about food!" he laughed. "I can't decide what you like more: baseball or bean burritos."

"That's a tough call, but probably baseball. What's your favorite restaurant?" I looked at him expectantly and watched his eyes scrunch together in concentration. My, oh, my, did Acer have a gorgeous profile under that backwards ball cap. He glanced towards me and flashed a smile that made my stomach tighten.

"You're probably going to laugh," he said.

"Try me."

"You know my family has a sky box at the dome?" I rolled my eyes and nodded. "Well, there is this place around the corner from our seats that makes the best hot dogs. Like out-of-this-world good!"

I snickered a little. "You mean to tell me that your favorite restaurant is a stadium hot dog vendor?" He nodded and then I burst into laughter. "Really? Ace you need to get out of Booneville! That's just sad."

"Told ya you would laugh," he grinned. "It's not my favorite restaurant though, just my favorite fast food type place. I really like this place we visited in Garden Grove, Florida called Clementine's. They have the best crab legs and seafood gumbo on the planet."

"Well, that sounds better than a hot dog vendor."

A bump jostled Bonnie awake and she raised her head from Acer's shoulder, and then turned towards me. Smiling with her eyes still half closed, she wrapped me in a hug. "I'm so glad you are going to the beach with us," she said, still groggy from sleep.

"I hope it's worth all the snoring I had to endure to get here," I joked.

"At least she didn't drool on your shoulder," Acer added tugging on his T-shirt sleeve.

Bonnie crossed her arms in a huff and sat bolt upright. "I don't snore and I definitely don't drool!"

"How would you know?" Acer followed up with an obnoxious snore that sounded like a cross between a pig and a train whistle.

"That's not right, Ace," I interrupted. Bonnie smirked at her brother, thinking I was taking her side. "It was more like this." And I gave my own imitation. We both laughed and Bonnie scowled.

"Ha-ha!" she returned sarcastically. "I can't believe you two!" She glared at me and continued. "I am starting to regret your coming with us now that you're tag teaming with my brother!"

"Oh, Bonnie," I squeezed her shoulder, "you know I don't mean it! I'm just teasing you."

She laid her bald head against my shoulder. "All right, I guess I forgive you."

"Well, I'm *not* sorry!" Acer nudged her.

She turned and slugged his shoulder. "I'll deal with you later."

Acer turned off the main road and headed over a sandy trail that was lined with wild sea oats. I watched with anticipation as the sand gave way to the most incredible sight I'd ever seen.

The midday sun at Surfside Beach was bright, high in the sky, and the dark blue water shimmered in its reflection. We drove down close to the water's edge and parked with the tailgate towards the ocean. I stared out the back window at the rise and fall of the sea. It was a beauty that left me stunned. Sure, I had seen beaches on television or in the movies, but none of them compared to what I was experiencing firsthand at that moment.

I continued staring, completely mesmerized by the rolling tide. "The water goes on forever," I breathed. "It runs right into the sky."

The cab grew quiet as I became immersed in the view before me. Gently beyond the pier, the waves rocked, but as my eyes followed their journey to the shore, the blue peaks turned into huge white caps that violently crashed into the sandy beach only to softly return to the ocean. It was a constant ebb and flow of waves rolling in and out from the sky. After a moment I turned my gaze away from the breathtaking view and found two sets of azure eyes, twinkling at me in amusement.

"Sorry, just trying to take it all in right now," I explained.

Their faces wore mirror imaged lopsided grins. Bonnie's cheek dimpled at her upturned mouth, otherwise they were identical with their bald heads. I smiled back. It hadn't taken long for me to get used to seeing them both without hair, although I think it still freaked out their mother.

Bonnie refused to wear a wig. For her, it was very freeing. She had even talked about tattooing her head and never having hair again, but I don't think she was really all that serious. At least I hoped she wasn't that serious.

"That's all right, Scout," Bonnie said. "It's nice to be reminded that God has given us a beautiful world to live in and we should take the time to notice it once in a while."

"I've never seen anything like this," I said "It's so beautiful."

They joined my study of the ocean beyond the truck for another quiet moment. It was like they too saw something fresh and new in what had become bland and redundant in their own eyes. Bonnie sighed quietly next to me and squeezed my neck.

"Surf should be good," Acer broke the silence. "We can catch some great waves today."

"Well, have fun with that," Bonnie replied. "I plan to sit on the beach with this big giant sun hat mom made me bring, and catch up on some reading."

"Same here, minus the big sun hat," I stated and opened my door.

Acer's face fell. "You mean you are going to spend your first time at the beach sitting on the sand!" he spoke in disbelief. "Not on my watch! You are going surfing with me!"

While I shouldered our beach bags, Bonnie eased herself out through my door and leaned on my shoulder. She was very weak, and just the effort to stand, holding her own weight, took much out of her. Acer rushed around the front of the truck to help me ease her gently to the sand.

"I can't surf," I replied when he rounded the corner. Acer put his arm around Bonnie's waist and took most of her weight.

"Neither can he," Bonnie retorted with a laugh and then winced in pain. "But he has fun trying."

"Hey! I can surf!" Acer argued.

Bonnie patted his cheek. "Keep telling yourself that, Bennie."

We walked arm in arm across the sand. It was surprisingly hard and thick, not soft and powdery like it looked from a distance. When we were about fifteen feet from the water, Acer took a large sheet and laid it on the sand, burying each corner. Bonnie leaned on me and watched as he jogged back to the truck and returned, carrying two lounge chairs, an umbrella, and a cooler. His muscles rippled in his arms, and I couldn't help but watch him move.

I distracted myself and spared a glance back out into the rolling waves. They seemed strong and there were a couple of surfers up the beach a ways, out past the sand bar. One of them stood up on their board and immediately wiped out. It made me shudder. I wasn't sure I could swim in waves like that and yet, Acer actually thought I could stand on a surfboard and ride a wave.

195

"I'm not that strong of a swimmer," I stated when Acer returned. "I'm not even sure I could swim in waves like that, let alone surf."

"I'm sure you would be fine," Bonnie said, as I helped her into one of the chairs. "The waves are not as big as you think here in the gulf."

"You're going surfing with me, Scout, and I'm not taking no for an answer!" Acer stated, and slammed the beach umbrella into the ground behind the two chairs.

I picked up Bonnie's beach bag and sun hat and handed it to her. "Well, I guess I'm going surfing, whether I want to or not," I muttered.

She thanked me and adjusted her hat as she took out her book, setting it on her lap. "Don't worry, Scout, you learn fast and I am sure you can figure this out before you drown. You might even find out you like it."

"Yeah, right," I said sarcastically.

"Bon-Bon, you need anything else?" Acer asked.

"Nope, you got it all right here for me, thanks." She smiled. He leaned down and kissed her cheek before standing and looking at me. "Wait here, Scout. I'm going to run up to the surf shop and rent you a board."

"Take your time." I plopped down in the seat next to Bonnie and leaned over. "He's really serious about teaching me how to surf, isn't he?"

She nodded with a wide grin. "'Fraid so, girlfriend."

"Be back in a few minutes," Acer stated and took off.

"Great!" I responded unenthusiastically. "Can't wait!"

It felt like five minutes had passed but Bonnie explained it was more like thirty when I commented on how quickly Acer had returned, carrying a long bright yellow surfboard. He staked it in the sand next to the blanket and retrieved his own from the back of his truck. I tried to act excited about my first surfing lesson, especially since Acer was grinning ear to ear, but I was scared to death that I would hurt myself or someone else and that fear escalated quickly, hovering just around panic. My legs shook and my stomach churned with nausea.

"Ace, I-I'm not sure about this," I stammered.

He reached out and touched my shoulder. "Don't worry, Scout, I won't let you get hurt. I rented you an eight-foot foamie. You can face plant on this baby and not break anything. And we will start out on baby waves," he assured.

As he spoke, his fingers trailed down my arm to my hand and he gently squeezed my fingers. It was a sweet and familiar gesture: one that I had used on him a few weeks ago to calm his own rising panic when Bonnie locked herself in the bathroom. My stomach fluttered at the memory and the feel of his thumb tracing the back of my hand. I tried to avoid his gaze, but he squeezed my hand gently and I raised my eyes. His blue eyes were serious.

His words were soft. "Trust me. You can do this. I know you can. You can ride a motorcycle. You can hit a baseball. You can do anything you set your mind to."

I exhaled slowly and picked up my board. He was right. I could do this. I was athletic. I was smart. I could swim, sort of. "Ok, let's go surfing," I said with determination. Tossing my hat into my bag, I headed towards the water, my confidence growing with each step.

"That's my girl!" Acer exclaimed.

My girl?

What on earth did he mean by that? My cheeks flushed, but I kept moving towards the beach, pretending I didn't notice his comment. "So what do I have to do?" I asked.

Acer stopped short of the water and laid his board in the sand. I did the same and waited for his instructions. After giving me a quick anatomy lesson of my board, we practiced the key fundamentals of surfing. It seemed pretty easy, but of course we hadn't made it to the water yet.

For my first ride, Acer led me away from the beach, far enough out that the whitewater was not as rough, and showed me how to ride a wave while laying on my stomach. It looked easy enough, so after watching, I tried it myself on the next wave that came in.

I positioned my body just as he had shown me, and started to paddle a little bit. The wave picked me up and glided me towards the shore. Then all of a sudden, I felt my feet lift over my head, a second before my face slid off the front of my board and slammed into the pounding wave. My forehead hit the sandy ocean floor and the wave washed over, spiraling me into a feet-over-head flip that landed me on my back in water that was thigh deep.

Wipeout!

Disoriented and embarrassed, I tried to stand, but the tug of my board leash yanked my foot out from under me and dragged me towards the beach. I was in knee-high water now, but the force of the next wave crashed on top of me just as I inhaled which filled my mouth with salty water and I sputtered and coughed as I got back to my feet. This was a disaster!

Acer hustled back to me, a lopsided grin on his face. "That is called a pearl!"

I had no idea what he meant and didn't care. It was a face plant into water and there was nothing fun about that. I coughed, feeling a little spark of anger in my chest as I watched his smiling lips. "I thought this was supposed to be easy, Ace! It's fun! I'm going to love it!" I imitated his waving arms and enthusiastic tone. He started laughing which was the biggest mistake he could have made because it ignited a fury inside my chest reminiscent of daddy's funeral.

I passed him carrying my "foamie" sloshing back towards Bonnie. He grabbed my arm to stop me and with reflexes fueled by anger, I grabbed his upper arm under his shoulder and body slammed him into the ocean. He hit the water with a hard smack. It surprised me as much as it did him, but I immediately offered him my hand in apology. The shock in his eyes was overshadowed by the silly grin that crossed his lips as he took my offered hand and let me pull him to his feet.

"I'm sorry," I apologized gruffly, still angry that he could find humor in all of this. "That was pure reflex."

"I knew you had quick reflexes, but I didn't know you had a black belt in karate," he laughed. "Remind me to never sneak up on you." He worked his shoulder. "At least, it was my left arm."

"Sorry." Idly, I brushed some seaweed off his shoulder. "I can't do this, Acer," I said seriously.

"Since when did you become a quitter?" he returned and I looked away. He reached up and pulled a clump of seaweed out of my hair. "You'll get the hang of it. That was just your first try. Try it again and this time arch your back when you feel the wave lift you up. You just had too much weight on the nose; that's what caused you to pearl."

"I don't want to," I returned.

"Try it one more time," he stated flatly. "If you quit because you failed on your first ride, I will lose all respect for you."

"You don't respect me anyway!"

"Oh, yes, I do," he said, "but I won't if you quit. If you quit now, I will know the truth that you are just like all the other girls who think they can hang with the boys."

I scowled at him. "You're a jerk!"

He smirked, "Maybe, but I'm not a quitter."

Angrily, I grabbed the rails of my board and stormed back out to sea. This was so stupid! Why did I let Acer talk me into this? I didn't want to learn how to surf. Now I had to go out there and prove to him that I could surf just as well as any boy. Man, did he know just which buttons to push to bring out the fire in me.

I ranted until I saw a wave that looked smaller than the first one and got into position. It lifted me and as I started to feel the force pushing me to the shore, I arched my back, like he said. That slight adjustment put more weight on my thighs, and lo and behold, it worked. I stayed planted in place and my board glided faster and faster the closer we came to shore. The acceleration was gradual, but powerful and...I loved every minute of it.

As I neared the beach, I sat up and straddled my board, my feet grazing against the sandy floor until I stopped. Acer sloshed over to me, wearing the same smirk and patted my shoulder.

"Not bad," he said. "Let's give it another couple of practice runs and you can try to pop up on some bigger waves." I rolled my eyes at him and he grinned even bigger. "Told you, you could do it."

I stood and playfully punched his shoulder. "Yeah, you did."

Sometime in the middle of learning how to surf, Jose, Rachel, and some other people I recognized from school joined our group. Two of them were wake boarding and the rest were floating around in the waves close to shore, while Acer worked with me on popping up. Like it or not now, I had an audience and I was determined not to make a fool of myself, but it was hard to do when I was wiping out more than popping up.

Popping up, which was just the transition from lying flat to standing, was easy, but the staying balanced while standing was a lot harder. Over and over, I fell, but Acer wouldn't let me quit and so after about five or six wipeouts, I rode my first wave all the way into the shore. I know it was a baby wave, but I finally rode a wave and didn't wipeout. My face broke out into a smile and I did a mental fist pump. I had learned to surf. A girl from middle America had learned to surf!

The cheers I received from our companions made me feel great and I heard Bonnie whoop from the shore. I turned to look at her mummified form, sitting under the umbrella and gave her a wave before turning back out to surf again. Suddenly, I felt Acer engulf me from behind in a bone-crushing hug, and the force of his embrace knocked me off my board. We splashed into the salty water. Acer landed in a push-up position hovering just above me as a wave came crashing into us and bowled him over. He jumped up and offered me an apology as he pulled me to my feet.

"You did it!" he commented. "You rode your first wave!"

"Thanks to my surf instructor," I replied.

He raised his eyebrows at me. "You want to go again?"

I nodded emphatically, "Oh, yeah!"

"Then, let's go."

We paddled out together this time going out beyond the sand bar. I tried to ride the first wave I saw and couldn't paddle fast enough to catch it. Instead, I turned around, straddled my board, and watched as Acer caught the next wave with ease. Despite what Bonnie said, Acer could surf. I was no expert, but he looked good to me. He popped up smoothly each time and had had only one wipeout, but that was because he was trying to avoid a collision with me.

I rode about five more waves before my body couldn't take it anymore and I had to head back to shore. As I walked up the beach with my board heading towards Bonnie, Acer caught up with me and draped his arm around my shoulder.

"Hey surfer girl, you giving up?" he said, very close to my cheek.

"No, just need a break." I glanced at his hand dangling just over my shoulder and inhaled sharply. It felt so natural to walk next to Acer like this and I fought the urge to wrap my free hand around his waist. The audience that we had on our little excursion today helped with that. My hand stayed clamped tightly against my leg.

"Thanks," he said and I felt his breath against my ear.

"For what?" I questioned.

"For going surfing with me."

"It was fun, Ace," I returned with a grin. "I'm glad you made me do it."

We staked our boards in the hard sand and automatically turned towards each other, just like magnets. Awkwardly, he leaned around his board and brushed a strand of curls out of my face. "I didn't want you to miss out on all the fun just because you were scared." He smirked.

"I wasn't scared," I stated and looked down and drew circles in the sand with my toe.

"You sure fooled me." He leaned in closer and rested his hand on my shoulder. "I don't think I have ever seen you this intimidated."

Heat rushed to my cheeks. I wanted to duck away, but his smoldering eyes wouldn't let me go. For a moment our noses were inches apart and the flush that I saw on his cheeks, I am sure, mirrored my own. Clumsily, we both took a step back, smiling in embarrassment. "You're a good teacher, Ace." I slugged his arm.

He brushed imaginary sand off his shoulders. "I am, aren't I?"

"And so humble too!" I added jokingly.

He trailed his fingers down my arm. "Are you hungry?"

My stomach growled at the mention of food and we both laughed. "Yeah, apparently I am."

"I'll go grab us some food." He gave my hand a squeeze and took off towards the shops up the beach. I watched him go then started walking towards Bonnie. She was studying me over the top of her sunglasses, a sly smile playing at her lips.

As soon as I sat down, Bonnie turned to me. "Spill it."

"What?"

She slapped my shoulder. "You know what! What's going on between you and my brother?"

"Nothing," I averted my gaze.

"Come on, Scout. I know better than that. I can practically feel the energy rolling off the two of you when you get within a foot of each other!"

I thought about the energy that surged through me every time he touched me and quickly hid the smile that came to my lips. "I promise you. There is nothing going on," I returned evenly.

"Oh, yes, there is. I was only under house arrest for two weeks. I can't believe I missed out on that much! Now, spill it!" she demanded.

"Why don't you ask your brother?" I retorted.

"Oh, believe me, I will, but I want to hear it from you first."

"Bonnie, I really have no idea," I began. "You know, a few weeks ago, we were at each other's throats. Then Coach Mac handcuffed us together for the afternoon and the next thing I know, Acer is at my doorstep every morning giving me a ride to school, and asking my brother-in-law if he can take me out to the beach!"

"Woah! Wait a second! Back up! Handcuffed?" she asked.

"He didn't tell you about that?" I questioned.

"No, that must have slipped his mind," she snickered.

"Figures."

I summed up our afternoon side by side and the last two weeks leading up to this morning. "I can just picture both of your faces when Coach Mac slapped on those handcuffs!" she laughed.

"It was not funny!" As weak as she looked, her laughter was strong and contagious. I found myself giggling too. "I just kept praying that neither of us had to go to the bathroom!" We laughed even harder.

"Oh, that would have been bad!" she said between laughs.

"I was glad that it was your car we had to figure out how to drive together. I mean what if it had been my motorcycle?"

"That would have been nice and cozy!" she commented, and we started giggling again.

Our laughter finally faded and I stared idly out to sea. When I really thought about it, the signs were plain as day. Acer and I had grown pretty close the last few weeks and it wasn't just because of Coach Mac and baseball. We were growing closer because of Bonnie. Acer and I were a team in both her care and her entertainment. We were the shoulders she cried on when the pain was too much to bear, and we were the ones who made her laugh when everything got too serious. It was a joint effort, and in some ways, we had been there for each other too.

"Apparently, Coach Mac knew what he was doing," Bonnie said with a lopsided grin that looked exactly like her brother's. "Bennie has never taken this much interest in a girl."

I frowned quizzically. "He's never had a girlfriend?"

She shook her head. "Nope, he has never had a girlfriend. He took Kiley to the Oktoberfest Ball last year, but he only did that because I made him."

"Why would you do that?" I asked with a scowl.

"I know, right," she started. "Sam Hardy asked me to go and I really wanted to go with him, but I didn't want to go out with him by myself. I knew that Kiley really liked Bennie and if he asked her then we could go on a double date. So we did and it was the worst date ever."

"How bad was it?"

The look on her face turned to disdain. "First of all, Kiley wore this extravagant strapless number and anytime she moved, her boobs threatened to escape, and Sam was so enthralled with watching Kiley and her peep show that we hardly even talked. Secondly, Kiley was all over Bennie the entire night. I mean really all over him. She sat in his lap whenever we were sitting and when we were dancing, it was like she was a pole dancer and Bennie was the pole. I mean, that's my brother for crying out loud!"

"I bet he thoroughly enjoyed that."

"Uh-uh," she shook her head again. "Bennie was completely embarrassed! He was so mad at me for making him go out with Kiley that he refused to talk to me the entire way home, but when we did get home he was like a volcano. It was the biggest fight we ever had. We were yelling and throwing stuff. He kept saying that when he was ready, he would find his own girlfriend without my help and she would be a lot less hands on the first date. My mom and dad finally came in and calmed us both down, and we ended up laughing about the whole thing." She was thoughtful for a moment. "But I wouldn't mention to him that I told you about this. I'm not entirely sure he would like that."

I tried to avoid thoughts of Kiley most of the time. I couldn't walk by her at school without hearing some comment about being a lesbian or, recently, a member of a motorcycle gang.

"You don't have to worry about me mentioning anything to your brother. I can't stand to talk about Kiley. Really, I can't even picture the two of them together. She doesn't seem like his type."

She tilted her head and looked at me with contemplation. "Come to think of it, Scout, you are exactly my brother's type. You are fun to be around, but not overbearing. You speak your mind, but not all the time. You love sports, but you are not fake about it. You are beautiful, but you don't even know it. You are exactly someone that would attract him."

"Like magnets," I said softly, "that need to be…"

"Flipped," she finished and grinned. "He told you my theory." I nodded in response.

The magnitude of her revelation brought both dread and excitement to the pit of my stomach. It was true. Acer and I had come to the point in our relationship where the line that defined friendship blurred into something more complicated. If Bonnie was right, and she always seemed to be right, Acer saw in me what he wanted in a girlfriend, and secretly, I knew he was what I wanted in a boyfriend.

I guess it was easy to deny all of my true feelings for him when we were arguing and butting heads on the baseball field, but now we had this new found camaraderie, and denial was difficult. I thought about our awkward little exchange a moment ago. I knew I had feelings for Acer. Every time he touched me, my stomach quivered and blood rushed to my cheeks, and if he felt the same way about me, then we were in deep trouble.

I looked at her seriously. "Bonnie," I said, "I…we…Acer and me, can't cross that line right now."

"Why not?"

"We are a battery, teammates," I explained. "It would screw up everything! We're finally getting along. We can finally complete a game without it ending in a shoving match." I exhaled slowly. "I've worked too hard to gain the respect of my team and this town. I just…I just can't let my feelings for your brother ruin that."

"So you do have feelings for him," she stated.

I was trapped. She had caught me and there was no point in denying it now. "You know the last two weeks have been a whirlwind of emotions and Acer has been like a rock. I have seen a side of him that I didn't know existed. He has so much potential as a player and as a friend, and I want to help him reach that potential. I want to help him be more than he ever thought he could be, and I don't want to screw that up."

"Do you love my brother?" she asked me.

I choked back the breath I was inhaling and my cheeks grew hot. Her question was so unexpected and bold, and I didn't know what to say. Love was a word I had never used outside of family. It was a strong word not to be taken lightly, reserved for those in my life who truly meant enough to me to love. Bonnie and Acer probably fell into that category. It just seemed so premature to make a declaration of love to Acer.

"I don't know," I sighed. "I know I like him a lot, but love, that's so strong."

"Do you think you could ever love my brother?" she pushed.

"Yes, I could," I relented.

She didn't speak for a moment and then through her thoughts, she whispered softly, "Maybe you are the answer."

"The answer to what?" I asked.

She shifted beside me, adjusting the blanket so that she sat cross-legged facing me. "You know, since this is my third time with cancer, I've really been thinking a lot about death." My panic face must have

206

shown up again because she gently patted my knee as she continued. "I know it's morbid, but what I have come to realize is that I am not afraid of dying. In fact, I really am looking forward to meeting Jesus Christ face-to-face, but I'm afraid of what my death will do to the people I love, especially Bennie.

We are closer than most brothers and sisters. Part of that is because we are twins, but part of it is also because of our circumstances. It seems I have always been sick and Bennie has always been there to help me; and at the same time, I have always been the one pushing and encouraging him to keep going because he really doesn't see how great he is at anything.

The last few days, I've been praying that if God is taking me home this time that he would make sure Bennie had someone who could help him stay on track and be everything that he was meant to be."

Another God thing.

I really wasn't comfortable with this line of conversation. Daddy's death was still too recent and thinking about Bonnie dying and me being the answer to her prayers for Acer, it was too much.

Before the tears could start falling, I laughed. "Well, that's funny, Bonnie," I said, "'Cause I've been praying too and I've been praying that God would remove your cancer for good this time."

She returned my smile and squeezed my leg. "Then I guess between the two of us, we've got it all covered."

I squeezed her hand. "Bonnie." I found my eyes drifting up the beach, watching as Acer made his way back to us with an arm full of food. "Please don't mention any of this to your brother. I don't want to encourage him to pursue anything with me beyond friendship."

"I won't. But are you going to deny everything when he finally gets the courage to open up to you? Because you know he will."

I had no idea how to handle that, but I would just have to cross that bridge when I got to it. "Probably not," I answered honestly, "but in the meantime, I'm going to try not to encourage him."

"Okay," she answered and then added, "Just be careful with his heart. It's really pretty obvious how you feel towards each other and if he ever becomes brave enough to make a move, you could crush him if you acted like there was nothing there. It would be better if you were honest like you were with me, and just tell him it is all too complicated right now."

"You don't think that would hurt him?" I asked.

"It will hurt him either way, but it would be easier for you both in the end if there was no room to wonder how the other was really feeling," she responded.

Wise girl, that Bonnie. She seemed to know exactly what to say and when to say it. "I'll keep that in mind," I whispered and hugged her neck.

At that moment, Acer made it back and stood on the blanket. He handed Bonnie a bag of food, but kept the other bag hidden behind his back as he turned to me with a grin. "I've got a surprise for you, Scout."

"What kind of surprise?"

"This!" he said and my eyes lit up.

He handed me a small plastic bag and as I looked at the emblem on the side, I knew exactly what was inside.

"You bought me bean burritos!"

"I found a place around the corner," he stated proudly as I practically ripped the bag from his outstretched hand. "Refried beans, sour cream, shredded cheese and tons of hot sauce wrapped in a homemade flour tortilla."

"You remembered!"

"Not exactly," he explained. "I forgot which kind of sauce you liked so I just got some of everything."

Without thinking, I wrapped Acer in a hug and then immediately withdrew. "Thanks, Ace."

Angela Geurin

"Consider it a reward for getting an A in surfing class today."

We all laughed and as I sat back down to enjoy my special lunch, Bonnie leaned over and whispered, "You ought to think about having that talk sooner rather than later, Scout."

Chapter Thirteen: Dangerous Ground

S pring break turned out to be a big turning point for the Bearcats and for Bonnie. Heading into the middle of April, we were leading the district. Acer had successfully completed his last seven outings and had even earned Player of the Week honors. Things were definitely looking up.

Things were not so good for Bonnie, though. They were unable to schedule her splenectomy after spring break like they'd hoped, due to complications from her treatment. The chemo was making her so sick that she had lost a lot of weight. She looked like flesh and bones, a walking skeleton. I visited her as often as I could, but because of her poor immune system, those visits were limited and she was under house arrest indefinitely.

Acer was holding up well. Baseball had become a form of therapy for both of us. Together we were an incredible team and when things with Bonnie became too much, we could get away and find comfort on the baseball diamond. I think he also found solace in hanging out with Danny Joe. Their mutual love for cars and engines had brought them together nearly twice a week as they worked on whatever engine they could find. My brother was really more like a big kid, so the age difference didn't seem to matter.

Danny Joe settled into the garage apartment while he tried to earn enough money to get his own place, so whenever there was down time, Acer would show up at the house and talk shop with my brother.

I was grateful for their close connection because that gave Acer someone to turn to besides me. He and I were getting closer and closer and the flirtatious comments were becoming more frequent. I wanted to talk to him like Bonnie suggested, but we were always interrupted. *Not really.* If I was truly honest, I hadn't tried to talk to him because every time I tried, I got cold feet. I was afraid of hurting him and losing my friend.

It wasn't until the middle of April that Bonnie finally got the news that her white cell count was stable enough that they could proceed with the splenectomy. Her surgery was scheduled for the week before the regional play-offs, which was great news for Acer since he would have to donate plasma and blood before her surgery.

The night before she had to go to the hospital in Houston for her pre-op, Bonnie asked me to come over and hang out. I helped her pack her suitcase, making enough room for her pink terry cloth robe. We ate dinner with her family and went through some more of her photo albums.

It was just before sunset when Bonnie decided to go swimming. She had told me to bring a suit, and since I still didn't have one, I reluctantly borrowed one of Mary's again. I chose the same one I'd worn on our beach trip. It was solid black with low rise bottoms and a halter neck top and out of all of the swimsuits in her closet, it covered the most skin. Bonnie's suit was a Hawaiian print, one piece that looked huge on her frail little frame.

I felt exposed even with my towel wrapped firmly around my chest as we walked outside to the patio. Acer was hanging out with Danny Joe and I was glad that it was just the two of us in the pool. Bonnie slipped out of her cover up and gently stepped down into the warm water, submerging her entire body. When she surfaced, I was still standing at the side of the pool with my towel wrapped around me.

"Something wrong?" she asked.

"I wish I had a T-shirt to wear over this suit," I muttered.

"It's just us," she stated.

"I know, but this suit is not something I would ever pick out on my own. It just shows way too much."

"So what! Mine shows my shunt. Quit being silly and get in!"

"All right," I groaned and let my towel fall to the ground and immediately jumped in the water.

The heated pool felt like bathwater and the underwater lights gave everything a purple hue. I tread water for a few minutes and watched as Bonnie swam all over, gliding as smooth as a dolphin through the water. You would have never thought she was so sick. When I asked her about that, she explained that the water was really easy to move in because it took away all the stress of gravity on her sore joints and muscles. She said she always felt good when she was swimming.

After about twenty minutes, we climbed into the adjoining hot tub and relaxed, gazing at the stars above. A minute or two passed before Bonnie finally broke the silence.

"What are the odds that this surgery will actually cure my cancer?" she asked me.

I really didn't know how to respond to that question and since we had spent the entire evening talking about everything but the surgery, I was afraid to say the wrong thing. "I don't know," I answered honestly. "What do your doctors think?"

"They say about eighty percent chance that it will slow the progression," she said.

"Then I'd say odds are probably pretty good. Are you scared?"

"A little. I'm not really scared about the surgery. It seems so routine. I'm really just ready to get this over with so I can see what I need to do next. You ready for the play-offs?"

212

"Oh yeah," I said enthusiastically. "The team is looking great. I think we really got a shot of taking it all the way."

"That would be awesome! Think about how bad the team has been in the past; this is like the biggest turn around in history and they will owe it all to you."

I laughed. "Hardly! If it was all because of me, I wouldn't need eight other guys out there."

"Well, I know one of those guys who would not be standing where he is right now if it weren't for you," she slid a sideways glance my way.

I smiled fondly, thinking back to the first practice I had with Acer. "Yeah, Ace and me have come a long way."

She wiggled her eyebrows playfully. "And still so much further to go!"

I splashed her. "What is that supposed to mean?"

She splashed me back and laughed. "You know what I mean!" She leaned her head back and then stretched her arms up to the night sky. "I need to get out of this hot tub before I fall asleep. I am going to head inside and change. Are you going to stay in a little while longer?"

"If you don't mind, I think I will go for another swim," I answered.

"Oh sure, take all the time you need. I'll be back down in a minute."

I watched until she made it all the way inside the patio doors before I climbed out of the hot tub and dove into the pool from the top of the rocky formations that served as a barrier. The slightly cooler water glided along my skin, caressing it like satin sheets as I swam the length of the pool. Swimming was so relaxing.

Suddenly, I felt a hand wrap around my ankle and tug me backwards. Immediately, I stopped and bent my knee trying to pull lose, but my foot wouldn't come free. Still underwater I tried to surface for air, my lungs starting to burn with the need to breath, and my body started to glide back the other direction. My foot hit a hard muscled chest and I flipped onto my back and kicked out with my other leg, connecting with a shoulder.

My face finally broke the surface of the water and I gulped a lung full of air before regaining my balance and lunging at Acer, pushing his head underwater. "That was not funny!" I shouted. "You scared me to death!"

"Hey, take it easy! Take it easy!" he hollered his voice sounding garbled as I pushed his head under several more times. "I'm sorry! It was a joke, Scout! I'm sorry!"

"What are you doing here?" I asked, deciding he had been punished enough. "I thought you were playing cars with my brother."

He laughed. "Is that what you think we do?"

"Am I wrong?"

"No, I guess you're not."

We were treading water, our heads and chests bobbing up and down and I suddenly felt my cheeks flush as I caught his eyes sliding down to rest on my chest. *Stupid bikini!*

I splashed his face and then let my body slide further down under the water.

"Is it OK if I join you for a swim?" he asked.

Heck no!

Unable to think of a reasonable excuse, I nodded. "Sure, Bonnie went in to change. I'll probably get out when she comes back down."

He smirked. "Well then, I'll race you to the end of the pool!"

"You're on!"

We took off. Halfway to the other side, I glanced over and saw that I was pulling ahead of him. Suddenly, I felt him wrap his arms around my waist. His body briefly stretched out against mine as he tackled me underwater. Just as I stretched my arm out to touch the wall, he lunged over the top of me, launching himself like a bullet and slapping my hand away at the same time that he reached the wall.

214

"Hey, you cheated!" I protested by splashing a wall of water in his face.

He playfully splashed me back and as I tried to retaliate with a bigger force, he grabbed my hand. My heart stopped as he held it, refusing to let go. Intently, he gazed into my eyes, his expression shameless as he laced our fingers together. Reflexively, I tried to splash with my other hand and he grabbed that one too, our fingers lacing automatically this time.

I needed an excuse to get out of this pool. It was getting too cozy for just two friends. "I probably need to check on Bonnie," I said, but he didn't let me go.

"No, you don't," he whispered and then tugged me towards deeper water. We swam together, holding hands until finally he led me to a built-in ledge in the side of the pool.

Trying to make my escape, I hoisted myself onto the ledge, leaving my feet to dangle in the water. He folded his elbows and rested them on my lap. His touch sent a tremor racing across my thighs.

In an attempt to distract myself from the butterflies in my stomach, I turned my eyes towards the night sky. "Look at all those stars," I breathed, "just beautiful."

"Beautiful," he echoed, resting his chin on his arms.

"We don't usually see this many stars in Kansas City," I rambled, trying to keep my breathing steady when all I could feel was the fluttering of my racing heart. "I can see why Bonnie likes to sit out here so much."

At the mention of her name, his hands clenched into fists against me, and then he unfolded his arms, resting them on either side of my body. His chin nestled in the space between my legs. I shifted slightly trying to put some distance between us, but he refused to move.

I rubbed his silky smooth head. "How are you holding up?" I asked and then gently maneuvered his chin off of my lap and slid back into the water. It didn't result in the escape I was seeking. Now, he had me trapped between his arms, with my back against the wall.

"I don't know," he answered honestly, his words full of emotion. "Nervous. Angry. Hopeful. Take your pick." He flashed a lopsided grin, but didn't move his arms.

"I like hopeful," I said nudging his arm with my elbow. "Hopeful is good." His arm didn't move.

He grinned and wrapped me in a hug, only to quickly release me. Keeping one arm around my shoulders, he rested his back against the wall next to me. "It makes me nervous when Bonnie talks about dying. I know she is fine with it, but I'm not. I'm not ready to let her go," he shared.

Let me go.

Tears filled my eyes as my daddy's dying words echoed through the depths of my mind. "I know what you mean," I whispered. "Letting go is the hardest part."

He must have sensed the change in my demeanor because he pulled me into his side, turning me towards him. Unable to hold back the floodgates that were triggered by his words, I buried my face against his chest.

"Hey," he said gently, "what's going on, Scout? I've got a feeling this isn't just about Bonnie anymore." He stroked my hair and rested his chin on the top of my head. "Talk to me."

I took a deep breath and let it out, slowly contemplating what to say. Acer was trustworthy, I knew, but I hesitated to open up this much to him about something so personal. Nuzzling his neck with my nose, I coaxed my head out of the crook of his arm.

"I haven't talked to anyone about this before because it's so painful to relive," I started slowly. He waited patiently for me to continue, his eyes full of concern. "I was with my daddy when he died. Not just in the same building or just outside the door. I was right there." I paused and closed my eyes. I could see it all so clearly in my mind, and felt hot tears run down my cheeks.

"I crawled into his arms and lay there next to him until he stopped breathing." His arms wound tighter around me and I choked back a sob and continued. "He was ready to go home, but I wasn't ready to let him go. I didn't want to let him go. I wanted him to go to the hospital and get fixed, but he knew his journey on earth was finished. He just knew. The last words he ever spoke, they were to me, and he said 'Let me go.' And that's what I did. I let him go." I sobbed.

"Oh, Scout," he whispered against my hair as I continued to cry softly in his arms. Gently, he pressed his lips against my forehead. I didn't flinch away or try to resist his touch; I reveled in it, needing the comfort and warmth of his embrace. His lips were tender and delicate against my skin. He breathed my name again, "Scout."

Methodically, he ran his fingers through my tangled wet hair, down my arm and back up again, this time tracing his finger along my neck and jaw until he hooked my chin and tugged it up so that I was looking in his face. Our eyes locked, and there was no escaping their azure depths this time.

Before I could protest, his lips covered mine, soft at first, but finding no resistance, he deepened the kiss and parted my lips with the tip of his tongue. Half-heartedly, I tried to step back, but his hand threaded into my hair and held me firmly against his mouth and for just a moment, I gave into the desire that I had buried so deep inside myself. I couldn't help it. His caresses were so tender and his lips so warm that I could not deny myself this pleasure any longer. I needed to feel this kind of acceptance, this kind of love. So I returned his kiss fiercely. I wound my hands around his waist, feeling our chests crash into each other which sent a whole new wave of sensation coursing through me.

All the while, my mind and my emotions were at war.

What are we doing?

You can't do this. You've got to stop!

But it feels so good! You know if you weren't teammates, you would welcome this openly.

I know, but we can't do this. It's got to stop!

Unfortunately, logic won out and woke me from my state of bliss. I knew I had to end the foolishness. "Acer, stop!" I spoke through his roving lips. "Acer, stop! We can't do this!" Either he didn't hear me or he chose to ignore me and continued exploring my neck. I started to give in again when his lips touched a particularly sensitive spot behind my ear. My knees buckled and he held me up. With our close height our bodies melded together so tightly, I could feel his heart beating through his chest, or maybe it was my heart pounding in my chest— either way there was another rush of butterflies in my stomach. It hit me so hard, my thighs tingled.

I had to get control of myself before it was too late. Pushing against his chest with enough force to send him back a step, I shouted, "We can't do this, Acer! Just stop! I don't want this!"

He released me and leaned back against the edge of the pool, confused by the mixed signals I was giving him. "What do you mean we can't do this?" He ran a hand over his bald head, and with fire in his eyes he began to protest. "Yes, we can, Scout! We just have to quit living in denial, that's all!"

"No," I returned evenly. "You're my teammate and my pitcher. That's it. I can't be your girlfriend too. It would mess up everything we have worked so hard to achieve this year!"

"You know, Scout, there are more important things in life then baseball," he muttered. He stood up and reached for my hand, lacing our fingers together. "Look, I know that this is not exactly what we planned, but I know our feelings are real. Don't try to deny it! I've seen it in your eyes too many times."

"Well, you're wrong, Acer. I don't want you! I don't need you! And I'm not in denial. You're nothing but my teammate and my best friend's twin brother! If you read something more than that, then you're just a fool!" I spat.

Anger and humiliation sparked in his eyes then, and he jumped up out of the pool, half running, half stomping, to the back patio doors. He grabbed his towel from the rack and whirled around to face me again. "You mark my words, Scout Rose! You're going to want this moment back. One day soon, you're going to regret every word you just said and when you realize it, it will be too late, because I'll be gone."

He wrapped the towel around his waist and strode off toward the door, slamming it behind him. All too late, I called after him. "Wait! Wait, Ben! Acer! That's not what I meant! Come back!" I pleaded.

Tears streaming down my face, I quickly gathered my things and toweled myself off as I headed down the stone path to the side gate just as Bonnie had stepped outside.

"Scout, what's going on?" she asked.

"Bonnie, I'm sorry. I got to go. I'm sorry."

"What? Why? What's going on? You have an hour until curfew."

"I-I have to go. I can't talk about it now!" I hugged her neck and she held me tight. Tears filled my eyes again. "Good luck with the surgery tomorrow," I said through my tears. "I will call you after school if you are up and can talk." I hugged her one more time and did not wait to listen to her protests; I just turned and left as fast as I could.

Chapter Fourteen: Advice

Three days later, I still had not been able to talk to Bonnie. She was in a medically induced coma as a result of the uncontrollable bleeding during her surgery. Mrs. Acer said that she had to have several blood transfusions. They wanted her to heal without inadvertently injuring her wound, and for now, visitors were limited to family only.

My heart ached for her. It felt like my dad all over again. Something so routine and simple had quickly turned life-threatening and serious. My life was on repeat and I just didn't understand why God was allowing this to happen to such a sweet person like Bonnie. I found it harder and harder every day to feel anything but bitterness. There were no diamonds to be found.

Well, maybe there was one. I still had not had to cross paths with Acer since our night in the pool. He was not at school on Friday because of Bonnie's surgery and we had the weekend off from baseball, but the play-offs were this week. I wouldn't be so lucky tomorrow and I really didn't know what I was going to say to him.

By Sunday afternoon, I was beyond miserable as my thoughts were consumed by guilt over hurting Acer and leaving Bonnie bewildered and alone when I had promised I would be there for her. I let them both down and I just hoped I would get the chance to apologize.

Finally after reading the same line from my history book ten times, I resigned to giving my bike a tune-up. I had been putting off the routine maintenance since baseball season picked up and it was really overdue

After a couple of hours in the garage, I had changed all of the oils and filter. I was in the process of returning the fork seal to its position when I heard footsteps coming down from the apartment upstairs. Danny Joe rounded the corner.

"Hey, Sis," he said and stomped towards me. He was wearing his typical blue collar work shirt unbuttoned and open to his white undershirt and dark pants with his big clumpy untied work boots. "What are you doing there?"

"Just changing the fluids," I responded.

"Wow, changing the fluids! I'm impressed!" He commented, walking around appraising my handiwork. "This is such a beauty. I'm still jealous that Dad gave it to you," He squatted down next to me. Then he pointed to the fork seal I had just put into place. "You've got that on backwards."

It looked exactly the way it did before I had taken it apart. "Are you sure? It looks right to me."

"I spent two years in juvi as a grease monkey," he said. "Trust me. I'm sure."

I handed him my tools and watched him go to work.

After tinkering in silence for a minute, he stated, "Ace hasn't been around in a while, what's up?"

I wiped the grease off my hands with a towel and sat cross-legged next to him. "He probably won't be around for a while."

"How come?" He asked as he continued to tighten bolts and shift pieces around.

"For one, his sister is in the hospital. And two, I said some things that really hurt him. I doubt I will ever see him again outside of school and baseball."

"Ta-da! That's how it should go," he boasted, pointing to the correct position.

"Wow, you did that really fast!" I said, handing him a towel.

"What can I say? I'm a grease monkey." He toweled the oil off his hands as he asked, "What did you say to Ace that was so bad he won't come around anymore?"

I hesitated. I didn't want to get into all of this with Danny Joe. Acer was his buddy, sort of, and besides, Danny Joe was not the smartest guy when it came to relationships. "It's just silly teenage stuff."

"What? You think I don't understand silly teenage stuff either? I swear, Scout, I really do have some ground to make up with you," he teased.

I studied the fork and suspension on my motorcycle. "It's not so much what I said, but the time that I said it."

He waited expectantly with his eyebrows raised.

I shook my head and sighed, "I don't want to get into this with you! It is too embarrassing!" He continued to stare at me with the same expression. Exasperated, I rushed through my response. "We were talking about Bonnie and Daddy and I started crying. We were just comforting each other and Acer kissed me, and I pushed him away, said I didn't need him. Now he won't talk to me. I should have told him months ago we could only be friends. Now we can't even be that much."

"So Acer kissed you? Like on the mouth?" he queried. My cheeks flushed and all I could do was nod my head. "Atta boy, Ace!" He nodded his head in approval, grinning broadly.

"Hey!" I glared, punching him the shoulder.

"What? You didn't like it?"

"No, it wasn't that I didn't like it," I interrupted him, "It's just that we can't do this whole boyfriend-girlfriend thing. We're teammates."

"Oh, so you're afraid."

"No! Ugh! Why am I talking to you about this? You are not exactly the best person to give relationship advice."

"Actually, I am," he said, sitting next to me on the floor of the garage, his legs stretched out in front of him. "I know exactly what it takes to screw up a relationship, so if you want a relationship to work, don't do anything that I do." I had to laugh at his logic. "I understand mistakes because Sadie and me have made a lot of them. You and Ace pushing each other away like this? Big mistake."

"It's not like that. You just don't get it!"

"Believe me, Sis, I get it. I really do. You have worked hard to show everyone that you can be one of the boys, and from what I've seen, your team and your coaches, well, they see you that way. But that's all you let them see. You and Ace are closer than that and you've actually showed him that you're not all vinegar. He is the only one that you've given a chance to see you as more than just the homerun crushing catcher. To him you're like…a homerun crushing diva."

"He said that?"

"No, not those exact words, but he's got it bad for you," he returned.

"He told you that?"

"Not exactly," he said. "He didn't use your name, but I knew who he was talking about. Besides, it's not so much what he said. It's the way he acts around you that gave it away. Same with you for that matter. I just don't get why you are so afraid."

"I'm not afraid!" I argued.

"Oh, yes, you are. You're afraid of what everyone is going to think about you and Ace being together. That's the part I don't get. Sis, you never cared about what other people thought before. Why the change? What happened to all that confidence?"

"I didn't have an entire town looking for any excuse to say I don't deserve to play baseball anymore," I answered. "If anyone thought that Acer and I were more than just friends, they would use that against me, and say that girls and boys can't play on the same field."

He sat up and wiped my cheek with the towel. "I bet most of your team thinks you two got together a long time ago. I know I did, until Mary straightened me out."

"But up until the other night we were dealing with just rumors. He crossed the line. Now some of those rumors are true and everything has changed. "

"How's baseball changed? Has any of the time you spent together off the field hurt the team?"

"No," I answered. "In a way it kind of helped the team because in the beginning we hated each other. We fought all the time and it was a constant battle on the field between my stubbornness and Acer's temper."

"Then why would you and Ace dating off the field be a problem now? Unless you two start making out in the dugout, I don't see how anything would change." I blushed. "You earned your spot on that field because of your ability. Believe me everyone respects that. It's not every day that a girl can crush a baseball 400 feet." He shook his head and then his expression grew more thoughtful. "Let me ask you this. If there was no baseball, and you and Ace were just kids at a high school, would you go out with him?"

"Yes," I blurted out and then felt my cheeks flush as a result. "I mean, maybe…"

"Then don't be afraid," he cut me off. "It's not worth it. My fear has driven Sadie away every time and my pride has kept her there. You and Acer could be whatever you want to be because you both respect each other and you have each other's backs. Just don't be afraid of what everyone else thinks. That's not who you are, Scout."

"You know, Danny Joe, sometimes you make perfect sense."

"Don't worry. I won't let it go to my head." He stood and then helped me up off the floor. "Come on," he said, "It's dinner time. Let's go see what we can scrounge up."

Monday morning came and went. Mary let me take my motorcycle to school for the week, so I didn't have to worry about the awkward ride, or lack of an awkward ride, from Acer. Especially since I still hadn't seen or heard from him. In fact, it wasn't until our afternoon practice that we even saw each other. He wasn't exactly friendly, but it wasn't as hostile as our first practice either. Our conversations just involved pitching and our upcoming series against Coronado. He never gave me an opportunity to talk about anything else, not even Bonnie. We only spoke when it was necessary. This was so much worse than our first practice.

The next two days were more of the same, but Thursday as I pulled up to school, I noticed Acer hanging out by his truck. When I pulled off my helmet and shook my hair out, I saw that he was walking towards me. Hoping that I would finally get a chance to talk to him about last week, I looked in my rearview mirror, combed out my locks with my fingers and then met him half way across the parking lot.

"Hey, Acer," I greeted him, trying not to seem too eager.

"Hey," he said coolly, his eyes avoiding my face. "My mom wanted me to tell you that they have moved Bonnie out of ICU and into her own room."

"That's great news!" I said excitedly.

"She's still in a lot of pain," he said seriously. "Mom thought that having you there might help take her mind off of it," he informed me and then quickly turned to leave.

I reached out and touched his shoulder. "Acer, wait." He stopped, but didn't turn around so I dropped my hand and apologized to his back, "I'm sorry for what I said last week. I'm just scared and I…"

"Visiting hours are over at 9:00," he said evenly and strode off.

I guess I deserved that.

Our first game of the best of three series was at Coronado that afternoon, which was only thirty minutes from the medical center where Bonnie was staying. Coach Mac agreed to let me leave the game with Mary and Brian instead of riding back with the team so that I could visit Bonnie afterward.

We won 9-7 and that is all that I could remember about the game because I floated through it in a haze. Acer wasn't pitching so I was the designated hitter. It was the worst hitting performance of my career. I don't remember how many times I struck out, but the only good contact I made was a line shot to the shortstop for the last out of the eighth inning.

Acer couldn't avoid me completely in the dugout, but he didn't go out of his way to find me either. Danny Joe was right. Acer and I spent so much time together on and off the field that apparently people did think we had gotten together weeks ago. The coldness between us seemed to draw more attention than any of our previous actions. Three different people at some point during the game casually asked if Acer and I were having a fight. The more I thought about it, the more I realized that no one would have noticed anything different about Acer and me if I hadn't pushed him away. It was my fault!

I had to fix this. I missed my friend and my team needed their all-star battery back.

As I left the dugout after the game and found Mary, I was surprised to see Acer standing with her. I froze as I realized he was riding with us to the hospital.

The three of us headed to the parking lot. Acer and I didn't make contact nor did we speak unless spoken to directly. If Mary noticed, it didn't stop her talkative nature as she continued to drone on about everything from the game to the many wonderful intricacies of being five months pregnant.

After the longest thirty-minute car ride ever, we arrived at the children's cancer hospital at the medical center. They dropped us off and went to park the car, and Acer led me through the front doors. As always, he ushered me through the automatic doors ahead of him, but I didn't feel his typical touch at the small of my back and I really missed it.

We headed to the bank of elevators on the far side of the lobby; and other then his casual request for me to punch the button for the fourth floor, he said nothing. The elevators opened to a large room that was full of toys, televisions, two huge fish tanks, miniature and adult-sized tables, and brightly painted murals. It was so inviting; it didn't feel like a hospital at all.

"What a fun place!" I commented.

"Yeah, if you're five," he returned drily.

To the left of the open area was a huge nurse's station with four short hallways that branched off behind it. Without a word, Acer strode purposefully toward the hallway on the right. Bonnie's room was all the way at the end. I noticed many of the doorways and walls were decorated with cards, children's drawings, and balloons. Most of the doors stood wide open and each seemed to be occupied by a child with a bald little head and sunken eyes just like Bonnie's. It seemed there were no other teenagers, at least down this hallway.

When we arrived at Bonnie's room, the door was closed and I heard her cry out in pain. Acer winced at the sound. I placed my hand on his shoulder, but he didn't acknowledge it, nor did he shy away from it, so I left it there. He started to open the door, but then stopped, leaning his ear close and listening.

"I think we need to wait," he said. "It sounds like they are having a hard time with her IV again."

"Again? Doesn't it stay in her arm?" I asked.

"Her veins are too fragile so they keep breaking and when they break they have to put in a new IV."

"Well, can't they just put the meds through her shunt?" I asked.

"I don't know! What do you think you are—a doctor now too?" he yelled.

"What is that supposed to mean?" I returned heatedly.

"Forget it," he spat.

"Fine!" I huffed and leaned my back against the wall outside her door and stared out the window at the end of the hall.

We stood in seething silence for a few more minutes, both of us cringing at the sounds of Bonnie's screams until finally she was quiet again and the door opened. A young nurse in pink scrubs covered with little white rabbits walked out briskly, shaking her head. She didn't acknowledge either of us as she moved down the hall, pushing her little cart in front of her.

Again, Acer ushered me through the door ahead of him in his ever present gentle way. I stepped around the curtain and gasped at the sight in front of me. This was not my friend! She wore a pink stocking cap. Her petite body was so frail and thin that her head looked like a giant basketball. Her skin was pasty white except for her arms. Her arms were completely covered by mammoth-sized purplish black bruises. She lay back on the pillow, and her sunken eyes were closed and her face was contorted in pain.

I took a step back and bumped into Acer. Gently, he steadied me on my feet and nudged me forward. It was then that Mrs. Acer realized we were even in the room.

"Oh, good!" she said, walking to the foot of the bed and wrapping us both in a hug. "You kids were able to make it after all. I sure appreciate Mary bringing Ben along."

She took my hand and walked me over to a chair by Bonnie's head. Gently, she reached out and stroked her cheek. "Sweetheart," she said leaning in close. "You have visitors."

Bonnie opened one blue eye, but didn't move. Her lips moved slightly and then I heard her scratchy voice say, "Hey girl."

"Hey yourself," I gently wiped a tear off of her cheek.

"Thanks for coming," she croaked out.

"Sorry, it took me so long," I answered. She reached out and grabbed my hand. Afraid that I might damage her already fragile skin, I didn't squeeze it, but I held it firmly.

Acer came alongside me and reached out, brushing his hand down her arm. "Hey Bon-Bon, do I need to beat up a couple of nurses for you?"

"Yeah, that'd be great." She tried to laugh, but it sounded more like a cough. "How was the game?"

"We won." he said wirily. "Scout struck out three times."

I shot him an exasperated look, but otherwise didn't take the bait.

"Everyone has an off day once in a while," she commented. "It's about time Scout had one."

Suddenly, her face twisted in a pain and she inhaled sharply. Her eyes were shut tight, and a lone tear slid from her eye and trickled across the bridge of her nose. She gripped my hand hard and I tried to resist the urge to pull away as she crushed my fingers in her grasp.

"Bonnie, hon, you need something?" her mother said gently.

"No!" She screamed, shocking us all. She sat up abruptly, crying out as loudly as she could. "I don't need anything from anyone!" She cried out in pain as tears streamed down her face. "This is not living, Mom! This is dying a very painful and slow death! This surgery was supposed to make me live longer! I could have died at home without all this pain! I could have lived for months without the constant nausea and weakness of these treatments! I'm so sick of fighting cancer!"

I looked at her mom and Acer, helplessly watching tears well up in their eyes as Bonnie continued her rant. "Why won't you just accept it? I am going to die before I graduate high school, before I get married, before I grow up! But look at the life I have had. Is that not enough? Why won't you listen to me? I'm not getting better this time! Just let me die!"

Acer rolled his eyes and muttered, "That's the meds talking."

"I'm so sorry, honey," Mrs. Acer whispered. "We just did what we thought was best. I'm so sorry. Excuse me." She choked back a sob and ran out of the room. Acer turned towards me and I saw the tracks of tears below both of his eyes. Slowly, he turned and followed after his mom.

I sat down in the chair next to Bonnie's head, never letting go of her hand. After a few moments of silence, she relaxed and asked quietly, "What happened between you and my brother?"

I leaned forward and responded deliberately, "We kissed in your pool."

The corner of her mouth raised in a slight smile. "I figured that was it. Guess you never had the talk with him."

I shook my head. "I wasn't very nice to him afterwards either."

"It makes sense now." She took a deep breath and let it out slowly. "He's really hurt."

"I know. I'm sorry. I know the timing is terrible, but I promise you, I will fix this. I'm sorry I ran off the other night."

"He loves you, Scout," she stated seriously. "Not the artificial teenage love. He really loves you and will probably wait until you figure out for yourself that you love him like that too."

"Now, I know the meds are talking," I teased.

"You'll see, Scout," she answered, but her eyes were closing. She was drifting off to sleep, succumbing to the pain medicine.

We sat in silence, still holding hands until finally she fell asleep. After a while, her hand relaxed enough that I eased out of her grasp. Bonnie had given me a lot to think about, especially after my talk with Danny Joe. I found myself grappling for an excuse to argue what they were both implying, but I couldn't. They were both right. Somewhere along the way Acer and I became more than friends in spite of ourselves. Everyone saw it happening but me. As I looked down at Bonnie sleeping peacefully, my thoughts were driven back to the reality of how terribly sick and hopeless she was, and my heart ached for her.

I needed to go for a walk and clear my head before it exploded.

Quietly, I crept out of the room and walked slowly down the hallway towards the waiting area. Along the way, I passed an elderly woman with dark gray, curly hair. She was wearing a pink jacket that indicated that she was a hospital volunteer, but what caught my eye was what she was doing. At each room, she would reach out and touch the room number. She was in total view of the nurse's station, so obviously no one looked at her as a threat or concern, but there was something very odd about her behavior.

As she was moving onto the next room, our eyes met and she smiled sweetly at me and then fluttered her fingers in a little wave. In an automatic response, I did the same, then swiftly moved down the hall. I reached the waiting area and spotted Mary and Brian sitting on either side of Mrs. Acer. Mary's arm was draped around Bonnie's mom and she was leaning her head back against my sister. Her eyes were swollen from crying, as were Mary's.

I then realized that Mr. Acer was on the other side of my brother-in-law. The two weren't holding each other like Mary and Bonnie's mom, but they were red-eyed, obviously having shed some tears together. I was reminded of what Bonnie had once said about Mary and Brian being the nicest people in town. From what I was seeing at that very moment, they really were.

Once again, I was struck in awe at how wonderfully God had orchestrated my life so that I was constantly surrounded by people who not only understood God's love, but lived it out in a very genuine way. Bonnie's words of "God is so good!" echoed in my head, and it made me angry.

Diamonds in the Dirt

Oh really? If God is so good then why is your best friend lying at the end of the hall dying from cancer? It's absolute cruelty to allow someone so young and so undeserving to suffer such a horrible thing like this! For that matter, why would God take both of your parents with the same ugly disease and then bring you to Booneville only to watch someone else you care about die again from it? There was no goodness in that!

My thoughts went wild and the anger and bitterness welled inside me as I raged internally. I stormed over to a chair and plopped down, tears of bitterness stinging my eyes. I grounded them out with my fists.

When I lifted my head again, the little elderly woman I saw down the hall was standing in front of me. Startled, I gripped the edge of the chair and stared questioningly at her peculiar expression. Without introduction, she opened a little black leather bound book that I recognized immediately as a Bible and read:

"And we know that God causes everything to work together for the good of those who love God and are called according to His purposes. Romans 8:28," she said. "The Holy Spirit led me to remind you of that."

My lips could not form words. I stared at her in bewilderment. Was she for real?

"Who are you?" I finally asked. "What were you doing down my friend's hallway?"

She pointed to the shoulder of her jacket where her name badge was attached. "I'm Ruby. I volunteer in the hospitality room on the twenty-fourth floor. There are thirty-one floors in this building, and every day when my shift is over, I pray for each patient on one of the floors of this hospital."

I gestured to the empty chair next to me and she sat down. "Every patient on the entire floor? That must take hours. What does your husband think about that?"

"My husband has been dead now for twenty-five years," she replied. "I like to think that he is happy with what I am doing with my

232

life. You see, when you get to be my age, you learn to slow down and focus on the important things that fulfill the purposes of God." She grew thoughtful for a moment and then continued. "Prayer is a very important activity and the patients and their families in this hospital need lots of prayer, whether they realize it or not."

I found myself feeling cynical. None of the prayers for my dad had done any good. There were so many people who were praying for him. Our church had even set up a twenty-four hour prayer chain and his cancer never stopped spreading. There was never anything positive that came out of all of those prayers for him. It all just seemed like a waste of time.

My expression must have shown my pessimism because she cocked an eyebrow at me and said, "'For everyone who asks, receives. Everyone who seeks, finds. And to everyone who knocks, the door will be opened.' God still hears our prayers and He is still in the miracle business."

"But there were many who prayed for my dad and he still died. And my friend down there has people praying for her and she is suffering worse than before. This is the third time she has had cancer."

"Prayer is not a formula," she responded gently. "Prayer is seeking the heart and will of God. Did you get everything you ever asked for from your dad?"

"Well, no," I answered.

"And your dad knew that you would be better off without some of those things. It's the same with God. He always answers our prayers; we just don't always appreciate the answer right away." She pointed up. "God is our heavenly Father. He understands us better than we understand ourselves. He created us, formed us in our mother's womb and gave us exactly what we needed to accomplish the purpose He has given us. God does everything for good. So as we pray in God's will with all of those truths in mind, we can be peaceful no matter what the answer is because we know it is God's will, and He loves us and He wants what is best for us."

Diamonds in the Dirt

"How could losing both of my parents to cancer and then watching my friend die from cancer be the best thing for me?"

"Maybe it's not about you. Maybe it's to benefit the life of someone else. I know that if my husband would not have died, I would have never volunteered at this hospital and the gifts of hospitality that God had given me would never have been shared outside my home. I would have never felt that I could spend hours a day praying for people I don't even know."

The faith of this woman was incredible. It was as if she took a tragic thing like death and found the diamond in it, and then not only acknowledged it, but turned it into a beautiful diamond necklace. The amount of hours she must have spent serving and praying for people that she didn't even know was staggering; it made me feel so inadequate.

"You know, I could never do what you do. I could never pray like you do. I wouldn't even have the words," I mumbled.

"Prayer is just talking, that's all," she said gently. "You don't have to pray longwinded elaborate prayers for God to hear you. You just have to say what's on your heart. I have a feeling that you are really good at speaking from the heart." She slid her eyes towards me with a grin. If only she knew the truth behind those words. "Besides, when we don't know what to pray, Scripture tells us, the Holy Spirit will help us: 'The Holy Spirit prays for us with groanings that cannot be expressed in words.'"

"Kind of like you coming over and reminding me that God is good, no matter what my mind argues?" I asked.

"Exactly!" she said and abruptly stood. "Now we have come full circle. I've got three more wings left and you need to spend time with your friend."

"Ms. Ruby, thanks for talking to me," I said, "and thanks for praying for my friend."

"Don't thank me. Thank my God," she answered. "He crossed our paths tonight."

She turned and left.

As I sat back and absorbed everything Ruby had just shared, I wondered if God would save Bonnie this time. If I prayed for her, would God really let her live the rest of her life cancer free?

I looked around the waiting room and there was no sign of the Acers or Mary and Brian, so I headed back down the hall to check on Bonnie. When I silently opened the door and walked around the curtain, I saw the four of them and Acer standing around Bonnie's bed. Their heads were bowed and their eyes closed, and I realized that Mr. Acer was praying for Bonnie's healing.

It was beyond coincidence and I was startled at the reality that God had just set up this divine appointment with Ruby so that my heart would be prepared to walk in and join them in prayer for Bonnie. Five minutes ago, if I had walked in on this scene, I would have turned around and walked right back out, believing that prayer wouldn't heal Bonnie. Instead, I walked over and stood in between Mary and Brian. Mary slid her arm around my shoulders. After a minute or two, Mr. Acer's prayer ended and it was quiet.

I felt a persistent push in my chest and I opened my mouth, took a deep breath and spoke from the heart. "God, we are asking for a miracle and your word tells us that everyone who asks receives. We are asking you to heal Bonnie. Remove every cancer cell from her body. Restore her bone marrow so that it will make the type of blood cells she needs. We are asking you for a miracle because the doctors here don't know what else to do to help her, but You do. You made her. You know every part of her. Only You know what needs to be fixed. Even though Bonnie is ready to meet You, selfishly I want her to stay with us a little longer. I just met her and I want more time to get to know her when she is not so sick. But if it's Your plan to take..."

Emotions welled up inside me and then overflowed into my voice. I had to stop, unable to speak anymore because of the tears. Mary wrapped her arms tighter around me and I felt Brian grab my hand. Then, I heard Acer's voice pick up where I had left off. "If it's Your plan to bring her home to You, we will be happy for her, but please give her some relief from her pain. Heal her wound from surgery so she can get out of this hospital bed and enjoy her last days here with us. Give us all the strength that You have already given her to let go of everything here for what waits for us in heaven. Until You take her to be with You, we are going to continue asking for a miracle. In Jesus' name we pray. Amen."

Chapter Fifteen: Apology Not Accepted

B all game!" the umpire yelled.

Our home field crowd erupted in cheers as I tossed him the ball and ran out to congratulate Jason on the save. This morning's game was tough. Acer struggled to hit his targets and his ball was dead. We had jumped out to an early lead, scoring five runs in the first inning. He kept them scoreless until the fifth when he gave up a run, but then in the sixth, he imploded and gave up three more runs before Coach yanked him. Luckily Jason was able to spread Coronado's hits out far enough that they could never get any kind of offensive strike going.

Acer and I were still just tolerating each other and going through the motions on the field. We didn't argue. We just didn't laugh much or joke around like we usually did. It was all business between us. Although, we had gotten the job done today, there was no fun in it. We did what we had to do to get by. Everyone seemed to notice our distance, but they were smart enough to stop asking about it.

"Nice save!" I patted Jason's back as we jogged off the field.

"Thanks! Great call on that screwball on that last hitter!" he replied.

"I just call them like I see them."

"Can you believe we are going to state!" he yelled playfully, patting my helmet.

With that win we had punched our ticket to the state play-offs, and for the first time in over a decade, the Bearcats would have the chance to play for a state title. I was excited, but as everyone celebrated around me, I found my thoughts drift to Bonnie.

After we had left her hospital room a few nights ago, and drove the long hour back to Booneville, I used that time to talk to Mary about my encounter with Ruby. I had told her about all the skepticism I felt about prayer, because of daddy, but that Ruby had given me hope, and then seeing everyone gathered in prayer around Bonnie, had bolstered that hope.

I just had to see Bonnie today. Eagerly, I waited for Coach Mac to finish his speech and send us on our way so that I could head to the hospital. When he finally finished, I sat down on the bench and started packing up my gear as quickly as I could. I switched into my tennis shoes just as Jose plopped down next to me.

He stared at me for a long moment and when he wouldn't speak, I finally asked, "What?"

"What's happened between you and Acer?" he asked.

I hesitated in the middle of looping my shoelace. "Boy, if I had a dollar for every time someone has asked me that over the last week."

He put his arm around me as I sat back against the bench. "I know that it's more than just worry over Bonnie. So spare me that lame excuse. Something has happened."

I glanced down to the other side of the dugout and spotted Acer throwing his bag over his shoulder and walking up the steps. "Just drop it, Jose," I said. "Something's happened, but it can't be fixed."

"You need to fix it! You two kept the game fun. You kept the team loose," he stated. "Between your joking about the hitters and your pregame hackysack rituals, this team was having fun and winning."

"We're still winning! We're going to the state play-offs."

"Barely. If Acer and you were on the same page like you had been weeks ago, Coronado would have never came this close to beating us. If you two don't get it together, we won't make it past the first round of the tournament. We need you two."

"It's just a game, Jose. They are more important things besides baseball."

"Not to you, there's not!" he returned. "You love this game more than anyone I know! So much that you'd put up with a bunch of boys just to get the chance to play!"

I sighed. "Look, I've tried to fix this, but he won't let me. He won't give me the time of day off this baseball field and on it, it's all baseball."

"Then you're just going to have to get his attention and make him listen," he answered.

"How do you suggest I do that? Hit him over the head and lock him in the garage?"

He looked thoughtful for a moment and then his eyes lit up. "Come to the spring dance tonight. We'll get Acer there and you two can have all the time in the world to talk. We will make sure of it."

"Sorry, Jose; I don't do dances. Besides, Bonnie is still in the hospital. I plan to be there the rest of the day."

Jose argued. "Then go see Bonnie and ask her what you should do. I know she would tell you to go to the dance. Rachel told me how disappointed she was that she wasn't going to get to make it. She'd tell you and Acer both to go. I know she would."

"I don't know, Jose."

"Trust me. Get to the dance tonight. It starts at 8:00." He stood and pulled me to my feet. "I know this will work."

"I don't even have a dress!" I yelled at his back as he turned and headed up the steps.

"I'm sure you can find something," he called over his shoulder. "It's not a formal, you know. It's just a dance."

"I'm not going!"

"Yes, you are! See you at 8:00."

Idly, I picked up my things and headed out of the dugout. What kind of hair-brained scheme did he have in mind? Even if I did go to the dance and by some miracle he was able to get Acer there, he couldn't make him talk to me. Acer barely looked at me off the field! He might look at me more and ease into a conversation, if I really got his attention. Appealed to his...Oh my gosh! That was Jose's plan! Get Acer to notice me and make him forget that I'd hurt him. It would never work!

I rounded the corner of the dugout and walked out the gate, shaking my head slightly. Suddenly I came to a halt. "WH-What are you doing here?" I asked in surprise.

My sister Ruth wrapped me in a tight hug. "Surprise!"

I noticed as I hugged her back that she stood at eye level. Normally she was at least five inches shorter than me, but apparently her wedge sandals made up the difference. Her hair, which was the color of my dad's in his younger days, was dyed blonde. It was a completely different look for her, but it matched her sun-kissed tan.

"You look amazing, Ruthie! Florida must have been really good to you."

"Thanks, Scout. Just thought I would try something different."

My brother-in-law, Julio, hovered in the background, his dark eyes twinkling in amusement. He had grown a goatee since the funeral and apparently had bulked up too. His arms hung at his sides and the muscles bulged beneath his black T-shirt. Releasing Ruth, I reached over and hugged him and said, "*Bienvenidos a Tejas!*"

"*Gracias, mija!*" he returned. "Good game."

"Thanks."

Ruth put her arm around me and we headed to the parking lot with Julio trailing behind. "It appears that we are going to see a lot more of each other. Julio has been picked up by the Richmond Vipers. We are house hunting this weekend."

"Get out! Really? First Danny Joe, and now you two!" I was shocked. It was like some kind of family reunion. All we needed was David and Emily to move down here and we would be one big happy family.

I spotted Mary waiting at the gate. "Sorry," she apologized. "I had to go to the bathroom for the tenth time. That's all I do now is drink water and go to the bathroom! I swear sometimes I'm carrying a bowling ball. If it's not swollen feet, it's…"

"Easy, Mama Mary," I interrupted her. "You're going to hurt Peanut's feelings."

She immediately stopped her rant and rubbed her round belly. It was her cue to stop complaining. Brian had started referring to her as Mama Mary a month ago and it always made her smile and after seeing the first ultrasound that resembled nothing of a baby and everything of a peanut, I started calling the baby Peanut, which Mary also found endearing. In combination, Brian and I found that we could diffuse Mary's brooding over being pregnant in one quick swoop.

"Is there anything else I should know, Mary?" I raised my eyebrows questioningly. "Are David and Emily here too?"

She laughed. "Not that I know of, but the way things are working out in the Rose family, I wouldn't be surprised if they were sitting in our driveway when we got home."

"You are still taking me to the hospital, right?"

"What's wrong?" Ruth asked, removing her arm and staring at us. "Are you hurt?"

Mary abruptly shook her head as I turned to Ruth. "Not me, but my best friend is dying from cancer." My eyes filled with tears, and I blinked them back.

Ruth wrapped me in a hug. "That's right, Mary told me. I'm so sorry." Over her shoulder I could see Julio looking confused at the sudden change in the mood."

"*Mi amiga es en un hospital.*" I explained in the best Spanish I had learned from two semesters of classes.

He nodded in understanding. "*Lo siento. Cuál es el problema?*"

I hesitated as I tried to translate the question. Then at last took a stab at answering appropriately. "*Esta* cancer.*"

"Scout!" Ruth exclaimed. "Your Spanish is really coming along!" Then she turned to Julio and rattled off a further explanation of which I could only catch a word or two.

Julio wrapped me in a bone-crushing hug and said something to me in which I could only understand *Lo siento*, I'm sorry. "*Gracias,*" I answered, getting the gist of what he said.

"Go, see your friend, Scout," Ruth stated. "Julio and I have two days to find a place to live before we fly back to Florida and start packing, so we will catch up tomorrow. We are still on for lunch, right, Mary?"

"Yes, 1:00 tomorrow," she replied.

"We will see you then," Ruth responded and exchanged hugs with Mary. "Love you." She turned to me then and hugged me too. "I'm so glad we got to watch you play. We will see you tomorrow. Love you."

"Love you too," I said.

Mary and I waited until they drove off in their rental before leaving the parking lot. After a quick stop at home to eat some lunch and change clothes, we headed to the downtown Houston medical complex. It was an hour drive and since it was just Mary and me in the car, I decided to get her advice on Acer. I had never completely told her the details of the pool, just that we had had a fight and sensing that it was a touchy subject, she never brought it up again, so I decided to tell her the whole story.

When I finished my recount, she nodded thoughtfully and then smiled. "Danny Joe already told me about that."

"That punk!" I shouted.

"It shouldn't surprise you! You know he can't keep his mouth shut," she answered. "Although, he did make it sound like there was a bit more than kissing going on."

"Figures," I said smugly. "He exaggerates everything." After a minute I asked, "What should I do? He won't let me talk to him about anything but baseball."

"He's hurt, Scout," she answered gently. "He's probably afraid of feeling that rejection all over again. Guys are so ego-driven and I'm sure that your response really bruised his. You are going to have to build him back up before he is going to trust you again."

"How do I do that?"

"You have to make him feel good about himself. You know, compliment him. Tell him how great he is."

I laughed. "In other words, blow a bunch of smoke at him!"

"It's not smoke! Look somewhere behind that wall you have erected, you like Benjamin—a lot. If you didn't we wouldn't be discussing this. Just remember a gentle word turns away wrath, but a harsh word stirs up anger. So for every harsh word you say to him, you are going to have to say about ten kind things to make up for it," she explained.

"I have a lot of ground to make up then," I retorted.

"Start looking for the diamonds in his personality, make a list if you have to and then every time you see him, tell him one of those things, but be prepared for him to reject it and doubt your sincerity. He's hurt so he's probably not going to trust anything you say because he is so used to all the negatives."

"You use this kind of thing with Brian?"

"Of course," she glanced over at me and grinned mischievously. "How do you think we have stayed married this long?"

It was after 2:00 by the time we stepped out of the elevators onto Bonnie's floor at the hospital. My stomach felt queasy, thinking about the last time I saw her and the sallow look of death that had encompassed her presence. I didn't know if I could handle it if she had worsened through the night, so I opted to stay with Mary to park the car so that we could go in together.

The door was opened as we approached and laughter could be heard drifting out. Knocking gently to announce our presence, we walked in and rounded the partially drawn curtain. As I steeled myself for the worst, I studied the floor and entered, but when I finally looked up, the sight before me brought an immediate smile to my face.

Ms. Acer and Bonnie were both snuggled up together in her hospital bed, a huge photo album spread across both of their laps. They were laughing together as they skimmed through the pages. Bonnie was wearing her pink terry cloth robe and a striped beanie on her head. Her skin was now back to its usual peach color and her eyes did not have the heavy dark circles under them anymore. They sparkled as they met mine.

"Hey girl!" she greeted me.

I could not stop smiling. This *was* my friend: bubbly, healthy, beaming. "Bonnie!" I rushed to the opposite side of Ms. Acer and wrapped her in a hug. "You look so good!"

"I feel good. Better than I have in a long time."

Thinking about my previous visit and the miraculous turn she had taken overnight, I felt an unspeakable joy. "God is so good!" I whispered.

"All the time, God is good," she answered.

Ms. Acer slipped out of the bed and walked over to Mary. "Oh my, I haven't stretched my legs in a while. Mary, care to check out the hospitality room with me?"

"You know I can always use a snack." Mary walked over to hug Bonnie and then she patted my shoulder and grinned. "Prayer is pretty powerful, isn't it?" she whispered.

Tears of joy filled my eyes and a lump caught in my throat. All I could do was nod. I waited for them to leave before I turned back to Bonnie. "I just can't get over how quickly you have turned around."

"Neither can my doctors. The blood work they did this morning came back all normal. My white cells are normal; my platelets are normal. It's almost like I have new blood running through me," she explained. "They are even talking like I might be able to be home by Monday."

"Wow!" I shook my head in amazement and thanked God for answering our prayers. He gave us a miracle just as we had asked. He healed her blood, her bone marrow; He fixed her. I wondered if this was what it felt like to watch Jesus heal the sick or raise Lazarus from the dead. Never before had I felt this close to God. It was amazing!

"Enough about me though," Bonnie interrupted my thoughts. "What's happening with you? How was the game?"

"It was OK," I said nonchalantly as I settled into a chair. "Acer couldn't finish the game, but Jason stepped up and we are going to state."

"Scout, that is awesome news!" she beamed and then her face fell, as she noticed my lack of enthusiasm. "Why aren't you excited?"

"I am."

"You could have fooled me!" She studied me intently for a minute. "It's my brother, isn't it?" I didn't respond. "You two still haven't talked this thing out."

"He won't let me, Bonnie! Besides, we both have kind of been preoccupied with something a little more important." I tilted my head in an indication of her and her hospital room.

"Well, that's been taken care of now, hasn't it?" She narrowed her eyes. "I can't believe he let this go this far! If he were here right now, I swear I would strangle him!"

"I am surprised he is not here." I asked curiously, "Where is he?"

"He told mom that Rachel had called him almost as soon as he got home, desperate for help tonight at the dance. Whoever she got to fill in for me is sick and she doesn't know who else to ask. So he is helping out this afternoon and tonight at the dance."

Jose was not kidding around. I chortled in amusement and Bonnie stared at me in confusion. I straightened a little, still giggling and then explained Jose's talk with me after the game. "It's like he thinks I can walk in and sweep him off his feet and then ride off with him into the sunset." I chuckled again.

"He's right. You have to go, Scout!" she exclaimed.

"I don't do dances," I protested.

"You do now!" she said forcefully. "Here is your shot to get Bennie in a position where he can't run away from you. And with the added bonus that he will see you in something besides your jeans and T-shirt. Think about how much attention he gave you the last time he saw you in something other than typical Scout attire."

I blushed involuntarily at the thought of me in Mary's halter-topped bikini. I groaned, "Bonnie! I don't want to go."

"I don't want you sitting here at the hospital all night with me! My mom can do that. Besides, I'm doing much better now and I don't need a babysitter."

"Bonnie," I pleaded. "You don't understand. These kinds of things are so awkward. I hate dancing! I don't even have a dress!"

"Then don't dance. That's not why you are going anyway," she retorted, "Mary can help you find something."

"What am I going to help you find?" My sister questioned as she and Ms. Acer strolled through the door.

Bonnie and I spoke at once.

She said, "A dress."

I said, "Nothing."

Bonnie glared at me. "You can't visit me tonight. You have other plans."

"What other plans?" Mary asked.

I closed my eyes in exasperation and then turned to Mary. "I need a dress," I groaned and then sighed. "Not a formal dress, just a nice dress for the spring dance at school tonight." Mary's response was a definitive "yes," but her expression of delight and anticipation of getting to play dress up with me was much stronger. I rolled my eyes. This was definitely going to be a disaster!

"Scout, hold still!" Mary demanded.

"You're going to poke my eye out with that thing!"

"She will if you don't hold still," Ruth returned.

I looked up at the ceiling. This was so ridiculous! As soon as we were back at home, Mary started rifling through her closets of clothes until she found a short dress in a deep shade of green. Not five minutes later, Ruth and Julio showed up. They'd found the perfect temporary apartment for their relocation earlier than they had thought. Everything after that was a blur of cosmetics and clothes.

Seated in front of Mary's gigantic vanity, wearing only a form-fitted cream-colored slip and nude pantyhose, I was helpless to the treatments provided by my sisters. Ruth stood behind me with a long curling iron, twirling my auburn hair strand by strand into tiny ringlets. Mary stood directly in front of me, applying layer upon layer

247

of creams, powders, blush, and now mascara. I was getting a complete overhaul.

The enthusiasm with which my sisters transformed me was overpowering any annoyance I was feeling. It was like they finally had permission to make me look and feel like a woman, and they were not leaving anything undone.

Finished with my eyes, Mary then turned her attention to my lips and began applying lip liner and then at last the only cosmetic product I would occasionally sport: lip gloss.

She placed a tissue in between my lips and instructed, "Blot." I obeyed and she quickly began removing the small diamond stud earrings that I rarely took out and replaced them with silver hoops the size of half dollars.

Ruth set the curling iron down on the counter. "What do you think, Mary? Up or down?" she asked.

Mary studied her work for a moment and then responded, "Down, definitely down, but maybe pull the sides back from her face." She opened a drawer and handed her two beautifully designed silver combs with floral engraving along the tops. Mary quickly scooted out of the room and Ruth took her place in front of me, placing the combs on either side of my head.

"Beautiful," Mary murmured as she returned, carrying the dark green dress. I wasn't sure if she was talking about me or the dress. "Now step into this and I will help you zip up the back."

It was a simple, but short form-fitting scoop neck dress that had a front slit. As Mary zipped the back, I stared at the mirror, trying to absorb the fact that the tall gorgeous red head staring back was really me. I was completely stunned at how beautiful I had become. Mary and Ruth stood to either side of me, pleased with their work.

"Amazing, isn't it," Ruth commented.

Mary nodded. "She looks just like mom." I swallowed a lump in my throat. "OK, I know you are not into heels." She raised a hand and halted my protest before it could start, "but you can't wear a dress like this with flats."

"Or combat boots," Ruth added.

"Or combat boots," Mary included. "So here are some pumps. They aren't as high as the funeral shoes." I winced at the reminder. "Will you at least try these on before you throw them at me?"

Julio and Brian dropped me off in front of the school gymnasium on their way to pick up dinner at Frosty's for the rest of my family. I was actually relieved when Brian offered to drop me off. I could only imagine what kind of embarrassment Mary, Ruth, or Danny Joe would have caused me. It was bad enough that when I walked down the stairs into the living room Danny Joe had yelled, "Scout's smoking hot!"

I wobbled my way across the parking lot, trying to maintain my balance. After about five steps, I was starting to get the hang of it and then suddenly my heel slipped and I nearly landed on my backside, only saved by my hand gripping the door. "I'm going to break my ankle in these stupid things!" I muttered.

Straightening, I opened the door and stepped into the hallway. The music was already pumping out through the closed gym doors. There were about ten or so people mingling around. Casually, I walked over to the check-in table where Beth from my English class and a girl that I didn't know were sitting, collecting entrance money.

They studied me curiously as I approached the table. "Hey, Beth," I greeted.

She stared at me for a moment without saying a word and then as recognition hit her, she sat up in stunned disbelief. "Scout? Wow!" she gushed. "I didn't even recognize you, I swear! You look amazing! I love your hair. I don't think I have ever seen it down like that, and your dress is gorgeous!"

My cheeks started to flush with embarrassment. I turned around to head to the nearest pay phone to get someone to pick me up, when Jose sidled up next to me. He threw a five dollar bill on the table. "I got this," he said and then guided me to the gym. He was dressed in black pants and a bright electric blue silk shirt.

"You clean up nice, Jose," I commented.

"So do you. I couldn't decide if that was you when you walked in the door. You look like a model."

I nudged him with my elbow as I blushed again. I took a deep breath. "So where have you stashed Acer so I can get this over with?"

He opened the door to the gym and ushered me inside. Immediately the deep thumping base and deafening music hit me like a wave. Leaning next to my ear, he shouted. "You're going to love this! Rachel has him taking money for pictures."

The inside of the gymnasium was completely transformed into a giant disco. Colored lights flashed in time with the music, streamers hung from the rafters, and a DJ with a full sound table was situated on a stage under one of the elevated basketball goals.

I scanned the crowd as Jose led me in the direction of the picture booth. We walked through the middle of what served as the dance floor and I spotted Kiley and her circle of lemurs staring openmouthed at me. When my eyes connected with hers, the shocked look transformed into a hard glare, and she quickly turned back to her inner circle.

Before we reached the other side of the dance floor where the pictures were being taken, we passed Cade and his buddies laughing and knocking each other around. He raised his eyebrows and sneered in my direction. I turned my head away in disgust, but then as I walked in front of him, he reached out and grabbed my arm and pulled me close.

"Hey, baby, want to dance?"

As I spun around, he pulled me to within inches of his face. With reflexes that surprised even me, I grabbed his hand and twisted hard until he was bending under the pressure. "I warned you to keep your filthy hands off of me!" I shouted.

He winced in pain and his friends backed away. I put pressure on his shoulder and had the satisfaction of hearing him cry out in pain. His friends were stunned as I pushed him to the floor into a kneeling position. His eyes were anxious as he stared up at me.

"You lucked out tonight, Cade, on account that I'm wearing my sister's expensive dress and shoes," I shouted over the music and then released his arm giving his backside a hard nudge with my foot which sent him sprawling to the floor. Swiftly, I spun on my toe and strode after Jose.

He was looking around trying to find me, realizing for the first time that I was no longer at his side. When I finally caught up, he leaned in close to my ear. "Where'd you go?"

"Got a little distracted, that's all," I shouted. Not wanting to give Cade a seconds worth of my time, I changed the subject. "Tell Rachel, she did a great job. This is awesome! You wouldn't even know that people played basketball in here most of the time."

Jose pointed in the direction of the table sitting in front of a black backdrop that flashed intermittently with the lights from a camera. Acer was seated in front of it, staring idly at the dance floor. He didn't notice us as we approached, but I felt my heart jump at the sight of him. Heat rose to my cheeks. He wore a simple collared shirt in a shade of red with khaki pants, nothing I hadn't seen him wear to church, but whether it was because the flashing lights or the pure anticipation of telling him the truth about my feelings, he took my breath away.

"Acer," Jose called. "I brought you some company."

He glanced up at us then, and did a double take before our eyes locked. A multitude of emotions crossed his face in a matter of seconds as we studied one another. At first his eyes were wide in surprise as it took a moment for him to realize it was actually me standing in front of him, and then they softened into a luster of happiness as recognition hit him. His eyes quickly smoldered with desire, and just as swiftly changed into a hard, cold, angry glare. The defiant stare that settled over his features said it all. This was not going to work. He knew exactly what I was trying to do, meeting him here looking like this and he wasn't falling for it.

Jose nudged me forward and before Acer could protest I took the empty seat next to him, stumbling awkwardly into the chair. "I'll come check on you two after a while," Jose grinned and walked off.

Acer crossed his arms over his chest, refusing to look at me. The muscles beneath his shirt strained against the fabric. I waited to see if he would say anything and when he didn't, I decided to break the ice.

"So, pretty amazing about Bonnie, huh?"

He nodded, but still did not look at me.

"I saw her after the game; she looks almost normal!"

"What are you doing?" he spat. "You are not dressed like *that* to talk to me about Bonnie!" He glanced at me and then quickly turned away. "I'm really surprised that you of all people would stoop to this level."

I eyed him in feigned innocence. "What? You don't like my dress?"

He tried unsuccessfully to hide the color that sprung to his cheeks. "I didn't say that." He paused and then turned to face me. "You know you look gorgeous, but it doesn't matter. It's not going to make a difference."

"I know it won't make a difference and I tried to tell Bonnie and Mary and Jose and everyone else who helped to encourage this plan, but that's how desperate I am to fix what's happened between us. I am *this* desperate." I gestured with my hand, indicating my impromptu make over. "I'm wearing heels for crying out loud!"

He stole a glance down my leg to my foot before leaning back in his chair. "You wasted your time. What happened that night, it's all over. You just need to move on. Forget it ever happened. It was just a mistake."

Angela Geurin

That stung and I no more believed that then I did that the moon would crash into the earth tonight, but I remembered Mary's warning that he would reject me at first and so I pressed on desperately.

The music changed to a slower, softer song. I took a deep breath and let it out. "Acer, that's the thing about this," I responded. "I've tried to forget it. I've tried to move on, but I can't." Urgently, I reached out and took his hand. "Acer, I'm so sorry. You were absolutely right. You said I would regret everything I said to you and I do. I wish I could take it all back. All of it! I didn't mean any of it. I was just scared. Terrified of what other people would think and say. I was so stupid and I am trying hard right now to make this right."

His hand sat limp in mine and he was completely unmoved. Determined to lay it all out on the line with him, I leaned in close to his ear so he would be able to hear me above the music. "Benjamin Acer, I love you and I have since the moment you walked through that bull pen gate months ago." I stared at our hands. "Ace, I don't want to lose you. I want to move forward. We are so much better together then we are apart. I want you. I need you. I need you in my life."

He turned towards me and his eyes were soft at first, but turned hard and cold. "This is just an illusion, Scout. We got caught up in the emotions of the moment. You're just my catcher and my sister's best friend, nothing more."

Ouch!

There was a burning in my throat as the tears rose to the surface. I couldn't hold them back and as I choked on the sob that escaped my lips, my own words echoed back through my head. It cut deep and I felt as if my heart was bleeding as my chest burned with the blow of his rejection.

It was really over. He had openly given me his heart and I had crushed it beneath my cleats. Now, in my efforts to restore what I had so insanely rejected, he had returned the favor in kind. I knew I deserved it, but I was hoping for so much more.

Hiding my tears, I nodded slowly and released his hand. The need to run away took me by surprise and I found the urge too strong to ignore and rushed out of the gym side door. As the tears poured down my cheeks and my shoulders heaved with uncontrollable sobs, I collapsed to my knees in the soft grass of the football practice field.

This hurt. I was used to pain by now, but this hurt worse than anything else I had experienced this year: even worse than losing my dad. Danny Joe was right, I had opened up more to Acer than I had to anyone else and this coldness that I felt between us was devastating.

I don't know how long I knelt in the grass bawling, but before long, I realized that I was not alone. There was a rustle of footsteps behind me and I turned around desperately hoping it was Acer, but as my blurry eyes focused, I realized all too late that it was Cade.

His hand rose before my instincts could register the movement and with a lightening sharp blow, his fist struck hard against my temple. It knocked me to the ground and I felt him grab a fist full of my hair and yank my head up to stare into his evil, uncaring eyes. His face inches from mine. He spat, "Not such a tough girl now, are you?"

Chapter Sixteen: Survival

His breath was hot against my face and it reeked of alcohol. Everything around me started to fade to black and I forced my eyes wider in an effort to stay conscious. Desperately, I tried to get out of his grasp, reaching around to claw at the hand that was threaded in my hair, swinging with my other hand trying to connect with any part of his body. With his free hand, he grabbed my flailing arms and pinned them painfully behind my back. My legs were folded, the heels of my shoes stuck to the hem of the dress, preventing me from freeing them. Each time I tried to raise up, he would yank my head down by my hair.

Roughly, he shoved me backwards and slammed me into the ground, falling on top of me. I tried to kick him off, but his weight was too much. My head was pounding and I could feel my eye swelling, but I continued to fight. He held my arms above my head and spread my legs apart with his knees. I kicked violently, but despite my strength, I was trapped. Nothing I did slowed his advances and I knew I needed help.

"Get off me!" I screamed at the top of my lungs and kept screaming until his mouth covered mine in a rough attempt at a kiss. I bit down on his lip hard until I tasted blood. Immediately, he jerked his mouth free, leaving warm blood trickling down the corner of my lips. In disgust I coughed and spit the coppery taste out of my mouth, spraying his face.

He released one of my arms and then reached back and hit me again with the heel of his hand. My cheek erupted in white hot pain. I could feel blood pool in the corner of my nose and my vision exploded into stars, but with one hand free, it was all the momentum I needed to

255

fight harder. I clawed at his face, digging my thumb into his eye socket and then, I raked my fingers across his cheek. He howled in pain and raised his face away from my reach. I raised my head and balled my hand into a fist then swung with all my strength, but he ducked away at the last second and my hand connected with his shoulder. The blow didn't even knock him off balance. He was nothing but a solid wall looming over me.

I tried once more to free my legs, kicking wildly, but felt his body press into me harder, forcing me back to the ground. He regained control then and pinned one of my arms above my head. With my free hand, I grabbed one more time at his face and dug my nails in deep before he finally pried my fingers away, forcing my arms together above my head. I jerked both of my arms in a last ditch effort to free myself, but his hold was too strong. He held my wrists in an unbreakable hold. It was getting hard to breathe and my cries and screams for help were becoming a struggle. He pushed me further onto my back until I could feel every inch of him pressing into my body. Roughly, he grabbed both of my wrists in one hand and reached between our bodies. His hand fumbled down my chest towards the waistband of his pants.

"No!" I panicked, knowing what was coming next. "No! Get off me! Please, No! Help me! Somebody help me!"

He leaned into my ear. "What's the matter? I thought you liked it rough." I started to sob as he continued to taunt me. "No one is coming to help you. No one can hear you, Red. You are about to learn that I always get what I want."

My breathing became shallow and too quick to satisfy the ache in my lungs, but I refused to relent to his abuse. Ignoring his taunts, I fought him with every muscle in my body and silently prayed for God to help me. Send someone wandering back here to this dark field.

"Oh, God! Help me!" I screamed. "Please, Cade, stop! Please stop!"

"Shut up!" he yelled and he smashed his head into my jaw.

I could feel his fingers beneath my dress, painfully digging into my thigh. A rush of fear washed over me and I felt a sudden surge of adrenaline before jerking my hand free and balling it into a fist. I punched him in the chest, knocking the wind out of him. Rage flared across his face and he reared back for another blow, but before he could connect with my cheek, a shadowy figure caught his arm in mid-swing and swiftly yanked him away into the darkness.

As soon as I felt freedom, I rolled over and scrambled across the grass on my hands and knees. Terror shook my body as I raced away from my attacker. I saw a bright light shine across the field and headed towards it. I tried to stand up, but whether it was from shock or blows to my head, I fell back to the ground dizzy, hovering at the edge of consciousness.

My head lolled over to the side and my gaze followed the beams of light to the spot behind me in which Cade and my savior were wrestling. All at once I saw a red shirt and a nearly bald head and knew that it was Acer. He had pulled Cade off of me. He had come after me. God had sent Acer! My heart leapt, but it soon turned to panic as I realized that he was shaking Cade like a rag doll and pummeling him with his fists.

"You sniveling little sack of..." Acer's voice registered as he repeatedly slammed Cade's head into the ground.

Cade's body was limp in Acer's hands, but he didn't stop beating him and smashing him into the ground. I stood on shaky legs and tried to run back to him to make him stop before he killed Cade, but I stumbled and had to crawl the distance between us.

"Acer, stop!" I shouted. "You're going to kill him!" He continued to pound him until I jerked his shoulders with all the strength I had left. "Stop it!" I fell backwards, taking Acer with me.

We landed in a heap of arms and legs and I choked as the air rushed from my lungs. Immediately, Acer rolled off of me, but I still couldn't catch my breath as my entire body shook. I lay on the ground—stunned, gasping for air, unable to move. My vision was getting darker and I knew that at any second I would black out. Acer's face was coming into focus and I locked onto his piercing blue eyes, anchoring my consciousness to him.

His lips were moving, but my ears were ringing and I couldn't make out what he was saying. I felt my eyes roll back and my vision close, but I made myself focus on Acer. His beautiful blue eyes filled my view.

Gently, he gathered my body in his arms, pulling me into his lap. I felt completely limp, unable to move anything, yet unable to stop the convulsions that were racing across every muscle. With a strength that I didn't know he possessed, Acer stood bearing our combined weight, cradling me like an infant. He grunted under the stress, but began slowly walking and I tried to move my arms one more time. This time they obeyed and I locked them behind his neck.

I could hear muffled shouts and strange voices, but the only words that registered were Acer's. "Stay with me, Scout. I've got you. It's all over. I'm going to get you some help." I was gasping for air. "Calm down. You're OK now. Just breathe, honey. Just breathe."

My body continued to shake and my breathing still came in shallow painful breaths, but his soothing words gave me focus and as I snuggled against the warmth of his swaying embrace, I felt his chest rise and fall in a steady pace that I tried to match with my own, filling my lungs to capacity before exhaling.

Gradually, my breathing returned to normal, but the shaking continued. I felt cold, freezing cold. My teeth chattered violently and my lip along with the entire left side of my face throbbed with pain. I closed my eyes and heard a pitiful cry, one filled with pain and fear. The sound echoed in my head and I wondered who else had gotten hurt. I started to ask Acer if someone was helping the other girl and then suddenly realized that the heart-wrenching cry was coming from me.

"It's OK, Scout. It's over. He's not going to hurt you anymore," Acer soothed. I felt him stumble and I winced as my cheek banged into his arm. "I'm sorry, Scout. I'm so sorry. Hang in there. We're almost there," he whispered against my hair, brushing his lips across my forehead.

"The ambulance is on its way," I heard a woman say. "Take her into the training room."

"Benjamin, let me take her," a man said, and I tightened my grip around Acer's neck.

"Don't let me go," I whispered.

"No, I've got her," Acer stated flatly. "Just open the door."

The woman spoke again and it registered that the voice belonged to Ms. Appelbaum, the assistant principal. "Lay her down over here."

My eyes fluttered open and the artificial lights stung. I felt Acer sit me on the padded surface of one of the tables and my body started to shake wildly as the warmth of his body moved further away. Fear, suddenly and surprisingly, took hold and I gripped his shirt collar.

"Acer," I croaked, "Acer, don't let me go." I tried to scramble back into his arms. "Acer, please!" I pleaded, still convulsing all over my body.

"OK, Scout. I'm right here," he replied and wrapped me in a hug. "She hasn't stopped shaking since I got to her," he said to Ms. Appelbaum.

Ms. Appelbaum was a short woman with long brown hair that was always elegantly twisted into a bun at the base of her neck. Like always, she was dressed in a navy blue suit of which I am sure she had a closet full. Her long narrow chin ended with a small cleft and her eyes were always very serious behind her wire-rimmed glasses that rested low on the bridge of her nose.

Her eyes softened as she gazed at me and gently reached out and brushed my hair out of my eyes with the back of her hand. "I'm sure she is in shock," she spoke sadly. Calmly, she walked across the room to a metal closet and retrieved several items as Acer gingerly sat next to me on the table. His warm embrace never left me. I leaned into his shoulder and circled my arms around his waist.

Ms. Appelbaum handed him a blanket and he wrapped it around my shoulders. It was scratchy and smelled like mothballs, but it added some warmth. Acer pulled me to his left side and rubbed my arms vigorously. I laid my head on his shoulder again and squeezed my eyes shut, the action drawing a groan and twinge of pain from my swollen face.

I felt cold pressure from an icepack that was placed on my left cheek. "Here, Benjamin, help her keep this over her eye." He moved his left hand up my shoulder until it rested on the ice pack.

Ms. Appelbaum pulled a chair over in front of me and with gloved fingers began cleaning the cuts on my knees that I didn't even know existed until the alcohol swabs stung them. My breathing became easier. The only part of me left shaking was my hands so I locked them together around Acer's waist.

The room was deathly quiet as she worked on cleaning me up, and at last I felt safe again. Until Ms. Appelbaum finally asked the question I knew would come, "Can you tell me what happened, Scout?"

My body shuddered as my mind flashed back to the attack. Acer tightened his hold on me giving me the confidence to speak. "I-I went outside to get some fresh air and I thought I was alone. I didn't even… realize Cade was there until he…hit me." Acer squeezed my arm. "I fought back as hard as I could, but before I knew it he was on top of me trying…he tried to…" I choked on the word. I knew what Cade was trying to do. I just couldn't bring myself to say it.

"Benjamin, why don't you leave us alone for a moment," Ms. Appelbaum suggested, thinking I must be uncomfortable talking about this with him in the room, but she was so wrong. I needed him with me right now more than ever.

"No!" I shouted dropping the ice pack and gripping his hand. "Stay, Acer! Don't leave me!" Then turning my attention back to Ms. Appelbaum, I pleaded, "Please, don't make him leave me!" I started hyperventilating again. "Please don't make him leave!"

260

Acer laced our fingers and leaned his forehead against my temple. "It's OK, Scout. I'm not going anywhere."

I leaned against his shoulder and relaxed as my breathing slowed again.

"Acer, you saved me! Ms. Appelbaum, he pulled Cade off of me," I continued softly. "He stopped him…He stopped him from… from…" I still couldn't say it or even think the word. "He saved me. If he wouldn't have come out there when he did, things would have been a lot worse."

That was reality. Never before had I been more scared. I was never afraid to walk around outside in the dark. Heck, I got up every morning before the sun rose and jogged by myself. It's what I did in Kansas City and wandering around in this small town by myself didn't scare me, until now. Most people found me intimidating and would never attempt something like this, especially with so many people in such a close proximity. It was a clear sign to me that Cade was out of his mind.

"Did you have any indication that something like this could happen?" she asked. "Did Cade say anything that would make you think that he wanted to hurt you?"

"He has harassed me since the day I came here," I said, and sat upright thoughtfully. "But so have a lot of people. Tonight at the dance, I think he was drunk or something. He grabbed me when I first arrived, and I humiliated him in front of a bunch of his friends. It must have set him off, but no, I never thought he was capable of…that."

I could feel Acer tense next to me and he muttered something that I didn't quite hear under his breath. Ms. Appelbaum studied my face for a moment and picked up the ice pack. She handed it back to me, and when I didn't accept it, Acer sighed in exasperation and took it from her. Then he placed it over the left side of my face again, holding it there with his right hand. I felt his lips soft on my forehead before he rested his chin against my head.

"You don't have to be the tough girl tonight, Scout" he remarked drily.

"Yeah, I'm a real tough girl," I choked. "Got myself beat up and nearly…raped."

There, at last, I said it. I said exactly what his intentions were, but I burst into tears as the admission brought on a new wave of fear. Acer rubbed my shoulders and kissed the top of my head. "It's over, Scout. He can't hurt you anymore. You're safe now."

Ms. Appelbaum looked closely at Acer's right hand. "You're going to need to get some ice on that hand, Benjamin."

"It will be fine," he said. "Just take care of Scout."

"You may have broken some fingers."

"On your pitching hand, Ace," I muttered. "You broke your pitching hand?"

"It's not broken, Scout. It's fine. Cade's nose is another story." He snickered, but I couldn't even smile. I know that Cade deserved to have a lot more than a broken nose for what he did to me, but I just wanted it all to go away.

A tall gray-headed man that I recognized as one of the science teachers opened the door and crossed the room. Leaning down he whispered something to Ms. Appelbaum. She responded quietly, but not quiet enough that I couldn't hear her. "I don't want the police talking to her until her family arrives."

My family! My entire family would be here, well minus David of course, but Mary, Brian, Danny Joe, Ruth, Julio, and the police. "The police!" I squeaked.

Oh this was going to get ugly! I didn't even think about the police! Cade was going to be arrested. Acer could get arrested. Every detail of the past few months would be scrutinized. I would have to relive the attack over and over. The whole town would know what happened. His dad, being the mayor, would likely do everything he could to make it seem that I had provoked his son. Not to mention the fact that we would lose our starting second baseman right before play-offs. This was a disaster!

I groaned.

"Cade will be arrested," I stated quietly. "Acer, you might get arrested. What a mess! Why do we have to tell the police?"

"Scout, you have to report this. If Cade did this to you, he could do it to someone else too," Ms. Appelbaum reasoned. "It's the only way to make sure that he is held accountable for his actions and doesn't think he can do this again.

"But the play-offs. You could both miss the play-offs," I said to Acer.

It was a ridiculous argument and it sounded ludicrous in my own ears, but my mind was running through every possible excuse for not reporting this and it was the first thing that popped into my head. I couldn't think straight. At that moment I just wanted to rewind the day and erase the part where Bonnie convinced me to come to this stupid dance.

"Play-offs!" Acer exploded turning to face me. "For once, Scout, stop thinking about baseball! That little punk attacked you! He deserves to be arrested. He deserves to rot in jail! I was just defending you, and if the police arrest me for that then it will be worth every minute behind bars."

"Don't you see what's going to happen? Everyone is going to know what happened tonight! The whole town will know! I don't want this kind of attention, Acer! Everyone is going to see me as weak!"

Ms. Appelbaum patted my leg. "Scout, this isn't your fault, you…" she soothed.

Acer cut her off and grabbed both of my hands in his. "Scout, you are not weak! You are the strongest person I know. I thought my sister was strong until I met you. You have been knocked down so many times in the short time I've known you, and you still just get right back up and fight. You're not weak. You're strong."

I sniffed softly. "I don't feel very strong right now."

He leaned over until our foreheads were touching again. "That's why I'm still here. That's why I went looking for you to tell you just how stupid I have been acting. To tell you how sorry I am. Because you and me together, we are stronger than anything we'll ever face out there."

Briefly ignoring the fact that we were not alone, he brushed his lips against mine and sat back against the wall, pulling my head to rest on his shoulder again. I closed my eyes and let his strength engulf me like a warm blanket. He rested his chin against the top of my head and I wrapped my arms around his torso. I felt safe and as he gently placed the ice pack back on my cheek, I knew that Acer was back.

"I need to step out for a minute and speak with the police," Ms. Appelbaum said. I opened my eyes and watched her stride out of the room, leaving the door partially opened.

Acer began idly stroking my arm. I felt him adjust his weight and kiss my forehead before saying, "I am so sorry, Scout. I shouldn't have let you go. I should have listened to you, but I let my pride get in the way and look what happened." I patted his cheek. "I love you, Scout. I have for a while now and I should have told you tonight."

I smiled and stared into his face. "Let's just chalk this up to the fact that we are like magnets that need to be…"

"Flipped," he finished and gently kissed my lips.

Four days later as I headed for baseball practice, I forced myself to take my usual route across the football practice field even though it would lead me to the place of the attack. It was my first day back at school, my first practice since that night of terror. My mind immediately flashed back as I neared the exact spot that I had laid pinned to the ground beneath Cade, praying for someone to help me.

Angela Geurin

Suddenly, my legs were trembling and I stopped in my tracks, unable to take another step. Panic filled me and my heart raced within my chest, my lungs grew tight and constricted. Fear began to overtake me, but I refused to relent.

My physical wounds were healing well. The deep purple bruises on my cheek had turned a light shade of green, and my nose was back to normal since the swelling was gone. However, my emotional wounds were laid open and raw. Before they could begin to heal, I knew I had to face down this anxiety and fear. I had to take back what Cade tried to steal from me: my sense of security and confidence. If I didn't, I would never be able to move on and live life without jumping at shadows. I had to do this, and the sooner I did, the better off I would be.

With shaking hands and wobbly legs, I willed my body forward. I took long slow breaths as I finally reached the spot. Gradually, I eased down into a crouch and brushed my fingertips across the grass. The shaking grew stronger and I closed my eyes. The memories of that night played before my mind's eye and tears began to trickle down my cheeks, but I forced myself to relive it all over again, just as I had when the police took my statement at the dance.

Once again, I felt the weight of his drunken body forcing me to the ground, his hot nauseating breath in my face. I felt his hand yanking my head back, the shock of pain through my face as he struck me, the sound of my own screams.

My inner voice told me to retreat from these painful memories, but if I had learned anything over the past year, it was that everything always happens for the good of those who love the Lord, and it is often through our deepest hurts that the greatest lessons are learned. So, I stood firm, accepting each painful memory as it came.

Calmly, I inhaled and exhaled, even and slow. Embracing every memory, knowing that each time I refused to retreat from my pain, the stronger I would become. My hands started to relax, my vision cleared, and I felt strong again. Not because of my own strength, but because of the strength that God gave me that night and at this moment right now. I smiled in satisfaction and breathed a prayer of thankfulness.

Diamonds in the Dirt

Mary and Brian had tried to convince me to stay home from school, to take a few more days off to recover, but I refused. Every time that I changed my life out of fear was a day that Cade won, and he wasn't going to win anymore. He had already taken so much of my security. I couldn't run alone anymore because I was afraid. I couldn't go visit Bonnie after dark unless someone else drove me. Darkness was now something I feared, and I didn't want to be his victim anymore. I wanted to move on. Returning to that spot was a huge step in that direction.

Cade was arrested and suspended from school for the remaining month. It was rumored that his dad had made arrangements with the judge for him to stay with his grandmother in Port Aransas. Being that he was a juvenile offender, he would more than likely serve out any sentence handed down at the juvenile hall three towns over. But given the fact that his dad seemed to know everyone, Cade would probably just have to pay a fine.

Cade's parents didn't press charges against Acer, which made me think that maybe they were decent people who just had a bad apple. Cade had received a concussion, a broken nose, and a skull fracture from Acer's blows, so they probably could have made everything a big ugly mess, but they didn't. It seemed that they wanted the same thing that I did: own up to the events that took place, pay whatever consequences were owed, and move on. Eventually, I would have to face him and I wanted to be strong when that day came, but I knew no matter what, I would never be alone.

A hand gently touched my shoulder. I felt the heat of another body squatting next to me and without even opening my eyes to look, I knew it was Acer. I gazed intently at him and sat back on my haunches. "What are you doing here?" I asked.

He eased himself to the ground and pulled me against his body. "I was about to ask you the same question. I thought you were going to stay home today. I saw you on the way to sixth period and I went to find you after class, but you had already bolted out the back door." He tucked a stray curl behind my ear. "You don't have to do this so soon, you know? Everyone would understand if you took some time off."

"Why wait?" I asked. "Every day that I avoid the truth is a day longer in my recovery. It's a day that Cade wins. I want to move on. I need to get past this or it will eat me up inside."

He kissed the tip of my nose. "I'm sure you do, but just don't do it by yourself. Let me and your family help you."

I thought about my family's reaction when they had arrived at school that Saturday night. It was like a giant cavalry walking through the doors. All of them came, just as I had feared: Brian, Mary, Danny Joe, Ruth, and Julio. They all came to be with me, to help me, to let me know that I was not alone. I had even spent half an hour on the phone with David on Sunday afternoon and we hardly ever talked.

A year ago, I would have thought of my family as my dad and I. The rest of them just showed up when they needed something, but now I saw my family differently. We were a mighty army, the legacy my parents had left behind.

Then, there was Acer. He was my constant support. He never left my side Saturday night. He stayed through the police questioning, the ride to the hospital, which was in the neighboring county. The only time he left was to excuse himself when the nurses at the hospital had to examine me more privately, but he came right back as soon as they gave him the all clear. He even stayed with me until I had finally fallen asleep that night.

I reached back and pulled his head down, lightly brushing my lips across his. "I don't think I ever told you thank you."

His brow furrowed and he reached out to brush his hand against my cheek. "Don't thank me. I was the one who put you in that position to begin with. I should have never said those things to you. If I just would have…"

"Let's not play that game." I interrupted and threaded our fingers together. "We both made mistakes. Let's just leave it like that. We are together now and we are so much stronger together than apart."

He kissed me. I reached back and rested my hand against his cheek. It was pure bliss and unashamedly my mouth danced in perfect time with his. We were so much more than pitcher and catcher now.

Thinking about baseball practice, I broke away from his kiss and saw his lips form a little pout in response. "You know, Ace; this is our first practice together since…you know our relationship changed."

"Yeah."

"Well, don't you think we need to talk about that? Figure out how we are going to handle it?"

"What's there to handle, Scout?" he asked softly.

"We could make this pretty awkward for our team if we aren't careful. I think we need to maybe set some ground rules."

"Like, let's keep baseball on the field and the kissing stuff in my truck afterwards." He leaned down and kissed me again.

I rolled my eyes. "I'm being serious, Acer!"

He kissed me again. "I am too."

"Well, what do you think?"

He leaned into my ear and whispered, "I think you think too much and like you always tell me, thinking only hurts the team."

I did not appreciate having my own words thrown back in my face, but he had a point. "So, let's just keep baseball on the field and everything else off the field and we'll be just fine."

"Mm-huh," he muttered and then started kissing a trail from neck up to my ear that ended at my lips. "Sounds like a good rule to me," he murmured between kisses.

After a moment, I gently pushed him back. "We need to stop. We've got a state championship to win."

He kissed me again. "We're not on the field yet."

I stood and offered my hand. He let me pull him to his feet and then leaned in for another kiss, but I ducked away. "Acer, it's practice time. We can finish this later."

He playfully tugged at my pony tail. "I'm going to hold you to that."

Chapter Seventeen: Blessings and Forgiveness

A week later, the team was headed to Austin for the five day 3A State Championship Tournament and waiting for us at the athletic complex was more than just the bus. Acer pulled into a parking space and I couldn't believe the crowd gathered there for the big send off.

"Wow!" I said, as I stepped out of the passenger side of his truck and shouldered my bag. "There are a lot of people here!"

Bonnie slid out behind me and linked our arms. She had tagged along so that she could take Acer's truck back home. This was her first week out in the real world, completely released for all activities; and now that she was living a normal, teenage life again, she could do things like drive, go to school, and watch us play baseball. When I thought back to how sick she had been and how good she looked now, especially since she had started to let her hair grow back, I couldn't help but thank God every time I was with her.

"It's been a long time since Booneville has had a team qualify for any state championship," she said excitedly.

"Yeah, but it looks like the whole town is here! We can't be the biggest news in Booneville today."

Acer walked around the back of the truck and reached behind me into the bed to retrieve the rest of our bags. "This is big news for a small town. We're hometown celebrities, win or lose." He hoisted a bag on each shoulder and kissed my cheek. "You should know that by now, Scout." He tossed Bonnie his keys. "Take good care of her, Sis and we'll see you in Austin."

She caught the keys and then hugged Acer's neck. "You take good care of *her* too," she said, gesturing in my direction. "Don't let her push herself too hard."

Even though the attack had happened over two weeks ago, I was still having occasional panic attacks, which the doctors had said was brought on by too much stress. Bonnie had been with me for my latest episode and it scared her to death. She knew I wouldn't let it stop me from playing, but she still worried about me.

"Good luck, girl," she said and wrapped me in a hug. "Take care of yourself."

"I will," I assured her.

Acer and I started towards the bus, but before we were halfway there, I felt him tense beside me and a second later, realized that Mayor Traylor and his son were standing in our path. I was momentarily frozen in place, my heart clenching in my chest, my lungs struggling to fill with air. Quickly, I shut my eyes and willed the panic out of my body with two long slow breaths. This was my second time to face Cade since that Saturday night and fear still seemed to be a knee jerk reaction, but the more I continued to move on and live my life, the easier that emotion was to control. Protectively, Acer moved in front of me, blocking my view of the two.

"What do you think you are doing here?" he spat angrily his fists clenched. "You are not on this team anymore!"

"Easy, Benjamin," Mr. Traylor put his hands up in a gesture of peace. "We are not here to cause any problems."

Gently, I pushed Acer to the side and stepped in front of him. Bonnie approached and stopped on my other side. She reached down to grab my hand. Acer, still tense, laced our fingers on my right side and held them securely. I was in a protective sandwich between my two best friends and I felt a wave of calm wash over me as I slowly raised my gaze to meet them eye to eye.

"Hello, Mr. Traylor," I said calmly, "Cade."

"Hi, Scout," Cade said quietly.

Cade and I hadn't spoken since he attacked me, so I was shocked to hear him respond at all, but he stared at the ground, completely avoiding my face. Although it had healed, and the scars that remained were so minor that you couldn't find them unless you were really looking for them, I couldn't help but notice how hard he avoided looking at me. It was like he couldn't stand to see my face, like it was something too painful for him to look at.

There was no trial since he pleaded guilty to the charges and I was not required to attend the sentence hearing; I had found something else to do that day and let Brian handle everything. To my surprise, Cade's dad didn't try to get him out of anything. He actually was sentenced to three months in juvenile detention and 120 hours of community service.

Acer thought he should have gotten much more and so did Mary, but I was actually okay with everything. The last time I had to face him, I didn't see any of the cockiness or arrogance that had always been present with him in the past. He actually seemed remorseful, and I honestly believed he was. I think he was as shocked as I was at what transpired the night of the dance. I don't think he ever thought himself capable of something so violent.

"So, what are you doing here?" I asked.

I noticed Mr. Traylor forcibly nudge Cade and he immediately looked up and finally met my eyes. His eyes were not hard or angry, they were soft and rueful. At that moment, he reminded me of a little child.

He sighed before he spoke, "I…uh. I know that, um, it probably doesn't mean a whole lot, but… I am sorry for what I did to you that night at the dance."

"You should be!" Acer shouted.

I jerked his arm and leaned over, quietly pleading, "Just shut up and let him speak." He bristled at my words and I squeezed his hand. "It's okay. I can handle this. I'm fine." I kept staring at him until his hard eyes relaxed. Bonnie let go of my hand and reached behind me to grab hold of Acer's arm. Then, turning my eyes back to Cade, I gestured for him to continue.

"I wish I could do something more to make up for it, but I'm just so sorry and you don't have to worry about me bothering you again. I'm moving to Port Aransas. I won't be in Booneville again for a long time."

It was so strange. I actually felt sorry for him because his life was about to be turned upside down and I had been in those shoes before. Just not by my own poor choices. I knew Acer would think I was crazy to be so forgiving, but I just kept thinking about the story in the New Testament about Jesus on the cross. He was hanging there, dying for all the sins that we had committed, completely innocent of any crime, and yet he showed compassion and forgiveness not only to the people who were mocking him, but also to the thief hanging next to Him.

I had already settled everything in my heart, but at that moment, I realized Cade needed to know that he was forgiven. He needed to hear that from me. He needed to feel the love of our Lord Jesus Christ through me.

I nodded my head. "Cade, I want you to know that you're forgiven. I spent a lot of time reliving that night and thinking about what you had done to me. But I keep going back to the fact that Jesus forgave the people who hurt Him and I couldn't call myself a Christ follower if I wasn't willing to forgive you." Tears came to my eyes, but I didn't let them fall.

Cade's eyes were wide with surprise. I felt Bonnie squeeze my hand and saw out of the corner of my eye, Acer shake his head.

"Goodbye, Cade," I said and pulled Acer and Bonnie towards the bus. A lump rose in my throat and I swallowed it down along with the tears that tried to fall.

"Wait!" he called after us and I slowly turned around. "Good luck this week. Bring Booneville back a championship."

I smiled slightly. "Thanks."

Cade turned to leave and Mr. Traylor sent him on towards their car, but quickly closed the distance between us. Looking at me in disbelief, he said, "I wanted my son to own up to what he did to you, but you didn't have to forgive him." I couldn't speak so all I did was nod. "That says a lot about your character. You are one special lady, Miss Rose. We were all so wrong about you and for that *I'm* sorry."

"Thank you," I managed through the lump in my throat.

"If there is anything, I could ever do, anything you ever need, please don't hesitate to ask."

I nodded my head once more and turned back towards the bus. A single tear slid down my cheek as the emotional tension began to overwhelm me. I tried to keep walking, but Bonnie stopped me in my tracks and wrapped me in a hug as the tears flowed.

"He's right, Scout," she said, wiping the tears from my cheek. "You are very special. There are not too many people who could have done what you just did." She cradled my cheeks in her hand and looked me straight in the eye, "I am so blessed to be your friend."

Acer stood behind me and then wrapped us both in his long arms. He rested his head on my shoulder and whispered in my ear, "You are amazing, Scout."

Simultaneously, Bonnie in my left ear and Acer in my right, they said, "I love you."

I laughed and whispered back, "I love you too."

"That's enough," Acer announced as I tossed him the ball.

I tucked my glove under my arm, picked up my water bottle, and met him halfway across the bull pen. His body was stiff as he slid his jacket over his throwing arm and his face deadly serious, very unlike Acer before a game. He was usually so relaxed, but his nerves must really be getting to him.

"Red Oak looks really tough," he commented anxiously.

Yep, he was nervous. I started to reach out and wrap him in a hug, but we were on the field so I was not his girlfriend, I was his catcher, but at that moment, it was hard not to throw my arms around him and kiss away all of his doubts and worries.

Instead, I nudged him with my elbow. "Just go out there and get into your zone. Throw your game. That's all you've got to do. You are on today; everything is working. You don't have anything to be nervous about."

"I don't know. Red Oak is good," he continued. "We haven't played *anyone* that looks that good." He opened the bull pen gate and ushered me through ahead of himself.

"It's the state championship, Ace," I pointed out. "Everyone we face looks good, but we're better. That's why we are sitting in the championship game." I noticed Coach Mac, waving at us to hustle. "Come on, I think they're getting ready to start introductions."

As we jogged up to the field, I shook my head in amazement. This college field in Austin was a beautiful place to play baseball, although it was a bit strange to play on artificial turf. Ground balls really took some high hops at times, but for the most part it had the look and feel of stepping onto a major league field.

"You two ready?" Coach Haywood asked as Acer and I hurried into the dugout.

Acer nodded but didn't look up.

I answered for him. "He's looking good today, Coach. We're ready."

Then, I turned just in time to see Acer bury his head in the trash can and release his stomach contents. Wow, was he nervous! I don't think I had ever seen him like this before a game.

After I was sure he had finished, I handed him my water bottle. His face was pale and after he had rinsed his mouth, he eased himself down onto the bench. He looked awful. Coach Haywood had walked away and missed Acer's show or else he might have questioned my appraisal of warm-ups.

A bit shocked and frustrated, I sat down next to him, keeping a little bit of space in between us on the bench. I didn't want to be too close if he threw up again. "What is your problem? You're nerves getting to you? I've never seen you act like...*this*!" I wrinkled my nose and nodded to the trash can.

"D-Did you see who was in the stands?" he stuttered.

I stood and stuck my head out of the dugout and scanned the faces in the crowd. It was nearly a full house, but after all, this was the state championship game and the entire towns of Booneville and Red Oak seemed to have shown up. I spotted Bonnie and the Acers sitting with my entire family. David caught my eye and gave me a wave. I still couldn't believe he and Emily had flown down to Texas for this. David had never seen me play before.

I waved back and continued scanning and then I spotted them. Dotted throughout the stands were obvious baseball scouts dressed in their representative program's shirt or hat, with clipboard in hand. I nodded my head in understanding. This was Acer's year to be noticed. Before, he didn't think he had a chance to go anywhere. He thought he would just walk on at a local college if he even decided to take his play to the next level, but now that he actually tasted championship play, his dreams had grown up.

We'd actually talked at length about this very subject a few days before. He had received a couple of letters of interest from some very small college baseball teams. Like me, there was plenty of money for him to go to any college that he wanted without having to earn some kind of scholarship, although, his parents wouldn't complain too much if he happened to get one. Then, the very next day, he received an invitation to one of the professional baseball scout tryout camps that would be held in the middle of the summer.

Acer confessed that deep down he had always wanted the opportunity to play professional baseball, but he never imagined he would actually get that chance until the letters arrived. Now, it had evolved from an unattainable dream into a plan, a goal for his life. It was obvious that seeing all of the scouts here to watch this game, he recognized the opportunity to start heading towards that goal.

"Looks like the table is set," I said lightly as I sat back down. "Here's the chance you never thought you would get."

"I just don't want to mess this up, Scout." He ran his hand through his hair nervously. "Red Oak is so good. I just don't want to…"

Suddenly, he paled again and abruptly stood. I was not about to watch him toss his cookies a second time. Grabbing his shoulder, I spun him around and took two fistfuls of his jersey and pulled until we were inches apart.

"You need to snap out of this!" I yelled. "Look at me! Look at me!" I waited until he finally met my gaze. "Now breathe!" He shook his head violently. "Breathe!" He finally obeyed and his shoulders started to relax although his breath still smelled like stomach acid and nearly made me gag. "You listen to me, Benjamin Acer! This is just like any other game. You don't pay attention to Red Oak. You don't pay attention to the people in the stands. You focus on me. It's just you and me out there, playing catch. God wouldn't have set this up for you without giving you the tools that you need to perform. You just have to trust Him and trust me."

"Like any other game," he slowly said.

"Any other game," I repeated.

"Just you and me," he stated with a little more energy.

"You and me, playing catch," I affirmed.

His anxious expression softened into hard determination, the Acer I was used to seeing. "You and I playing catch."

I patted his shoulder. "No more nerves?"

"I'm much better now. Thanks," he nodded.

"Just remember, you and I together are stronger than anything we will ever face out there."

"Now the starting lineups for your Texas 3A State Championship Game between the Red Oak Rangers and the Booneville Bearcats," the announcer boomed through the loudspeakers and the stadium erupted into cheers.

"Show time," I stated and spun on my heel to head toward the dugout stairs. Acer grabbed my hand and yanked me back a step. He rubbed his thumb along my palm and mouthed *I love you*. I squeezed his hand and threw him a wink before tugging my hand free. "I know," I grinned. "Now, let's go win a championship!"

It was a rare jewel in baseball when a pitcher completely shut down his opponent. No hits. No runs. No one on base. Simply put: the perfect game. Only a handful of the elite had ever accomplished perfection, and it represented not just a stellar pitching performance, but a stellar defensive performance. It was all around perfection.

Not one of Red Oak's hitters had reached first base in six innings, and as I stepped into the batter's box in the top of the seventh and caught sight of the scoreboard, it hit me: Acer was throwing a perfect game.

Completely distracted, I quickly backed out of the box and faked something being in my eye. "Time out!" I yelled.

As I began to brush the imaginary dirt from my eye with the back of my hand, I glanced into the dugout. Acer was hanging on the railing at the far end all by himself. Apparently, I was the last to realize what was happening because no one was even remotely close to him. He was in his zone and the rest of the team stayed away so as not to jinx the zone.

The signs were all there. The team knew it. Just three more innings and Acer would clinch a perfect game and a state title—all in one day. Idly, I wondered if that had ever happened in a state championship game. I also wondered if Acer had any clue what he was about to accomplish.

"You need some help?" the umpire asked, interrupting my thoughts.

"No, no, I think I got it," I replied and took a couple of practice swings before stepping back into the box.

We needed to score him some runs. Our offense had threatened nearly every inning, but stranded our runners in scoring position each time, but not this time. One base hit, that's all it would take for Luke and Jose to score. I took a deep breath.

Off!

The world around me closed until all I could see was the pitcher. I followed the ball through his windup. Time slowed as he released it and I could see everything perfectly: the slight downward rotation of the red seams on the ball, the diving motion as it slid away from me. I could even make out the swirling script.

Crack!

My hands exploded through the ball and sent it flying toward centerfield. It took one hop before smacking into the wall, dying at the warning track. I sprinted towards first and watched the centerfielder throw it in. As the relay snagged the ball and threw it home, I took off and dove into second base, turning just in time to see Jose slide across the plate.

"Yes!" Jumping to my feet, I pumped my fist in the air.

The crowd erupted into cheers. We had finally scored some runs.

Coach Mac flashed two fingers at me just as Bull stepped up to the plate. I flashed them back, signaling to him that I knew there were two outs. After two balls in a row, Bull took the next pitch to deep left field. I sprinted, never hesitating as I rounded third and dug hard for home. With two outs, I had nothing to lose by going for broke, but as I crossed the plate, Red Oak was headed into the dugout. The ball had been caught, for out number three.

We were back to the top of the lineup after the change over, but this would be Red Oaks's third time to see Acer. I had to call smart here or it could all be over. The leadoff hitter had struck out twice when we set him up for high fastballs. He just couldn't lay off them no matter how far out of the strike zone they were, but this time he wasn't so aggressive. Acer took him to a full count before he finally swung. The ball was hit sky high just over third base. It looked like it was going to drop in for a base hit when out of nowhere, Luke laid out and caught the ball right on the left field line.

I pumped my fist in the air and let out a loud yell. *That was close!* Acer was completely unemotional, a machine. He caught the ball and readied himself for the next batter. Looking poised and ready, Acer struck out the second batter, but started to struggle with the third one.

The three-hole hitter sent the first two pitches screaming down the left field line in foul territory. Having adjusted his position in the box so that he could catch Acer's breaking pitches before they had a chance to move, he was crushing each pitch that was thrown. Every curve, every slider we threw he was getting a piece of the ball. We tried a high inside fastball and he opened up and sent the ball banging into the third base dugout. Acer threw a curve and he sent it into the stands behind the first base dugout.

We were ahead in the count, but it was too risky to throw anything close with the way he was swinging. I called for a curve off the plate, signaling that I wanted it way off the plate. The ball moved away just like it was supposed to and the location was exactly like I had wanted, but somehow the batter reached far enough with his swing that he was able to get a good piece and the ball shot like a bullet off his bat back up the middle.

Angela Geurin

I held my breath and watched helplessly as the ball bounced by Acer and headed towards the outfield. Just when I had ceded that perfection had ended with a base hit up the middle, Jose snagged it behind second base, whipped around and from his knees threw a laser over to Kevin at first base who strode out into a full split to catch the ball, one step before the runner reached the base.

"You're out!" The first base umpire shouted, making a big show with his fist as he punched him out.

I blew out the breath I'd been holding and ran up the first baseline. I slapped Kevin on the back and wrapped my arms around Jose.

"That's how it's done!" I shouted. Acer jogged by me and I gave him a high five. "Keep it up, Ace."

He nodded solemnly and jogged into the dugout. That was close. Just two more innings left. We just needed to keep it rolling for two more innings.

Our offense threatened to score again in the top of the eighth, but was unable to push any more runs across. Acer still seemed oblivious to how close he was to achieving a perfect game. He sat alone at the end of the dugout, barely watching our hitters. I watched him for a moment in complete amazement, realizing just how far he had come this year. He was absolutely composed, relaxed even, in the middle of the state championship game with all those scouts watching him. There was not a hint of Postal in his demeanor.

He turned, catching me staring at him, and flashed me the lopsided grin that I loved. My cheeks flushed. If anyone would have told me that Postal would be my boyfriend by the end of the season, I would have said they were off of their rocker, but here we were. He threw me a wink and turned his attention back to the hitters.

In the bottom of the eighth with two outs, the third batter of the inning was a mountain. His biceps were massive boulders that sat upon his arms and as he stepped up to the box, I knew we were in trouble. He pointed his bat at Acer, determined to get on base. Whether his cockiness got to Acer or not, we got behind and before I knew it we were sitting on a three and one count.

"Come on, Acer, go get this guy!" I encouraged.

The batter fouled off pitch after pitch, sending the balls screaming down the third baseline, just barely foul. Nothing we threw at him was getting by. I started to call time out, but Acer was in such a good rhythm, I was afraid it would hurt him more than help and instead I opted, one more time, to try and jam this batter's swing by throwing a fastball on the inside corner. Again he made contact, but popped it up in foul territory towards the first base dugout, only this time, it was high enough that I had a chance to get to it. I didn't even try to take off my helmet, I ran and lunged fully extended, reaching for the ball.

Bang!

Just as my glove snapped shut around the ball, my head slammed into the dugout fence post. The impact stung every extremity. My head didn't hurt, but the pole had apparently jammed my neck. I felt tingly, but as I slowly tested each body part, I was rewarded with the proper response and breathed a sigh of relief.

Standing slowly in front of our dugout, I tossed the ball to the umpire and headed to the bench. Coach Mac helped me get my helmet off. "You all right, kid?"

"At least, I know my helmet works," I replied sarcastically and eased myself down.

As our athletic trainer completed her examination, Acer plopped down next to me. "You okay?"

I nodded as the trainer put an ice pack on my neck. "That's why we wear helmets, right?" I said. "Jammed my neck pretty good though."

I leaned back and closed my eyes for a moment, rubbing at the stiffness. Acer's arm rested next to my leg and his fingers barely brushed the side of my thigh. "Can you finish the game?"

I sat up straight and scowled. "Of course! You know it takes more than a bump on the head to keep me off the field."

He returned the grin and patted my knee. "Yeah, you are pretty hard-headed."

I punched him in the shoulder. "That was not funny!"

"Ow!" he hollered and then I saw him do a double take as he looked onto the field. Acer bolted straight up off the bench. "Scout?" he asked. "Has Red Oak had any base runners today?"

"No, Ace," I answered, "They haven't."

Immediately, his face paled and his breathing quickened. I could foresee another trash can episode if I didn't get him back in his zone fast. Laying my ice pack on the bench, I stood and grabbed his ear and yanked him back down next to me.

"Ow!" he hollered, glaring at me. "What did you do that for?"

"Sorry, but I thought you were about to lose it again and I refuse to watch you upchuck all over the dugout!"

"That really hurt!" he whined and rubbed his ear.

"I said I'm sorry!" I repeated and draped my arm around his shoulders. "You just have three more outs, Ace. The guys are behind you. Whatever you have been doing for the last eight innings, you just need to keep doing it. Don't worry about anything else. Just pretend like it is the first inning again when you struck out the side."

He nodded. "We're just playing catch."

"Just you and I." After glancing around to make sure no one was watching, I brushed my lips across his ear, and then stood as Jon popped up for the third out. "Come on." I offered him a hand. "Time to put this game in the books."

He handed me my helmet and we hustled out of the dugout.

We had the bottom of the lineup, but as expected, it looked as if we were facing three pinch hitters in a row. "Fresh meat at the plate, boys," I announced.

I sized up the first batter as he stepped into the box. He took the first pitch for strike one. Then I called for a high fastball. It was a beautiful pitch and tailed up under his bat as he nearly swung out of his shoes. Now we had him set up for the off-speed, but instead of taking another hack, he squared to bunt, catching us all off guard.

"Bunt!" I screamed as soon as I saw his hands sneak forward.

He laid it down perfectly back up the middle, neither corner had a chance to get to it. I was sick. To come this far, and lose it on a bunt to a pinch hitter with two strikes was awful, but that's when Acer sprung off the mound, scooped it up and tossed it to first, all in one motion. It wasn't even a close play.

I pumped my fist in the air. "One down! Atta baby, Acer!"

The next batter took the first pitch and the second and the third, until the count was two balls and one strike. His bat still hadn't left his shoulder and he took the fourth pitch for strike two.

"We got a window shopper, Acer; blow it by him!" I taunted.

The batter glared down at me as he stepped up to the plate. I called for a slider and had the satisfaction of watching his first swing pop up behind the mound. Jose caught it easily for out number two.

Next, Red Oak sent up a third pinch hitter, green and eager to impress his team. He had a lot of bounce in his step and his practice swings were precise. This would be a battle of the wills for sure.

Acer nailed the first pitch for strike one, but Mr. Peppy fouled off the next two. Then, Acer started to falter. He lost his slider in the dirt and we were sitting at a full count with two outs.

As much as I hated to, I called time out and jogged to the mound.

"What's up, Ace?" I asked.

"My arm is killing me," he said, pain evident on his face.

"On what pitch?" I asked, watching him clench and unclench his fingers.

"All of them," He tried to smile, but I could still see the pain in his face. "I think I must have strained it on that throw to first base."

284

"You've thrown a lot of pitches today," I commented. "You just need one more pitch. Dig deep one more time. I know you can do it. Just one more pitch, Ace. That's all we need."

He nodded seriously. "Make it a fastball. That one doesn't seem to hurt as much."

"You got it, boss." I winked and jogged back to the plate.

It all came down to this one moment, this one pitch that would decide a champion. This batter was determined to get a base hit, but Acer was just as determined to strike him out. Only one of them could be the champion today, and as that ball slipped by the bat and popped my mitt, in the back of my mind, I had known all along that it would be Acer.

"Strike three. You're out!" the umpire yelled behind me.

The entire season flashed before my eyes upon hearing those words. From my first meeting with Coach Mac, the tryouts, the editorials in the newspaper, the constant bullying from our opponents, the fights with Acer: after all of that, we were state champions.

Tossing my helmet and glove towards the dugout, I sprinted out to Acer pumping my fists and screaming in elation. He met me halfway to the mound and caught me in his arms in a ferocious bear hug.

"We're state champions! You did it, Ace!" I yelled. "You did it! You threw a perfect game!"

"No, we did it, Scout! You and I together, we did it!" He returned and in front of that entire crowd of people in the middle of the field he kissed me and for once, I didn't worry about what anyone else thought or said. I didn't shy away or get embarrassed, I just wrapped my arms around him and kissed him back.

Epilogue

Present Day

W ell, Ms. Rose," Charlotte Anderson spoke after listening to my story. "You have truly experienced some difficult times; yet you sit here before me, having accomplished much in spite of your hardships."

I smiled and ate the last bite of my raspberry tart. *Hardships!* Sitting on this side of my life, the word seemed a little strong. Compared to what Bonnie had gone through, what both of my parents had suffered, my troubles seemed pretty small in comparison. They weren't hardships. They were tools for the lessons I needed to learn. All those events, and so many others, had shaped me into who God designed me to be.

"I don't really think of them as hardships," I said quietly. "They are more like the dirt covering the diamonds along my journey. If I would have just quit living and focused on all the dirt in my life, I would have missed out on all the diamonds, the true blessings, that were there waiting for me to receive them."

She raised an eyebrow. "Exactly what diamonds did you find?"

"I am closer to my family now, especially Mary. She is so much the mother I never had and never knew I needed. That wouldn't have happened if I hadn't been forced to move under her roof for three years. Persevering through three years of high school baseball with everyone laughing in my face, taught me how to be humble and disciplined. I

286

would have never truly appreciated the gifts God has given me, if I didn't have to do something as desperate as play baseball with a bunch of boys, and I probably wouldn't have been a college All-American softball player." I paused and sipped my water. "I have such a strong prayer life now because I witnessed its power and purpose, and that never would have happened if Bonnie hadn't been so ill that only a miracle from God could heal her. I'm much more forgiving now because I understand what it takes to forgive and I never would have understood that if Cade wouldn't have put me in a position to need to forgive something so…horrendous." I smiled to myself as I added, "I wouldn't have learned to love unconditionally and irrevocably if I hadn't met Benjamin Acer."

She eyed me curiously. "So what has become of you and Mr. Acer?"

"Well, that's another story," I said with a smirk.

"One that I look forward to hearing very soon, Ms. Rose." She waved to the maître d' "You are a talented storyteller and you are exactly the right person for our department. My assistant will contact you and set up your appointment with Human Resources."

My heart leapt! Did she just say what I think she said?

"I-I got the job?" I asked in shock. She eyed me as she signed the check and then nodded slightly. "Th-Thank you! Thank you so much for everything, Ms. Anderson."

She handed the check to the waiter and then offered me her delicate hand. I shook it a little too hard, but she smiled perceptively at my enthusiasm and gently removed her fingers from my grasp. "Let's do this again sometime soon. I do look forward to hearing more of your story."

About the Author

Angela Geurin graduated from The University of Tulsa with two degrees in speech-language pathology. She has been a practicing speech-language pathologist for the last ten years. She lives with her husband and two daughters in Texas where she teaches Sunday school and coaches little league softball.

More Titles by 5 Fold Media

The Transformed Life
by John R. Carter
$20.95
ISBN: 978-1-936578-40-5

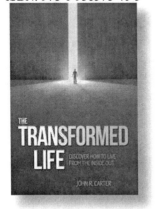

Personal transformation requires radical change, but your life will not transform until you change the way you think. Becoming a Christian ignites the process of transformation.

In this book, John Carter will teach you that God has designed a plan of genuine transformation for every person, one that goes far beyond the initial moment of salvation. More than a book this 10 week, 40 day workbook will show you how to change.

Luke, to the Lovers of God
The Passion Translation
by Brian Simmons
$14.95
ISBN: 978-1-936578-48-1

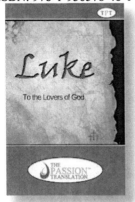

All four Gospels in our New Testament are inspired by God, but Luke's gospel is unique and distinct. Luke writes clearly of the humanity of Jesus—as the servant of all, and the sacrifice for all. In Luke's gospel, every barrier is broken down between Jew and Gentile, men and women, rich and poor. We see Jesus in Luke as the Savior of all who come to Him.

I highly recommend this new Bible translation to everyone.
~ Dr. Ché Ahn, Senior Pastor of HRock Church in Pasadena, CA

Like 5 Fold Media on Facebook, follow us on Twitter!

"To Establish and Reveal"
For more information visit:
www.5foldmedia.com

Use your mobile device to scan the tag above and visit our website.
Get the free app:
http://gettag.mobi

CPSIA information can be obtained at www.ICGtesting.com
Printed in the USA
LVOW12s1655020913

350608LV00005B/8/P